Marquesas Gold

J. Thomas Stovall

If you can read, you can do anything.

J. Thomas Stovall

By **J. Thomas Stovall**

The Cuban Sanction

Miracle at Indian Key (First in the CJ and Skye trilogy)

Marquesas Gold (Second in the CJ and Skye trilogy)

A Miracle for Tristan (Third in the CJ and Skye Trilogy)

Keys Publishing
Franklin, NC

This is a work of fiction. The events described here are imaginary. The settings, locales and characters are fictitious and not intended to represent specific places or living persons. They are the product of the author's imagination.

Library of Congress Cataloging-in-Publications Data ISBN: 978-0-692-49116-4

Acknowledgments

The second novel in the CJ and Sky trilogy is finished. As I wrote about the teens, they took me with them on their adventures, but I wasn't the only one along for the ride.

Diane Strickland, through her wonderful imagination, brought these two characters to life. Her editing skills, suggestions, and perseverance were the fundamental building blocks for this novel. You have my sincerest thanks and gratitude, Diane. I couldn't have done it without you.

We both hope you enjoy Marquesas Gold. It was a true labor of love.

Marquesas

Gold

Chapter One

Renaldo Rodriguez, an attractive, hard-working man, stood in his neat garage packing up his fishing gear for a weekend getaway from his nagging wife. He could not wait to get away from her. *The sooner, the better*, he thought. He picked up his gear and headed to his truck, not bothering to say goodbye. Once trim, beautiful, and vivacious, his wife had gotten fat, unkempt, and mean.

Fishing was his escape from his unhappy marriage, and he managed to get away almost every other weekend. Strangely, she never nagged him about his fishing trips. *I think she is as glad to be rid of me for a couple of days as I am her. How did I ever get myself into this farce of a marriage?* Unfortunately, both were devout Catholics, so there was no chance of a divorce.

Renaldo, in beige cargo shorts and no shirt, and wiping beads of sweat from his face, stood at the stern of his eighteen-foot Sea Breeze boat. He had a larger boat, but he favored the smaller Sea Breeze when he fished alone. He was fishing with a donut-shaped yoyo. It was what poor fishermen used in Cuba, his birthplace. Renaldo had a job selling high-end luxury boats, and he and his wife lived very comfortably. He could afford expensive Daiwa spinning rods, but he preferred his favorite yoyo because it reminded him of his roots. Tired and sleepy from his second long night of fishing, his deep brown eyes kept slowly closing. His boat was anchored south of Sand Key, about two hundred yards from a lighted tower that winked at him every eight seconds. Finally, wiping the moisture from his face, he glanced down at his waterproof luminescent watch. 12:33 a.m. *It's about time for me pack up and head home,* he thought, part with relief that he would get to sleep in his own bed, and part with regret that he had to face his fat, annoying, wife again.

A warm, humid breeze blew in from the west at six miles an hour caressing the glassy surface. Renaldo did not need a light. His boat was well lit by the full moon overhead.

Fully contented from a fruitful catch, he did not realize that within forty-three seconds he would no longer have to worry about his nagging wife. Renaldo Rodriquez would be dead.

Two eyes the size of large dinner plates quietly rose to the surface and lingered for a moment. The predator, analyzing its prey, moved within thirty feet of the boat. Hunger had driven the beast to the surface. Prey large enough to satisfy the predator's appetite was hard to find in these parts, especially in the warm, shallow, waters of the Keys. The need for food was overpowering, and the predator's instinct was to do what he had to do to survive.

Exhausted, but instantly alert, Renaldo turned when he heard the splash slam hard against the side of his boat, rocking it back and forth on the dark, glassy water. *What was that?* His heart skipped a beat. Focusing his tired eyes, he saw the predator, and he couldn't believe what he was seeing. Now fully awake, his eyes opened wide in terror. Fear instantly covered his handsome face, and his heart began racing wildly. *It can't be, not in this warm water! What the....!*

Before he could complete his thought, two lightning rod tentacles broke the surface, shot through the air, and entangled him. He saw them coming, but he was in shock and couldn't move. The rapid tightening grip of the massive creature forced Renaldo's eyes to bulge from their sockets. Struggling was useless. Blood ran down his cheeks like red rainwater. His heart felt like a freight train trying to escape his chest. Bright red blood squirted from his open mouth as he bit into the meat of his tongue. A hysterical scream welled up in his throat, but it was quickly silenced as he as viciously jerked into the sea.

Chapter Two

The day was sunny, humid, and very warm, and the water was unusual for this time of year. Sixty feet visibility was remarkable, particularly in the Gulf of Mexico. The temperature was a tepid eighty-seven degrees. Sediment from the Mississippi River, with three hundred tributaries flowing into the Gulf of Mexico depositing millions of tons of debris, made it the world's largest sauna.

CJ Jansen loved it. It was his world. Being on the water had been his life for as long as he could remember. Born and raised on Islamorada in the Florida Keys, he was in his element.

He and Skye Somers, his best friend, had pulled his seventeen-foot McKee Craft on a trailer from Islamorada down to Garrison Bight Marina in Key West, Florida. At eight thirty-eight in the morning, they launched the *Gator Bait,* parked his yellow 1973 Volkswagen Thing, gassed up the boat, and headed for the Marquesas Keys, twenty miles due west of Key West. The uninhabited islands, with a two-mile wide lagoon surrounded by mangroves, had been used for target practice by the military up until 1980. Now, known best for its excellent sports fishing, the islands drew the locals and tourists to the pristine beaches and waters for both onshore and offshore fishing.

The clear morning sun stood at a quarter high in the sky with winds from the south at barely five miles an hour, and the surface as smooth as glass. CJ's little boat, Gator Bait, skidded along with little effort during the twenty-mile trip that took less than forty minutes. Arriving at their destination, CJ, in teal and black Ocean Pacific swim trunks was the first to dive into the water. He was so excited, he couldn't wait. Eighteen feet below the surface, he investigated an isolated crop of niggerhead coral. CJ didn't particularly like the name. In fact, he found it downright offensive. He had no idea how a coral head growing in the middle of a desert of sand had gotten such a name.

He watched colorful fish swim by, their fins and tails moving lazily as if in slow motion. *There is so much beauty down here*, he thought. Starting to feel a little lightheaded, he knew he needed to get to the surface for more air.

Breaking the barrier between two different worlds, he blew water out through his snorkel and sucked in a lung full of fresh air. His dizziness from lack of oxygen quickly cleared as he looked around for Skye. He saw her holding on to the dive ladder at the back of the boat, cleaning her mask, preparing for her dive, C J kicked his way over to her.

"You should have seen that six-foot Moray eel down there!" he said with excitement. "What a beauty! It was solid emerald-green."

Cute and petite, Skye reached over with her small free hand, grabbed his mask, turned his head toward her, and looked through the glass at CJ's face.

"You can keep your beautiful green Moray eels, thank you very much!" She wanted nothing to do with eels. Never had, never would.

Her first look at the mouth full of sharp teeth had made Skye decide that she wanted to stay as far away from eels as she could. She was very adventurous, but she wasn't stupid.

Adjusting her face mask, she pushed off and away from the ladder. Her right hand held a Voit Swim Master Speargun. Heading for the bottom, she expertly reached out with her left hand, grabbed the surgical tubing, pulled it back, and cocked the gun, all in one fluid motion.

Still smiling at Skye's remark about the eel, CJ followed in pursuit, thinking about how opinionated Skye had always been. *Spicy is what dad calls Mom and Skye. Spicy, huh? More like volcanic, if you ask me.* Despite her minor faults, he knew she was the only one for him. Of course, he still hadn't told her how he felt.

They had been best friends for six years, since she was ten, and he was eleven. She lived in Connecticut and visited her Poppy in Islamorada every summer. He found out pretty quickly that Skye was very curious and loved adventures. The consequences of their adventures never seemed to bother Skye. Over the years, they had both been on restriction more times than he cared to remember. Skye always managed to talk him into one escapade after another, and for some reason he could never tell her no. *Life has never been dull when she's around, that's for sure.* His smooth face broke into a smile inside his mask.

Yellowtail and medium-sized hog snapper swam in and out around the coral head. At a depth of fifteen feet, Skye took aim at a strawberry grouper floating just above the sand. Delicious grilled grouper was Poppy's specialty, and her mouth was already watering at the thought of it. She heard the familiar click as the spear released. Then all hell broke loose as the spear penetrated the mid-section of the flailing grouper. *Phooey! Too close*, she thought as the spear and line passed completely through the fish. The grouper went wild as it tried to escape the line that held it captive. Sand and silt were swirling as it tried to break away.

Eventually, the line cut through the body of the fish while it tried unsuccessfully to make its way to the safety of the coral. Within seconds, the green Moray eel had the dying grouper clenched in its jaws and snatched it back into the darkened crevices of the coral head. Skye was horrified. Everything had happened so fast that she had had no time to react. She had planned to spear a grouper to take home for dinner, but her stomach still churned a little at the grouper's terrible fate. *Poor grouper, what a horrible way to die,* she thought, vowing again never to have anything to do with eels.

Swimming up to Skye, CJ touched her shoulder, pointing to something glittering on the bottom. Glancing down, Skye thought, *Wonder what that is?* Taking her mind off the vicious, hungry, Moray eel, she moved closer to get a better look at the sparkling object below her. She reached down and pulled up what appeared to be a thick gold chain. *It can't be real, can it?* She wondered. It had a large green stone hanging from its center with what looked like diamonds surrounding the mounting. *Oh, my gosh, it is real! It has to be!*

"We're rich! We're rich!" Skye screamed at the top of her lungs as she broke the surface of the water, gasping for air. CJ popped up beside her.

She held her arm as high as it would reach, but still the heavy chain hung in the water. "What a beautiful necklace! It's exquisite!" She had never seen anything like it. Little did she know that it had been in the water for several hundred years.

CJ reached over to examine Skye's find. "It's beautiful, Skye! I never realized how heavy gold could be. I hope it's real. Do you think that enormous stone in the middle is an emerald?"

"Oh, it's real all right." Then, looking closely at the large, green stone, she replied, "Yeah, it sure looks like an emerald." Skye retrieved the necklace from CJ and began making her way back to the boat. Looking over her shoulder, she asked, "Would you mind going back down for my speargun? My hands are full." She headed back to the *Gator Bait.*

CJ laughed. *Yeah, sure, her hands are full. She just doesn't want to let the gorgeous necklace out of her sight. Guess it's a girl thing.*

CJ realized that their day on the water was over almost before it had begun because of their find. They had planned to stay all day, but those plans were moot now that they had discovered the thick gold necklace. Frowning in disappointment, CJ remembered that Skye had brought a couple of her world-famous sandwiches and her homemade walnut brownies, but it didn't look like they would eat until they got home. *Bummer*, he thought, feeling his stomach grumble in protest.

Quickly retrieving Skye's speargun, CJ caught up with her before she made it back to the boat.

Ninety-five yards to the north of CJ's boat, an unattractive, unwashed, obese man, with his flabby belly hanging over a pair of filthy khaki shorts, stood in the shade of a few mangrove trees on Gull Key. He rested an old pair of binoculars on a tree branch to help keep his filthy, shaking hands from blurring his vision. His heart was racing like Dale Junior's number eighty-eight at the Daytona 500 last year. His breath wheezed from too much smoking and reeked from the odor of rotten teeth. With his one good eye, he stayed focused on the two young swimmers making their way to the boat. What had caught his attention was the heavy gold chain in the girl's hand. *Oh no! They found the gold. That's my gold, and ain't no kids gonna take it away from me.* Acid rose in his throat, and uneasiness pulsed through his body. He knew eventually he would have to decide what to do with the teens. He was not giving up the gold. *No way,* he thought.

Chapter Three

CJ had the *Gator Bait* at full throttle heading back to Key West. He and Skye were on cloud nine over their new find. As the small boat skimmed the smooth surface of the water, a thousand questions ran through CJ's mind. *Where did the gold come from? I wonder if it's from an old shipwreck.*

Luckily, he had remembered to mark the spot on his chart before getting underway. Now and then Skye would look over at CJ, flash him one of her beautiful, dimpled smiles, and then jump up and down in excitement as if she has just won the lottery. She held tightly to the center console to keep her balance.

CJ's forehead wrinkled in thought for a moment, and then he shouted to Skye over the roar of the outboard engine, "We should keep this quiet for a while. We need to talk with Poppy and my folks to see what they say. What do you think?"

Skye briefly considered his question. "Yeah, maybe you're right. What if this is part of Mel's Fisher's treasure? Will we get to keep it?" Her bright blue eyes danced with anticipation as she caressed her treasure. Skye had read Poppy's book on the history of the Keys the previous summer and had learned that the Atocha and the Santa Margarita both sank during a hurricane in 1622, off the Dry Tortugas, about seventy miles from Key West.

"I sure hope so," CJ said in response, his eyes shining with excitement with thoughts of the money they would get if they sold the necklace. "We'll have to sort it out when we get home."

Riding the smooth swells at just over thirty miles an hour, CJ preferred to stand instead of sit on the blue and white vinyl bench seat that held an ice cooler. His knees bent a little to absorb any pounding should the boat hull leave the surface. His six-foot-four-inch frame, filled out quite a bit from the previous summer, towered above the Plexiglas windshield that would have shielded most people of average height from the wind and salt spray. Unfortunately, with his height and the speed they were traveling, it was hard for him to breathe. It was as if the wind was trying to suck the air from his lungs.

Looking over at CJ as he maneuvered the boat, Skye smiled, and the dimples in her cheeks deepened. *It's so good to see CJ again,* she thought as she looked at his long lean body that sported a colorful swimsuit and a bare chest. *Wow, he sure has filled out since last summer.* His arms were muscular, his skin bronze from the sweltering sun. She was shocked at the strong attraction she felt for him. It had been almost a year since they had last seen each other. In fact, it had been last August when CJ had driven her up to Miami International Airport, so she could fly back home to Connecticut.

This summer was her sixth year coming down to Islamorada, and nothing in the world could keep her away. She was happy to be back again with the tall palm trees, shallow white sand beaches, and great seafood. She especially loved staying with Poppy, her amazing grandfather, who adored and supported her no matter what happened, and plenty had happened.

Of course, it had been a shock last summer when she had told him about the grumpy pelican, Flapper, and the show-off dolphin, Squeaky. It was still hard for her to believe that she had been able to communicate with them through telepathy, and also through talking to them. She still wondered how it was possible, and she looked forward to seeing them again.

She thought of Flapper with his wide brown wings that had

lovingly encircled her when she had visited him at the bird sanctuary after he had been injured, and Squeaky, who had pulled her across the channel to rescue CJ on Indian Key. She briefly wondered if they would still be able to communicate. She would be devastated if they couldn't. The two of them had become good friends and had saved both hers and CJ's lives the previous summer. Since she had only arrived in Islamorada the night before, this was her first day with CJ, but she knew that Flapper and Squeaky would find them sooner or later.

Shifting her thoughts back to CJ again, Skye knew her feelings for him had grown from last summer, but she was surprised that she felt such a strong physical attraction to him this year. Sadly, she couldn't let him know because she was afraid it would ruin their friendship, and she was certain that was all CJ wanted from her. He had never shown any interest in her other than being friends when she visited in the summer.

Up ahead, Fleming Key came into view. The south side of the key led to the entrance to Key West Harbor. CJ eased back on the throttle and backed their speed down to about twenty-five miles an hour.

As Skye gazed off into the distance, CJ, deep in thought, looked over and noticed her silhouette formed from the backlight on the horizon. It was the same image he remembered from her visit last summer. *She's even more beautiful than last year, if that's possible,* he thought. *Her hair is longer, and it's a little darker blonde this summer, but it always lightens up in the sun. She sure has filled out in all the right places too. Dad would say that she has bloomed since last summer. She's not that little pigtailed girl anymore. Hot is the only word I can think of to describe her now.* Just thinking about Skye that way made him blush pink in embarrassment.

Thinking back, CJ remembered the first summer Skye had come to visit her Poppy. She was a tiny, blue-eyed, dimpled ten-year-old girl with a flat chest and blonde pigtails, wearing flowered shorts and a sleeveless pink tee shirt. They had become fast friends that day. Her Poppy and CJ's parents lived in the same area on Florida Bay, and shortly after Skye arrived, he and his dad had gone to visit Skye's Poppy, Mr. Hudson. That day was the beginning of a summer friendship that had lasted for six years.

After years of being best summer friends, his feelings for Skye had begun to grow into something stronger last year. He was afraid if he told her how he felt, she would pull away from him. Since she had turned sixteen just after she left last summer, he had been worried that maybe she would begin dating while she was at home in Connecticut. He had even been afraid she might not come back to Islamorada again this summer.

Last year she had confided to CJ that her parents had told her that she could date when she turned sixteen. So far, she had not mentioned another guy at home, and he certainly wasn't going to bring it up to her.

———————

Radio waves travel at a hundred eighty-six thousand miles a second. A text message sent from Gull Key to Boca Chica took less than one microsecond to reach its destination, far ahead of CJ and Skye. When the recipient received the text, he walked from his shack, got into an old, dirty, white cargo van and headed for Garrison Bight Marina.

———————

CJ traveled up Key West Harbor Range until he came to Fleming Key Cut and headed for Garrison Bight Marina. He parked his boat next to one of numerous boat ramps. Skye jumped to the dock and helped secure the boat. The necklace, safe in a plastic baggie she had retrieved from the lunch cooler, lay on the seat next to CJ. Skye was an excellent line handler. She expertly secured two spring lines to cleats. Pleased with her handiwork, she put both hands on her hips, smiled, and waited for CJ to say something.

"Not bad," CJ grinned. "Once a sailor, always a sailor."

"Well, I had a good teacher."

"I'll teach you some more this summer."

Teasing him, Skye laughed and said, "I was thinking of Poppy."

Acting as if he was offended, CJ stomped off to retrieve his yellow Volkswagen.

With the *Gator Bait* finally loaded on the trailer, CJ revved the engine, slowly released the clutch, and at the same time eased off the emergency brake. The VW shook as its rear wheels began spinning, leaving a cloud of black smoke from burnt rubber on the damp, seaweed-covered ramp.

At the top of the ramp, Skye grabbed the door, jumped in and slammed it shut. On their way out of the marina, neither was aware of the filthy white cargo van parked discreetly in the rear parking lot.

The driver withdrew a pen from the glove box and jotted down CJ's license plate number. His grimy fingers pushed the key into the ignition, starting the engine. Moments later, the van pulled out, unnoticed behind the VW Thing, and followed the young couple.

Chapter Four

A loud pounding on the front door drew Poppy from a deep sleep. *Who in the world can that be at this hour?* He managed to raise his aging body slowly from the king size bed, with the covers askew. His aching joints were stiff from too much inactivity. He had been unusually sedentary for the past few weeks. Having just turned seventy-one, he had decided that getting old was no fun.

Of course, since Skye was here for the summer, he figured he would get back in shape, at least in shape for an old man. *Her adventures sure keep me busy.* He smiled as he remembered all of hers and CJ's exciting escapades the previous summer.

Poppy was still having trouble accepting the fact that his granddaughter could communicate with a pelican and a dolphin. He would never understand it, but he had seen Skye talking with the two of them on the dock last summer at her going away party. She had told him that both would be there, and both had showed up. One was perched on a piling, and the other was doing flips in the water.

She said she had promised them a bucket of fresh fish for saving hers and CJ's lives. He knew his granddaughter well enough to know she was telling the truth when she said she could talk with them.

The pounding on the door continued as Poppy stepped into his old worn slippers. He grabbed his wire-rimmed glasses, and with thinning, wispy white hair standing at attention, he shuffled down the stairs in wrinkled, blue-striped, cotton pajamas. Passing through the large, comfortable living room, he noticed that dawn was breaking. It shone through the white custom sheers as his eyes began to adjust to the early morning light. The persistent pounding grew louder as he neared the door. "For heaven sakes, hold your horses! I'm coming as fast as I can."

When Poppy finally reached the solid white door, he peered through the peephole. He saw no one, and the pounding had stopped.

Curiosity caused him to reach down and turn the doorknob, releasing the lock. Slowly, he cracked the door and peeked through the narrow opening, finding the entrance surprisingly empty. As he stepped out from behind the door, he heard the sound of running footsteps fading down the long driveway. He turned to go back inside and noticed a small note taped to the outside of the door. It was too difficult to read in the dim light, even with his glasses, so he reached up, jerked it off the door, and stepped back inside. *What in the world is this, and who was that running down my driveway?* he wondered. Yawning, he thought, *I need coffee.*

Comfortable and stretched from years of wear, his bedroom slippers made a flapping sound as he headed to the kitchen.

A creature of habit, when he reached the kitchen island, he pressed the start button on the coffeemaker that he had prepared for brewing the night before. Finally, he switched on the overhead island light. Squinting from the brightness, he adjusted his glasses and began reading the note printed in block letters.

STAY AWAY FROM THE MARQUESAS KEYS OR YOU WILL BE SORRY!

Poppy stared at the note, contemplating its meaning. *CJ and Skye!* he thought. *They're in danger! Someone found out about the gold necklace. But who could have known about it? Only Michael, Maria, CJ, Skye, and I know about it. Could someone have seen them when they brought the necklace from the boat?*

The previous evening, Poppy's house had been filled with excitement. Skye and CJ had showed up with the gold necklace they had found while diving. They had been jumping up and down enthusiastically, talking about how rich they were going to be. Poppy had immediately called Michael and Maria Jansen, CJ's father and mother, and had asked them to come over. He told them the teens had a big surprise to show them.

When CJ's parents arrived, Poppy already had a pitcher of Margaritas prepared for the adults. CJ and Skye were drinking Cherry Cokes from Poppy's specially installed soda fountain.

Maria, beautiful as always, her face still unlined at forty-nine, was in a sweeping, ankle-length, black and white cotton skirt and a sleeveless white knit top. Michael, sandy-haired, tanned and handsome, was dressed in dark blue shorts and a navy and white Hawaiian-themed shirt.

Skye began telling them about how they had discovered the necklace while spear fishing. "CJ pointed to the reflection on the bottom, so I went down, reached into the sand, and there it was, just lying there. Isn't it the prettiest thing you've ever seen?"

Smiling and nodding at Skye in agreement, Maria turned to Michael and asked, "What about salvage rights? Do you think that could be a problem?"

Michael looked around the room. "I think they'll be okay," he said. "A few years ago, Mel Fisher won a court case against the State of Florida. The state had to return all of the gold it had confiscated."

"Hey, Dad," CJ asked, "how much do you think this thing weighs?"

"I have no idea, Son," Michael answered. "Quite a bit, I'm sure. It's heavy, and that stone in the center looks like a big emerald with diamonds around it. The stones alone are worth a fortune."

Poppy's eyes lit up. "I just remembered something. I've got a food scale in the pantry." Excited, he got up and headed for the shelf on which he had stored it.

Skye couldn't keep her hands off the long chain. From the moment she and CJ had arrived at the house, the necklace had been her constant companion.

Poppy returned with the scale and sat it down in the center of the kitchen island. Everyone gathered around it.

Sliding the dazzling emerald setting off the necklace, Skye gently laid the beautiful chain on the scale. Everyone's eyes were straining at the digital readout. Skye felt the tension in the air as each of them waited to see the weight of the shining gold piece of jewelry.

"Seventeen and a half ounces," Poppy said as he looked at the others.

Big smiles brightened each face.

CJ's mind worked like a calculator as he came up with the value. "That's twenty-four thousand five hundred dollars in today's gold market," he said grinning. "Of course, that doesn't even count the emerald and diamonds, or the historical value. I'll bet the whole thing is worth at least fifty thousand dollars. Maybe even more," he told the group.

Skye threw her fist in the air, giggled, and did a little dance. "Let's go back tomorrow and look for more gold." Her blue eyes were sparkling. "Looking for gold is so much fun," she said, thinking about what new gold pieces they might find. *This summer is sure off to a fantastic start!*

———————

After reading the note again, Poppy immediately dialed CJ's house. Michael answered the phone. "Hey, Michael," Poppy said, his voice shaking a little, "we have a big problem. You and CJ need to get over here right away!"

"We'll be right there." Michael wondered what was going on.

Poppy didn't get upset easily.

Seeing her grandfather's worried look as she walked into the kitchen, Skye asked, "What's the matter, Poppy?" She had been upstairs in her room daydreaming about what she and CJ would do with the money from the gold. *Maybe I'll keep the necklace if we find more. I'll ask CJ what he thinks.*

Looking a little pale, Poppy pointed to the note.

The kitchen was silent as Skye read the note, her big blue eyes growing wider and wider.

"Oh, my gosh, Poppy," she gasped. "What are we going to do? Who do you think wrote that note? How could anyone else know about the necklace? I didn't notice anyone around when we left the marina."

"I don't know, honey. When Michael and CJ get here, we'll figure it out."

Chapter Five

Anxiously awaiting CJ and his dad, Skye opened the sliding glass door and walked out into the back yard. She did her best thinking while sitting on the edge of Poppy's dock, and she needed to think about who had written the threatening note.

The weathered dock was long with wide planks, and at the end a twenty-two-foot Sea Craft boat hung from its davits. Occasionally, her grandfather allowed her and CJ to take the boat out into deeper water to dive the reefs. CJ loved to drive it, but it was too expensive to operate on his meager budget, so they settled for the *Gator Bait* most of the time.

Skye sat quietly, thinking about the note, but she couldn't imagine who could have written it or why. Gaining no ground on solving that mystery, her mind drifted back to her visit last summer. She felt a warm glow as she thought about the adventures she and CJ had experienced. Her discovery that she could communicate with Flapper and Squeaky had overwhelmed her. It was still hard for her to believe, even though she knew it was true.

Then she remembered the horrific explosion on a houseboat and their rescue of Mr. Duncan, the rich oil executive who owned the boat. As a thank you, he had set up a trust fund at the University of Florida for both hers and CJ's college education, which had been a generous and pleasant surprise. John Duncan had told them that with the money in the trust fund they could attain the highest degree they wished to earn. Elizabeth Duncan, Mr. Duncan's young wife had been indicted for voluntary manslaughter, which had sent her to prison for ten years. She had hired a thug to set the explosion, and unfortunately for him, he had also died in the explosion.

And, of course, there was Indian Key, where CJ miraculously had been rescued from drowning by the spirit of an Indian chief.

Her mind started whirling with thoughts of what this summer's adventures would bring. *I just hope I don't get in as much trouble as I did last summer. I was afraid that Poppy would tell Mom and Dad, and they wouldn't let me come back down here. But on the day I left for home, Poppy whispered to me that it would be our secret, so I knew he hadn't told them. Poppy has always been there for me. I just want to make sure I don't ever do anything to hurt or disappoint him.*

As Skye waited for Mr. Jansen and CJ to arrive, she worried again about the note. Her mind raced with questions. *Who wrote it? Who delivered it? How do they know where I live? What is their connection to the gold necklace and the Marquesas Keys? Does the gold we found put Poppy in danger too?* The more she thought about it, the more uncomfortable she became. She finally decided that she might once again have gotten her and CJ, and maybe even Poppy, into something that could be dangerous.

Skye leaned back with her arms extended behind her and looked out to the horizon and the mangroves that lay in the distance. Suddenly, she saw a brown pelican gliding inches above the water. *Flapper*! she thought with excitement as she jumped up from the dock. Her heart raced with anticipation, happy to see her old friend.

The bird gained altitude, turned in her direction and drew closer. *There's Skye!* he thought, excited to see his human friend from last summer. *I had hoped she might be back down for her vacation by now. It's been so long since I've seen her.* Having no concept of time, Flapper had checked Poppy's house continually since Skye had left at the end of last summer, hoping he would see her there again. He had even lowered himself to ask, "that dolphin," Squeaky, if he had seen her. *To be honest,* Flapper thought, *I don't really care for him because he's such a show-off. But he is always there when Skye needs him, so I guess I'll just have to put up with him.*

"Flapper," Skye yelled, "over here!"

Last summer, without the phenomenon of her unique ability to communicate with Flapper and Squeaky, both she and CJ most likely would be dead. The pelican and the dolphin had saved their lives. The two had become friends of Skye and CJ, and she had looked forward so much to seeing them again. Ten months was a long time. Waiting at home in Connecticut, she hadn't thought summer vacation would ever come.

Flapper rocked his wings back and forth. He made a steep right turn, swooped down, and then landed on a piling close to Skye.

"My goodness, it's been such a long time," Skye smiled. She walked over, took Flapper's face in both hands, and kissed his beak.

"I've flown by here so many times hoping to see you, Skye. When did you get back? I talked to Squeaky last night, and he said that you and CJ were out at those islands where that glittery stuff is."

Putting aside her fears about losing her ability to communicate with Flapper, Skye quickly answered the bird. "I arrived here the night before last, and CJ and I were out there yesterday. You should see the gorgeous gold chain we found! It has a huge emerald surrounded by diamonds, and the chain alone weighs over a pound."

"A pound? I guess that's big, huh? I don't know what a pound is, but it must be a lot for you to be so happy. What's an emerald, Skye?"

Skye laughed and said, "Yeah, a pound is a lot for a gold chain. An emerald? It's a big green stone that costs a bunch of money, and the diamonds around it cost lots of money too."

"I guess money's good, huh? What exactly is money, Skye? What are you going to do with that gold chain?" Flapper was full of questions, and Skye patiently answered him.

"Yes, money is good." Skye smiled again at having to explain simple things to Flapper. "It buys a bunch of good stuff. I'm not sure yet what we are going to do with the chain. CJ and I have to talk about it and decide." She turned around when she heard the sound of CJ's VW pulling into the driveway.

Quickly standing up, she said, "I've got to run now, Flapper. CJ and his dad are here. Hey, I've got something else to tell you later. Stay in touch, okay? I may need your help."

Wonder what else she has to tell me? Knowing that he might be able to help Skye made him very happy. After all, she was his only human friend, and she could talk to him, which made him very happy. He liked CJ too. *He's nice to me, and if he is a friend of Skye's, he is a friend of mine.*

Chapter Six

Sitting on the drooping front porch of the old house, Jack Watson said, "So, what are we going to do with them?" he asked his partner Pete about the two kids who had found the gold. Sitting as far away from Pete as he could, he waited for Pete's answer.

"I guess we'll have to whack 'em," Pete Samuels answered in his heavy Conch accent. Born and raised in Key West, he had a deep Southern drawl with a slight Caribbean English patois. He reached down into an oversize ice chest and extracted the last cold beer. It was his eighth Miller Lite for the evening, and he wasn't feeling any pain.

As usual, Pete was grungy looking. His unshaved face was bright red from the heat and too much beer. His hands looked like he hadn't washed them in a week, and he probably hadn't. Taking baths was low on Pete's list of things to do. His wrinkled plaid shorts were wet from sweat that had slowly dripped from his torn, soaked tee shirt. An offensive body odor emanated from him. Because of the complaints from the guards and inmates in prison, a doctor had been called in to examine him. Pete had been diagnosed with TMAU, a metabolic disorder causing him to smell like rotten seafood. Sometimes he even smelled like garbage. He had lived with it so long; he didn't even notice the smell. Unfortunately, everyone else did and stayed away. Jack was the only one who stuck around. Pete didn't bother to bathe much because he knew even if he did, he wouldn't smell any better.

Jack leaned back in his lawn chair, casually put his hand over his nose and mouth to draw a deep breath. *One good thing*, Jack thought, *at least today is Saturday, and sometimes Pete takes a bath on Saturday. It doesn't help much, but the odor is a little less offensive.*

"I ain't so sure that's such a good idea," Jack cautioned. "We start whacking kids and the cops'll git involved. We'll never git the gold if that happens."

Pete's lungs wheezed as he took another drag on his cigarette. "So what? I don't care if the cop's git involved. How will they know who got rid of 'em? Hey, if it makes you feel better, we can just beat the crap out of 'em, and they'll never wanna go back to the place where they found the gold."

Relieved, Jack said, "You remember the time I caught those kids robbing my lobster pots? I ain't seen 'em 'round here since then. Yes, siree, I taught 'em a good lesson." In truth, Jack had just run the kids off with threats. He hadn't even touched either of them. They were both about thirteen years old, and Jack could be mean if things didn't go his way. He didn't particularly care for kids, but he was glad that he had talked Pete into not killing the teens. He had done lots of bad things in his life, even robbed and shot a guy, but killing a kid wasn't something he would ever do, unless it was in self-defense. *It just ain't right*, he thought. *Even a thief like me's got morals.*

Pete hefted his heavy frame up from the truck bench seat that served as a sofa on his front porch. He turned his one good eye toward Jack. He had lost his other eye in a fight in prison. The inmate who had caused him to lose his eye had died mysteriously in his bunk during the night a few days later. The guards found no apparent signs of foul play, and no autopsy was done.

"You go out there tomorrow and keep an eye on our claim. I know it ain't official, but what's ours is ours. I ain't gonna let those punk kids steal my gold." He turned and walked through the front screen door, letting it slam behind him. He needed to get some more beer to put in the cooler.

His gold? I thought we were partners. He had never completely trusted Pete, but he didn't want to give up his share of the gold either. Jack nodded to the slamming door and turned toward the setting sun. *Key West sure has beautiful sunsets,* he thought. Tourists came from all over the world just to enjoy and photograph this magnificent creation. Even the lowest dregs of society in Key West appreciated the view. Jack didn't realize it, but he and Pete were two of the lowest dregs of Key West society.

Jack had met Pete while they were in prison at Union Correctional Institute in Raiford, Florida, near Lawtey on US 301, where most everyone traveling through has been stopped for speeding at one time or another. It was known as Florida's number one speed trap by AAA since Waldo, formerly the number one speed trap, had dissolved its police force due to corruption by its police chief and another officer following an FDLE investigation.

Before Jack and Pete were incarcerated in prison, both had been young punks who thought they were untouchable. In separate robberies, one had shot a cop, and the other had shot a liquor store owner. Fortunately, neither victim died, but Pete and Jack were each sentenced to ten years for armed robbery.

When they got out of prison, Pete was heading back home to the Keys, and they joined up because Jack had no family to speak of and no other place to go.

Since they had returned to Key West, they had been robbing houses all over the Keys. So far, they had not been caught, but they had had several close calls. Obviously, from the way they lived, they weren't very successful in their chosen profession.

A couple weeks ago, Joe Spencer, another friend from prison, who had been in the cell next to Pete, had caught up with them. He had gotten out of prison a year after Pete and Jack had been released. He had been sentenced to five years for assault with a deadly weapon. They were all glad to be back together again.

After a night of heavy drinking, they had decided that the next morning they would go out on the water in the bonefish skiff.

Joe loved scuba diving. He had been born and raised in a little shack in the panhandle of Florida, close to Pensacola, where the beaches were like spun sugar, and the water was crystal clear. When his father wasn't drunk, he had taught Joe and his brother to scuba dive.

Though neither Pete nor Jack liked to scuba dive, they were happy to see Joe and decided to rent some scuba diving equipment for him. They fished a little and drank beer while Joe was diving. He hadn't been in the ocean since before he went to prison, and he was enjoying himself.

Late that afternoon, Joe came up to the surface yelling, "We struck it rich! We struck it rich!" as he held up a beautiful, heavy, wide gold bracelet. It was surrounded by rubies. All three men were ecstatic. Joe climbed into the boat and began dancing around. He told them he was going back down and would bring up all he could find. They agreed to split everything three ways. Joe went back down into the water, but Pete and Jack never saw him again.

Sitting in the boat and drinking beer, they waited over an hour for him to come back up, but he never did. Finally, realizing something had happened to Joe, they took the bracelet and headed back to the house, but not before marking the spot on a chart. The only thing they could figure out was that either a shark had gotten him, or he had drowned.

That's when the gold had become their gold. Both Pete and Jack had visions of all the money they would have when they got their hands on the gold that was in the water where Joe had been diving.

They needed to find another diver because neither of them could swim, much less scuba dive. They had been discretely asking around without giving out too much information and had been taking turns guarding the spot where Joe had brought up the bracelet. Pete was on guard duty watching their spot the day he had seen Skye bring up the necklace.

Jack sat quietly on the front porch stoop, looking to the west and thinking about the uncertainty that lay ahead. He was still worried that Pete might try to kill the two kids. *I don't trust Pete, and I don't like the prospect of gittin' rid of two kids. I wouldn't think twice if they were grown, but kids are a different story. They probably stumbled on our stash by accident. And besides, they'll never be able to find the spot again.*

Chapter Seven

Skye, CJ, and Flapper were seated at the end of the dock at Poppy's house, while Squeaky floated quietly in the warm lagoon below their feet. The north side of the island faced northwest, so for them to get a good view of the sunset they had to turn their heads to the left.

"Gosh, that's so beautiful," Skye said in awe of the picturesque sight. The beauty never ceased to amaze her.

Occasionally, Squeaky would playfully slap the water with his tail, splashing it onto the dock. His aim, which wasn't very good, mostly missed the threesome, but once in a while he'd luck out and spray them squarely in their faces.

"Why don't you tell that idiot to stop it? He's beginning to annoy me," Flapper complained.

"Now Flapper," Skye chided. "He's just happy to be with us."

CJ reached over and patted Flapper on the head, having an idea of what was happening. "It's okay, buddy. The spray feels good. It's hot out here."

After Skye had told Flapper what CJ had said, he had responded, still a little miffed, "Well, if you ask me, he looks like some sort of prehistoric creature that just likes to show off."

"Yeah, well, if you'd look down at your own reflection in the water, you'll see what a prehistoric creature really looks like," Squeaky snapped back.

"C'mon guys," Skye said. "Let's be nice to each other."

Changing the subject to ease the tension and calm her friends, she said, "Hey, what do you say we all go out to the Marquesas tomorrow and look for more gold?" She had told Flapper and Squeaky about their find, though neither of them was certain what it was nor understood the value.

"Sure, I'll go." Squeaky would do anything he could to make Skye happy. "Skye, what's gold?" he asked.

"Don't you know anything, you show-off?" Flapper snapped. Skye had told him what it was the day before, and his chest puffed out with importance because he knew something that Squeaky didn't.

Interrupting Flapper's tirade, Skye responded, "You know, Squeaky, it's that shiny yellow stuff that divers find in the water over in the Marquesas Keys."

"Oh, now I know what you're talking about. I can tell you where there's lots of that stuff," Squeaky said matter-of-factly. Of course, he didn't understand or care about the value, but if Skye wanted it, he would take her to it.

"Really?" Skye asked as she took hold of CJ's arm, her excitement rising. Her full attention was on Squeaky as she waited for his response.

"Yeah, but it's in deep water."

"What do you mean deep? The deepest water is only about thirty feet from here all the way to the Dry Tortugas," Skye said.

"Nope, not where I'm thinking," Squeaky answered.

"Well, just how deep is it?" Skye's curiosity and excitement heightened, and her heart raced in anticipation of his answer.

What is Squeaky saying to you, Skye? CJ wondered. He could tell from her conversation with Squeaky, and the look on her face, that something important was being discussed.

Squeaky rolled over and then righted himself. "It's about five times deeper than you think it is."

Skye did the math. "Five times thirty… Oh, my gosh, Squeaky! That's a hundred fifty feet! How do you know it's that deep?"

"By the pressure," Squeaky answered. "There's a crack in the bottom of the ocean, and that's where the yellow stuff is. What do you call that yellow stuff again?"

Impatient to get more information from him, she hurriedly said, "It's called gold, Squeaky. Do you mean to tell me that just off the Marquesas Keys there's a crack in the ocean floor, and no one has ever discovered it?"

"Well, I don't know about that because you're the only human I've ever been able to communicate with, but I can show you where it is," Squeaky answered, happy to see his friend so excited.

Skye looked at CJ. "Are you getting this?"

"I'm getting a little of it from what you're saying to Squeaky. I don't know what he's saying to you, though," CJ said, understanding that Squeaky was telling Skye something important. "Well," Skye said with authority, looking around at the others, "tomorrow we leave for the Marquesas. Is that okay with everybody?"

Here we go again. She asks and I follow. Wimp, he thought. "Sure, what time?" CJ asked. *How can I possibly tell Skye no?*

Though no one specifically asked him to join them, and he was still a little miffed at Squeaky for making Skye happy about the gold, Flapper said to her, "I might see you in the morning out on the water."

"Okay, Flapper. We should be out there pretty early. Come if you can." Flapper jumped from the piling, spread his wings, and took to the air.

Squeaky had given Skye some valuable information about the location of the gold. *I can't let that show-off get all the attention,* Flapper thought. He decided he would watch out for Skye and CJ anytime he could when they were in the water. Of course, he couldn't always be with them. *I can see a lot when I'm flying overhead, and I doubt that know-it-all will be around every time they're diving. They may need my help again this year like they did last year.* Satisfied with his decision, Flapper headed for his home in the mangroves.

Chapter Eight

Michael sat with Poppy at the island counter in the kitchen discussing the events of the previous day.

Michael was saying, "Poppy, I don't like the idea of our kids running off to the Marquesas Keys without any protection. What if they're confronted by the person who wrote the note? That person could be very dangerous, and the kids would be at their mercy. God only knows what someone like that is capable of doing, especially after writing that threatening message."

"I think we ought to find out who we're dealing with," Poppy said. "One of us should call Detective Callahan and fill him in on what's going on. Maybe he can find out who the note writer is. I'd feel better if Callahan was involved."

Michael reached into his pocket and pulled out his iPhone. "You're right. I'll give him a call," he said, hoping he had not deleted Callahan's number from last year. He had only seen Sean Callahan briefly a couple times in the past ten months.

His mind flashed back to CJ's miraculous rescue on Indian Key. Sean Callahan and Courtney Morgan had braved a storm to try to rescue Skye and CJ. *Yes, it was indeed a miracle*, he thought, remembering the sheer terror he and Maria had experienced, thinking they might lose him. And there was that unbelievable tale about being CJ being rescued by an Indian spirit that CJ finally convinced them was true, and which Callahan didn't deny.

So much had happened with CJ and Skye the past summer, but Michael knew he, Maria, and Poppy couldn't keep the kids on permanent restriction to keep them safe. They had to let them have fun, within limits, of course. He would talk to Callahan and see if he could find out any clues from the note. If they could find out who had written it, Callahan could put the creep behind bars where he belonged.

Michael sighed with relief as he located the detective's number in his phone. *Thank goodness I still have his number.* He pressed the dial button.

Moments later a voice answered. "This is Callahan. How are you doing, Michael?"

Of Irish descent on his father's side and English on his mother's, Detective Callahan was tall and well-built with thick black hair, light blue eyes, and very fair skin.

"How did you know it was me, Sean?" Michael questioned.

"It was easy. It's called *caller ID*. I'm not psychic, Michael," Callahan said and laughed. "What can I do for you? Don't tell me it's about those kids," he said and laughed again. "What have they gotten themselves into this time?"

"Yeah, it's about CJ and Skye," Michael sighed. "I need your help to make sure they don't get into any trouble. They seem to attract it like a magnet, don't they?"

When Michael had told Callahan about the teen's planned trip, the police officer smiled to himself. He looked forward to seeing the two of them again. They were good kids.

After talking with Sean Callahan, Michael had decided that he would check on CJ and Skye as much as he could and try to keep them close until they found the person who had written the note.

Michael had spent years with the National Security Agency, and he trusted his instincts. Right now his instincts were telling him that the kids could be in real danger.

Callahan had told him that he would check the note for fingerprints and see if he could come up with anything.

Lunch was always good at the Green Turtle Inn at Mile Marker 81.2 in Islamorada. It had been in business since the mid-1940s. After Hurricane Wilma in 2005, the restaurant had been rebuilt and had morphed into the landmark it is today. The white building, with green trim and covered with a tin roof, served breakfast, lunch, and dinner to the locals as well as travelers to the Keys.

It was one of CJ's preferred eating places. All the food was delicious, but his favorite dish was their turtle soup. The restaurant was always busy, but CJ and Skye managed to get seated.

The cute, curly-haired server brought the appetizer and drinks they had ordered. Skye sat across from CJ, sipping a Coca-Cola in the original green bottle, while CJ nursed an A&W Root Beer in its original brown bottle. The server returned to take their food order and quickly disappeared. The restaurant was crowded as it usually was at lunch and dinner.

Both sat in silence, disappointed that they had not been able to go to the Marquesas Keys. A quick moving front had come through the area during the night, and heavy winds had stirred up the water bottom, making visibility less than fifteen feet. They would just have to wait until tomorrow.

"Do you think Squeaky can find the trench?" Skye asked.

After eating nearly all of his turtle soup, CJ propped his chin in the palm of his hand, his elbow resting on the table. "I don't have any reason to doubt him. If he says it's there, then I believe it's there."

Pleased at his response, Skye sat across from CJ, fantasizing about finding a treasure chest full of gold.

As he finished his last spoonful of the tasty soup, the server brought their hamburgers and fries. CJ was already dashing his fries with salt and ketchup before the woman turned to leave.

"Gracious, you must be hungry," Skye smiled.

"Yep, I'm starved."

Skye and CJ did not notice the dirty-looking, dangerous, heavyset man come through the restaurant's front door.

Pete Samuels was passing by the Green Turtle, heading south to Marathon on the Overseas Highway, when he glanced over and saw the yellow Volkswagen Thing parked next to the building. He knew it was the kid's car. The kid who had his gold.

Without thinking, he spun his dilapidated van around and headed back up the road. He would soon regret his mistake. Parking in the lot, he lifted his heavy bulk from his truck and walked to the front door.

Samuels stood in the doorway looking around when he spied the young couple sitting at a table next to a window at the back of the room. His anger flared as he hiked up his wrinkled, dirty, orange plaid shorts and moved toward their table, absentmindedly tugging his much too small purple shirt over his flabby belly.

Within two seconds, he was looming over CJ and Skye. His strong body odor, bad breath, and rotten teeth made Skye wince when she looked up at him. She felt like she would never feel clean again. *Who in the word is that?* she wondered. Suddenly, her heart began racing in fear. *Could this be the man who left the note on Poppy's door?* Her big blue eyes opened wide in fright as she placed her hand over her mouth and swallowed back a scream.

CJ froze when he saw the unkempt, one-eyed man. His nose wrinkled at the overpowering odor. *Menacing and evil* were the stranger's description that came to CJ's mind. *Who is this guy? What could he possibly want with Skye and me?* Suddenly he knew. *The gold. It's got something to do with the gold.*

Samuels bent over and rested his large, greasy-looking hand on the table in front of CJ's plate. His fingernails were embedded with dirt, and his breath reeked so badly that CJ had to turn his face away. Samuel's left hand fell into his pocket as if he were holding something.

A gun maybe? CJ was sure he didn't want to see it, if that was what the huge guy had in his shorts.

"I ain't gonna say this but once," he said menacingly, "you kids had better stay away from them Keys, or I'll have your heads. You hear me?"

The restaurant was very crowded, and people had begun to stare at the fat, ugly, smelly man, wondering what he was saying to the teens. Skye and CJ didn't look like the type of youngsters who would associate with someone like Pete Samuels.

Michael Jansen stood at the entrance to the restaurant, watching the big man. He eased through the door and walked quietly toward the table.

Samuels roughly grabbed CJ by the top of his tee shirt at the same time Michael hit Samuels with all his might at the base of his head with his balled-up fist. The momentum knocked Samuels forward, and he landed on CJ. Both men went crashing to the floor, splintering CJ's chair. It was difficult to tell who came out worse, CJ or Samuels. Probably CJ, because Samuels had landed on top of him, and his reeking, heavy body made CJ feel like he was suffocating.

Skye screamed as she jumped from her chair, covering her mouth with her hand. "Oh, my gosh!" she yelled, her hands shaking as she grabbed Michael's arm. "Mr. Jansen, did you hear what that guy said? He was going to hit CJ!"

CJ fought to get out from under the dead weight when Michael reached down, grabbed CJ's arm and pulled him up. Half dazed, CJ struggled to his feet and finally regained his balance.

The man sitting at the table next to Skye and CJ thought, I'll *bet that's the boy's father. I was getting ready to get up and help the kid out myself. How did a creep like that get into this nice restaurant?*

Holding on to CJ, Michael looked over at Skye, and taking her hand, he said, "C'mon, guys, let's get out of here."

Chapter Nine

Back at Poppy's house, Michael sat at the kitchen island nursing his right hand. "Man, oh man. I think I broke it!" Michael moaned, rubbing his scraped knuckles and his swollen hand. He held his right hand up against his chest, his left hand covering his right, slightly rocking back and forth and fighting the pain, which seemed to have worsened in the past few minutes. *It's been a long time since I did something like that,* he thought. *It hurts like heck, but it sure felt good to knock the stinking thug out.*

"Let us take you to the emergency room, Mr. Jansen," offered Skye. "It looks awfully swollen. You may have broken it. It should probably be in a cast."

"Nah, it'll be okay," Michael said, a little embarrassed at his moaning and groaning.

"Thanks, Dad," CJ said, and then he walked around the kitchen island where Michael sat. He reached up and put his hand on his father's shoulder. "We'd have been in a heap of trouble if you hadn't showed up. That guy was big and mean, and his body odor was awful. Did you smell him? And his teeth, or what was left of them, were all rotten." Just thinking about the guy made CJ shiver. *What would we have done if dad hadn't showed up?*

"Yeah, he was pretty ripe," Michael answered, his nose wrinkling, remembering the stench.

Always a good host, Poppy brought a fresh pot of espresso to the table. "Y'all have a cup of this strong brew. CJ, you look like you could use a cup."

Smelling the aroma, CJ reached for a cup. "Want a cup, Dad?"

"Yeah, go ahead and pour your old man a cup."

To everyone's surprise, the doorbell rang.

"Who in the world could that be?" Poppy groaned, leaving the table to answer the door.

All eyes followed Poppy, curious to see who was ringing the doorbell.

When Poppy got to the door, he looked through the peephole. His forehead furrowed when he saw who it was.

"Hey, Detective Callahan," he said, opening the door.

"Hello, Mr. Hudson. Is Michael here by chance? I need to have a little chat with him and the kids."

"Sure," Poppy answered as he motioned to Callahan to come inside.

"Would you like a cup of fresh brew?" Poppy asked.

"No thanks, Mr. Hudson," the detective said.

"Detective," Michael said as Callahan took a seat at the kitchen island. "What brings you here?" He knew exactly why Sean Callahan had come.

Skye and CJ sat in silence, both wondering what was going to happen.

"There's a guy named Pete Samuels in the North Shore emergency room. He's suffering from a concussion, and God only knows what kinds of neck injuries. You wouldn't happen to know anything about that, would you Michael?"

Michael looked Callahan straight in his eyes. "As a matter of fact, I do, Detective."

Callahan glanced over at Skye. "What were you two doing in the Green Turtle?"

Skye lowered her eyes. "We were having lunch when this brute of a man came over to our table and started threatening us about going over to the Marquesas Keys."

Callahan's voice softened. "What did he say, honey?"

"Well," CJ started to respond.

"I'm not asking you right now, CJ. I'm asking Skye. I'll get around to you in a minute," Callahan admonished. He was immediately sorry for the brusque way he had spoken to CJ when he saw CJ's face turn red with embarrassment. He had forgotten how embarrassed he was one time as a teenager when his father spoke sharply to him in front of his girlfriend. He felt humiliated. *I'll have to watch that in the future*, he thought.

Skye was nervous and didn't want to say the wrong thing. "He said he'd have our heads if he ever caught us over there again. That's when he grabbed CJ by his tee shirt."

"Do you think it has something to do with the gold necklace?" Callahan looked at CJ for a response. Michael had told Callahan about the gold chain when he had spoken to him on the phone about the menacing message on Poppy's door.

"It has to be connected, sir. I think he's the guy that left the note on Poppy's front door."

"Sure you don't want some coffee, Detective?" Poppy asked. The tension in the room was palpable.

"No thanks, Mr. Hudson," Callahan answered.

"Michael, you know I can arrest you for assault and battery, don't you?"

Michael stood up and pushed his stool back. "Look, Callahan, all I was doing was protecting these two kids from being assaulted by that big hoodlum. As a father, I have every right, and you know it. You need to be over at the hospital right now arresting that creep."

"Well," Callahan said as he stood, "let's just hope this guy Samuels is okay. From what we know of him, this isn't the first time he's tried bullying someone. He has a rap sheet a mile long. He got out of prison about a year and a half ago for armed robbery. He shot a man, but the guy lived. If he regains consciousness, we'll question him about CJ and Skye, but cons like him don't usually talk. He could just be a big bully. Maybe he saw CJ and

Skye with the gold necklace when they got back to the marina. It could have been coincidental. Maybe he figured he would go out there where the kids had been to see if there was any more gold. Who knows? I can't arrest him until I find out if he's going to survive Michael's right fist." A little smile crossed his face.

"We spoke with several customers at the Green Turtle. No one heard what he said to CJ, except a guy at the table next to theirs, who told us that he was getting ready to get up and hit the guy himself. The problem is I can't arrest the creep for trash talking," he told the group. "If he had actually assaulted you," he said, looking at CJ, "that would be different, but your dad sent him to the hospital before he could do that, and it's a good thing your dad got there when he did."

Callahan stopped short and turned to Skye and CJ. "You kids had better be careful. I'm not saying you can't go there, but if I were you two, I'd stay away from those Keys, at least until we find out more about Samuels. He could be dangerous."

Callahan turned and headed for the door. Knowing Skye, and in spite of his warning, he knew there was no way she was going to stay away from the Marquesas Keys, and he also knew that CJ would follow. *I'll have to keep an eye on them and have someone watch Samuels when he gets out of the hospital to make sure they don't get hurt. They're fine kids, and I don't want anything to happen to them.*

Chapter Ten

Michael had insisted CJ accompany him to Tavernier Creek Marina to pick up a few boat parts he needed. CJ had been reluctant, impatient to get out on the water with Skye, but after a stern look from his father, he complied.

When they were ready to leave the house, CJ followed Michael out through the front door, thinking it strange they didn't go out through the garage as they normally did. He also thought it odd that his father hadn't wished him a happy seventeenth birthday. In fact, neither his mother nor his father had, and they both usually made a big deal about his birthdays. *I guess they forgot. Bummer.*

CJ sat in silence during the short ride up the highway to the marina. Michael made a left turn at Mile Marker 90, which was the entrance to their destination.

"How long do you think we'll be, Dad?" CJ asked. Eager to get going, he was sure Skye was anxiously awaiting his arrival at Poppy's house. Like him, she couldn't wait to get out on the water. He always looked forward to seeing her every day.

"Oh, this shouldn't take very long, Son." Michael smiled at CJ.

At the marina, Michael opened the front door for CJ and followed him into the parts department.

"Good morning, Mr. Jansen. Morning, CJ. You folks have a nice day, okay?" The sales rep smiled at the father and son. "Sure will," Michael responded as he continued to walk through the parts department and then out onto the docks.

CJ glanced down the dock and saw the boat he had been dreaming about ever since he had seen one at the Miami International Boat Show. "Hey, Dad, look at that Mako 204CC. Wow!" He began walking down the dock toward the boat. Michael followed, a little smile playing at the corners of his mouth. The Mako was loaded. It had a GPS, VHS radio, CB radio, depth finder, spotlight, and most importantly, a Bimini Top. The transom sported a new hundred fifty horsepower Mercury engine. "Think they'll mind if I step aboard?" CJ asked. "I'll be careful." *This is the most beautiful boat I've ever seen. One day I hope to have one just like this. It'll take a long time to save enough money, but it sure will be worth it.*

"I'm sure they won't mind, Son. Go ahead."

CJ's eyes widened in appreciation as he stepped down onto the deck of the Mako. Glancing up, he noticed a small group of people walking toward the boat. He recognized his mother walking alongside Skye, followed by Poppy, and his old friend Cap. All had broad smiles on their faces. *What are they doing here?* he wondered.

Ten feet from the boat, everyone broke out in song, singing happy birthday to CJ.

Puzzled, CJ watched each one of the group step aboard the Mako. Each one gave him a hug.

"Happy Birthday, Son. She's all yours," Michael laughed, reaching out and handing the key to CJ.

Stunned, CJ sat down on the bench seat, his hands on his cheeks, and his open mouth beaming in disbelief. "Oh my God, I can't believe it. I can't believe it," he kept repeating.

Skye sat down beside him and took CJ's hand. "Happy birthday, CJ," she smiled.

He reached over and gave her a hug. "Thanks, Skye. Isn't she beautiful?"

Skye just smiled at CJ, knowing how happy he was at receiving the beautiful boat for his birthday. "Now you don't have to borrow my Sea Craft," Poppy joked, gently punching him in the ribs.

"Oh, by the way, there's a trailer for her out in the parking lot. It's all set up and ready to go," Michael said grinning. *It's been so hard to keep the boat a secret from CJ, but it was certainly worth it,* he decided.

Maria bent down and gave her son a big hug. "Now, you and Skye please be careful with this thing," she warned. "Promise me?"

CJ looked up at his Mom. "Yes, Mom, I'll be careful," he said, reaching up to give his mother a kiss on the cheek. *I've got the best parents in the world,* he thought.

Cap took CJ by the shoulders. In his crusty old voice, he said, "Congratulations, Son. I think you just outgrew your little McKee Craft."

"What now?" Skye asked, looking at CJ.

He looked at her and grinned, "Let's load this baby on the trailer and head for Key West."

Chapter Eleven

Pete Samuels was furious. The longer he lay in the hospital bed, the madder he got. The neck brace he wore limited his mobility, but it sure didn't limit the curse words coming from his mouth.

Jack Watson straddled a straight back chair with his arms over the back across from Pete's bed. He had spent the entire morning listening to Pete's ramblings. He ranted on and on about how he was going to kill the guy. If he ever got near the jerk, he was going to break his neck with his bare hands. The diatribe continued for what seemed like hours.

"He sucker-punched me from behind," Pete grumbled. "I didn't even know he was there. That ain't right. It just ain't right."

"Whatcha gonna do about it?" Jack asked with a sly smile on his face. He knew he was egging Pete on, but he wasn't worried because Pete couldn't punch him even if he wanted to.

"Well, maybe I just might pay that little girl a visit one lonely night and scare her. That'll teach all of 'em." A nurse entered the room.

"Hey, honey, maybe we could go out one night on a moonlight cruise," Pete teased.

"Not in your lifetime," she shot back. *If he were the last man on earth, I would still say NO! I can't imagine this guy touching me,* she thought. Shivering in disgust, she couldn't wait to get out of the room, but as a nurse she had to at least act professionally.

"Mr. Samuels, you can go home now. The doctor said to keep that neck brace on for another seven days, and then he wants to see you in his office. His scheduler will call you with the appointment time."

Pete looked at the nurse in disgust. *Who is she to turn me down? She ain't as hot as she thinks she is.* He grunted as he lifted his two hundred forty pounds up from the bed. "Let's get the heck outta here," he said, wincing as he moved his head to the side.

Michael worried about CJ and Skye's safety, particularly out on the ocean. *These southern waters are the home of drug smugglers and pirates, and God only knows what would happen if they ran across some shady characters while they were out on CJ's boat.* After what happened with Samuels and CJ, Michael was worried about the teens going out on the water. *What if the guy is watching them?*

Michael had taught CJ how to shoot a twenty-five caliber Raven Arms. With Detective Callahan's help, he had managed to get CJ a carry permit even though he was only seventeen. After all, the previous year the Monroe County Sheriff had made Skye and CJ Honorary Junior Deputies. *Now*, Michael thought, *it's time to move him up to a little more firepower.*

Michael had called his old friend Sonny Mitchell with the National Security Agency and asked his advice about the kind of weapon CJ should have. Michael remembered the arsenal Sonny had shown up with when they had gone to rescue Maria from the kidnappers the year before. Sonny knew all about guns, and Michael trusted his judgment. He recommended a forty-five caliber Colt XSE automatic. Sonny had told Michael would stop an elephant in its tracks.

What in the world are those kids into this summer that Michael wants CJ to have a gun like that? Sonny thought maybe it was time for him to cruise down to the Keys and see his old friend.

Michael stood at the counter in Carbone's Custom Firearms in Key West. He stared down at the cold, deadly looking Colt XSE. "I'll take it," he said to the sales clerk".

Chapter Twelve

Still half asleep and yawning, CJ stumbled down the thirteen steps leading into the foyer. When he reached the hall, he glanced down at his watch, which showed 6:38 a.m. The aroma of fresh coffee perked up his senses. *It sure smells good*, he thought, taking a deep breath as he made his way into the kitchen. Like his dad, CJ needed at least one cup of coffee in the morning to wake up. *Two would be even better.* He smiled to himself.

Maria stood next to the stove. "Morning, sweetheart," she said lovingly. "Are you ready for another big day?"

"Yeah, Mom, Skye and I are going back to the Marquesas Keys to look for more gold." He pulled out a chair at the breakfast nook and slouched down into it. He stared at his mom. *She is the most beautiful woman in the world,* he thought. In white shorts and a red tank top, her shiny, black wavy hair hung loosely over her shoulders as she turned to CJ, offering him a cup of fresh black coffee. CJ seemed unaware of it, but he favored his mother. His wavy hair and his eyes were both dark like Maria's. His dad had sandy blond hair and light eyes from his Scandinavian ancestors. CJ got his height from his dad's side. Even though Michael was only five ten, Michael's father had been six feet three inches tall.

The door leading from the garage into the kitchen opened as Michael stepped inside. When he saw Maria standing by CJ, he smiled and walked over to give Maria a hug and a peck on her cheek. "Morning, sweetheart."

"What do you have there?" CJ asked curiously, looking at the box Michael held in his hand.

"Oh, just a little something," Michael answered. "Why don't you run upstairs and bring me your Raven. I've got something to trade with you."

CJ had a questioning look on his face, but without a word he got up from his chair and disappeared.

Michael turned and gave Maria another hug. "I love you so much," he said, looking deep into her eyes. She put her head against his chest and squeezed him hard. "And I love you too, honey." Maria knew that what they shared was unique and could never be challenged by anyone. Michael had given her everything she could ever have wanted. For a brief moment, she thought of their first son, Jeffrey, who at five years old had been struck by a police car, killing him instantly nearly twenty-two years ago. She would always miss Jeffrey, but she was very happy that she and Michael had been blessed with another wonderful son like CJ.

Two minutes later, CJ came downstairs, and he was slightly embarrassed when he saw his parents hugging. He felt as if he were interrupting them.

Reluctantly, Michael broke away from Maria and took CJ's pistol. Ejecting the clip and sliding the chamber open, he found it empty. *Good*, he thought.

CJ sat down in his chair to finish his coffee. Michael pushed the box in front of his son.

CJ looked up at his dad with a question in his eyes.

"Go ahead, open it," Michael smiled. "Your mother and I discussed it, and we both agree that you should keep this in your boat at all times, especially with everything that has happened since you and Skye found the gold."

CJ began gently opening the box, and then a smile crossed his face. "Whoa, Dad! Is this for me?"

"It's from your mom for your birthday."

Maria smiled and kissed CJ on the top of his head. "You be careful with that thing, okay?" she cautioned. Maria had lost one son to an accident years ago, and she didn't want to lose another one.

"I've been thinking," CJ said as he pulled the VW into Garrison Bite Marina, "maybe we should rent a space here to dock the boat instead of dragging it back and forth all the way from Islamorada. It would certainly be easier on the Thing," he said, looking over at Skye.

"That sounds good to me."

CJ pulled the Volkswagen onto the boat ramp, straightened the Gator Bait and began backing the trailer into the water.

In the back corner of the parking lot, someone in an old white van watched and waited.

Chapter Thirteen

Pete Samuels sat behind the steering wheel in the rusty white van. His neck was still in the brace, and he was still ticked off about it. He held an ancient pair of binoculars close to his eyes with both hands. A cigarette dangled between two grimy fingers in his left hand. He sat there watching CJ unload the new *Gator Bait* from its trailer. Pete's massive bulk against the steering wheel pressed his stomach too snuggly, which irritated the heck out of him. It felt as if it was cutting him in two.

"Looks like the kid bought a new boat," Pete mumbled.

Jack Watson sat in the front next to Pete. At just over six feet, Jack had slouched his hundred and eighty pounds down in his seat, thinking the kids wouldn't see him. He didn't stop to think that the van was too far away and parked under a shade tree, making it impossible for anyone to see inside the van.

"Yeah," Jack agreed. "His parents must have plenty of money. That boat must cost at least seventy-five grand loaded. Sure must be nice. Maybe we oughta hit their house. We could probably make a ton of money. They probably got at least three flat screen TV's and all kinds of electronics, plus the kid's mama most likely has a ton of fancy jewelry."

"Don't worry 'bout that. We're gonna make a fortune on the gold. Just keep your mind on that, and we're gonna have more money than we could ever spend." Just thinking about all the money made Pete's neck hurt a little less. He stretched out his arm, reached for the ignition and started the van. He jerked the gearshift into drive and pulled out of his parking spot. He slowly moved the van around the marina and finally came to a stop next to a bonefish skiff.

"Keep an eye on 'em, and call me if they find anything," Pete ordered. "Just be sure to keep your distance. I don't want 'em to see either of us."

Jack sighed as he opened the door and slid from the van. *Why do I have to be the one to go out in the boat and follow 'em? All Pete will do is go back to the house and drink beer. Must be nice.* For the time being, Jack knew he had to do what Pete told him to do. If he didn't, he might end up on the sharp end of Pete's knife. He had seen Pete when he was mad, and he didn't want that nasty temper turned on him.

CJ was thankful that his dad had switched out all of his equipment from the McKee Craft to the new Mako. As he and Skye slowly eased out of the marina, he turned on his GPS and pulled up the coordinates stored in the unit's memory. A real-life image popped up on the screen, and then a straight line appeared showing the course and distance to the spot where he and Skye had found the gold chain.

"Twenty-one point two miles. That'll take about twenty-five minutes," he said to Skye, glancing over at her. CJ was struck again by the change in her since the past summer. *She's so beautiful.* His heart did a flip flop.

As usual, Skye had her hair pulled up into a ponytail, held snuggly by her scrunchie. Dark sunglasses covered her big blue eyes, which matched the light blue two-piece bathing suit that accentuated her tiny but curvy shape. Touches of pale pink gloss on her lips made CJ yearn to lean over and kiss her. He had to force himself not to reach out and touch her. *She'd probably knock the bejesus out of me if I did.*

CJ drove the Mako like a spirited racehorse. The heavier boat rode the medium seas with ease. "This is nice"" Skye shouted above the wind and whine of the powerful Mercury engine.

CJ looked over at her and grinned. As he looked down at the GPS, he saw that they were going forty-seven miles an hour. They would arrive at the dive spot in twelve minutes.

He eased back on the throttle as they approached their destination. Finally, when the GPS showed that they were within a few feet of the spot, he put the engine in neutral and coasted to a stop.

Skye pushed the anchor over the side and let out about a hundred feet of line. In the distance, CJ noticed a small skiff moving fast, but it disappeared to the north of the mangroves. *Wonder where that guy's going in such a hurry?*

Skye moved back to the stern and began fishing out her dive gear from the storage locker next to the gunwale. She heard some high-pitched squeaks and looked over the side.

"Squeaky, you came!" Skye said, happy to see her old friend.

CJ was shocked when he saw Squeaky. *How did he get here so fast?* He knew dolphins were speedy, but he didn't know they could swim that fast.

Squeaky seemed all excited at seeing them. He came up to the edge of the boat and propped his snout on the low transom. "I figured you would be here," he said to Skye. "I wanted to show you the big crack in the deep water. I told you I would."

"How far from here is it?" Skye questioned.

"Not too far. You can follow me in the boat."

Skye looked over at CJ. "He wants to show us where the crevice is located."

CJ patted the dolphin on the head. "Good boy, Squeaky," CJ said with excitement in his voice. Even though he was a little apprehensive about the dive, the thought of finding more gold sounded wonderful.

Skye told Squeaky they would follow him.

"Good," Squeaky said, "let's go." And he swam off with the Gator Bait following closely behind.

Chapter Fourteen

Sweating from the heat as the boat slowed, Jack Watson eased the skiff around the north side of the Marquesas Keys. Once out of sight of the teens, he pulled back on the power and slowly made his way around to the west side of the mangroves. A shallow, narrow channel snaked its way inside the shrubs and trees, which afforded him a barrier from prying eyes. Gradually, he made his way to the south side of Mooney Harbor Key, where he drove the bow of his skiff up onto a small, sandy beach.

Walking forward in the skiff to the bow, he jumped ashore. Continuing his trek, he made his way up to the top of a sandy knoll, thick with some type scraggly brush, until his eyes could barely see the Mako out on the water. Surprised, he watched a dolphin put its head on the transom of the boat. A little puzzled, he thought, *Looks like the two kids are talking with that thing. That's ridiculous! There's no way they could be talking with the dolphin.* Lowering the binoculars and shaking his head at such a ludicrous thought, he finally put the binoculars up to his eyes again and continued observing the teens.

CJ looked down at his GPS. Squeaky was moving along at just under twenty-five miles an hour. *It's amazing how fast dolphins can swim.*

Skye noticed the water slowly changing color. "Hey, it's getting deeper," she shouted to CJ.

Suddenly, the water changed from light brown to what looked almost purple. Squeaky stopped, and before CJ realized it, he was almost on top of the dolphin. Seeing the boat rapidly moving toward him, Squeaky quickly dove deep to avoid being run over. As the boat came to a stop, he came up behind it, making all kinds of squeaking noises and shaking his head back and forth. It was obvious to Skye that Squeaky was very upset.

"Sorry, Squeaky!" CJ shouted, above the engine.

"What are you trying to do? Kill me?" Squeaky squeaked at CJ. Of course, CJ couldn't understand what Squeaky was saying, but he had a pretty good idea.

Skye jumped into the water and swam over to Squeaky, who was having a full-blown temper tantrum. She put her arms around his neck. "CJ is so sorry, Squeaky," she said soothingly. "You know he wouldn't hurt you for anything in the world."

Squeaky backed off a little, but he was still upset. "Just tell him to be more careful, okay? I don't want to end up shark food this morning."

"I'll tell him," she said, reassuringly. "Is this the spot?" she asked Squeaky.

"Yeah, this is it. It's pretty dark down there."

"Thanks, my friend," Skye gently said. "I owe you a huge bucket of fresh fish."

"Okay," Squeaky said, still a little miffed, but thinking about the yummy fish he would soon be eating. "I have to get back to my pod now." That said, Squeaky turned and headed back to Key West. *That was a close call. The thought of being shark food isn't something I want to find out about first-hand.*

Skye swam back to the boat. CJ lowered the dive ladder and gave her his hand, helping her aboard.

Handing Skye a towel, he said, "I'd like to troll around a while so I can get a feel for how wide and long this thing is."

"That's a good idea," Skye agreed, wiping her face.

CJ punched in their new coordinates on the GPS and then pushed the engine into drive. He slowly began moving the boat forward as he watched the depth finder. The depth changed from thirty to a hundred forty-three feet within a matter of seconds. And then less than a minute later, it was back to twenty-five feet.

"It's a pretty narrow crevice," CJ said.

"Let's see how long it is," Skye suggested.

"Okay." He turned the boat around. When he reached a depth of one hundred feet, he made a ninety-degree turn, trying to maintain that depth. Less than five minutes later, they were back at twenty-five feet.

"That's quite a crack in the ocean," Skye said.

"Yeah, I've never dived that far down before, not even with a tank," CJ confessed. *The water sure does look dark*, he thought, not looking forward to what he knew Skye would say.

"Well, I'm going to give it a try," Skye smiled, looking directly into CJ's eyes.

"Are you crazy, Skye? God only knows what's down there." CJ's voice showed his concern.

"Oh, don't be silly. If it's too deep, I'll turn back."

"I'm not comfortable with you doing this, Skye." *I can't let her dive that deep, but how can I stop her? Something could happen to her.* He shivered at the thought.

"Don't worry. I'll be okay," Skye said, reaching for her swim fins.

"Skye, wait!" Before CJ realized what was happening, Skye was in the water. She took several long breaths, paused, and on the third one she held her breath, bent forward, kicked her feet into the air, and was gone beneath the surface.

"Skye, no! Wait, please!" he said, scared for her and frustrated that he couldn't stop her.

CJ was shocked that she had the courage to dive into the deep crevice, not knowing what might lie in the dark depths. He wasn't sure he could do it. *Lord, please keep her safe.*

———————

The water is crystal clear, Skye thought as she went deeper and deeper. At thirty feet, she hit a wall of cold water and had to keep clearing her ears as she went deeper. Water pressure pushed against her facemask, forcing her to blow air out of her nose to equalize it. Shivering, she wrapped her arms around her shoulders, trying to ward off the cold. At this depth, her lungs were half the size they were topside. The deeper she swam, the darker and colder it became.

Suddenly, Skye felt uncomfortable in the alien environment. Blackness surrounded her, and she had never felt so alone. *What am I doing down here? What in the world was I thinking?* She decided to give it up and head for the boat. Below her was nothing except a deep black hole that was giving her the creeps.

Skye stopped her descent and looked up, which revealed tiny rays of light penetrating down through the water. She kicked hard toward the light. Her lungs ached from lack of oxygen. *I need to get to the surface now*! she thought. She knew that just needing air wasn't the only thing that had caused her to want to get back up to the boat. It was the first time in her life she had ever been afraid when she was in the water. The black hole looked menacing, and she was felt very threatened. But why?

Skye had no idea how long she had been down. She only knew she had to get some fresh air, or she would surely die in the cold, dark abyss. *Something just doesn't feel right down here.* She felt a shiver of fear rush up her spine. *What's that about?* Her heart began pounding, and her lungs were starving for oxygen. As she raced toward the light, her ears began hissing as the compressed air in her Eustachian tubes expanded when the outside pressure decreased. She felt dizzy as she approached safety.

About sixty feet below her, she suddenly felt the force of the water moving her, pulling at her, pulling her down. *What's happening?* Her heart felt like it skipped, and then it picked up more speed.

Glancing down, through her peripheral vision, Skye saw a glimpse of something that was enormous and moving very fast. *What in the world is that?* She quickly realized she didn't want to find out. She just wanted to get back to the safety of the boat and CJ. Terrified and unable to control her fear, she gasped, and water filled her mouth as she saw the huge, dark thing begin rising toward her.

Not looking down again, Skye started kicking so hard and fast that when she broke the surface, her body shot three feet into the air. Moments before she passed out, her lungs filled with fresh air. Gulp after gulp, her body began to stabilize. Her heart was racing in fear as she grabbed at CJ's arms, and he maneuvered her toward the swim ladder.

What seemed an eternity later, she was on the *Gator Bait*. *What was that? It was coming after me,* she thought, still frightened, her teeth chattering. Being very intuitive, Skye knew that whatever it was had wanted to hurt her. Or worse. She was in shock, and she kept staring down at the water, wondering if the enormous creature would pop up next to the boat and grab her.

Chapter Fifteen

The sky began to darken, and the wind started to picked up. *It looks like we're going to get some weather,* CJ thought. Pale and still trembling, Skye sat on the center console seat with a towel wrapped around her shoulders. She had not spoken a word since she had come out of the water. Now and then a shiver encompassed her, not so much from being cold, but from fear and thoughts of what she had just been through in the water. Her hands were still shaking from the rush of adrenalin as she had kicked in a panic to the surface.

Trying to calm herself, she sat quietly, debating whether or not to tell CJ about the huge thing she had seen. It frightened her just to think about it, but she was trying to rationalize her experience. *Did it really want to harm me? Did I actually see something, or was it just lack oxygen that made me think I did?* Skye kept remembering what she thought she had seen. *It almost looked like…what?* She dismissed the thought as ridiculous, but her mind kept going over and over what had happened on the dive.

"What happened down there, Skye?" No answer. "You want to talk about it?" Still no answer. "Are you ready to head home?" he asked. Her nod was almost imperceptible. *What is going on with her?* Realizing that she didn't want to talk about it, CJ started the engine.

He stood at the wheel. He had the *Gator Bait* going at a moderate speed over glassy water as they headed back to Key West. He would occasionally look over and see Skye gazing out at the water as if she had something on her mind. *She's not her usual bubbly self. She's been so quiet since she got back on the boat. Did something happen in the water?* CJ had become concerned, but he waited for Skye to tell him what was on her mind.

The evening sun danced on the western horizon, turning puffy clouds a warming orange. It was the time of day that CJ loved the most. Enjoying the beautiful view, he felt a small hand take his arm and gently tug. He turned and saw Skye looking up at him, a wan smile on her pale face. She motioned for him to stop the boat. CJ eased back on the throttle, wondering why Skye wanted to stop. *Maybe she's ready to tell me what's on her mind.* He brought the *Gator Bait* to a slow stop and shut down the engine. He took a seat beside her, unsure what was coming next.

As the boat quietly rolled in the shallow swells, Skye took a deep breath, turned her body to face CJ, took both his big hands in hers, and looked up into his soft brown eyes. She seemed a little embarrassed as she spoke softly.

"CJ," she said, "I have to tell you this. I can't wait any longer."

"What, Skye?" he questioned.

"I've never been more scared in my entire life than I was down there. It was terrible. I felt so helpless and alone. The darkness and the cold were so," she hesitated, "menacing. I felt encased in them. It was like being lost, and I guess I was until I looked up and saw the sunlight. It was almost as if it were a ray of hope that kept me heading for the surface." A tear rolled down the inside corner of her eye and onto her cheek. "There's something else, CJ. There was something down there. Something I felt was trying to hurt me. Something bad."

"What was it? What was trying to hurt you?" Emotion overwhelmed CJ. "What in the world did you see down there, Skye?"

CJ held her hands to his chest as he looked deep into her tear-filled blue eyes. He wanted to comfort her, but he didn't know how. He wasn't sure what she was talking about, so he just sat there listening, waiting on Skye to tell him more.

Hesitating, Skye lowered her head. "I'm not sure, CJ. I just know that it was big. No, not just big, it was enormous. I knew I had to make it back to the surface and into the boat so I would be safe. I felt like it was coming after me. I was so afraid down there, CJ."

Stunned, CJ just sat there, speechless for a moment. "Was it a big shark?" That was the largest thing he could think of in the warm waters.

"No, I don't think so. It was bigger than a shark. I got the feeling it was some kind of monster. I know that sounds crazy CJ, but that's how I felt down there."

"You can't go back down there again, Skye. If there is something dangerous in that big fissure, then we don't need to be diving in that area. We'll go back to the place where we found the big gold necklace. There will probably be more gold there."

They sat in mutual silence for several minutes.

Finally, Skye spoke. "After I got back on the boat, my mind kept saying, *never go back,* but after thinking about it for a while I realized I was letting fear control my destiny. I can't let that happen, CJ. I have to go back, or I might never dive again. Whatever it was, it's probably gone by now. I don't know, CJ, maybe I just let myself get all worked up from lack of oxygen. More than likely I didn't see anything down there. I've just never been down that deep, and maybe the depth and the cold got to me."

As he listened, CJ slowly nodded his head, but not in agreement.

"Do you understand, CJ?"

"I understand what you're saying, but there is no way either of us is going back down in that deep hole, monster or no monster. It's not safe free diving that far down. It's no wonder you thought you saw something." *Did she really see something*? The thought of losing Skye in the deep, dark chasm filled CJ with terror. *I can't let her go back down. I just can't.*

"I'm not a little girl anymore, CJ. I have to go back down there, and I need your support on this, okay?"

"Crap! I lost 'em!" Jack Watson screamed into the wind. He had watched the teens that morning until the girl had pulled up their anchor, and the boat started following the dolphin. He had to lie back out of sight to avoid being seen, and that's when they disappeared. He couldn't figure out where they had gone.

Jack had spent the morning scouting around the area, and then he had turned his boat west toward the Dry Tortugas until his fuel began running low. That's when he had to give up the search and turn back toward Key West. *If Pete finds out what I did, there'll be hell to pay. Pete has to be in charge, and I always end up doin' all the dirty work. He's pretty smart, though, a lot smarter and meaner than I am. For now, I guess I better do what he says. He's got a terrible temper, and I don't wanna be the recipient of his anger.*

Jack was holding his breath at thirty-five miles an hour. He almost felt that if he breathed, the engine would burn more gas. He kept hoping his gas tank wouldn't run dry. As he passed the south side of Crawfish Key, his engine died, and the boat came to an abrupt stop. "Crap!" he screamed for the second time that day. He stomped around the boat shouting obscenities as if that would bring him a load of fuel. *Now, I'm stuck. What do I do? Calm down,* he thought. *Yeah, just relax and throw the anchor overboard, he told himself.* His mind raced with what to do next. *Call Pete and have him bring some gas? No way. Not a good idea. Wait here for another boater? Hmmm, there's plenty of fishing boats coming in from a day's catch. Yeah, that's what I'll do. I'll wait for a tow.*

CJ hoped to make it back to Key West before sunset. Skye stood beside him, holding onto the center console rail as they sped around the southern side of Woman Key. As the Gator *Bait* straightened up for a new heading, CJ saw what appeared to be a bonefish skiff dead in the water. *What is he doing out here? There aren't any flats around here. That looks just like the boat I saw heading for the mangroves earlier this morning. Strange*, he thought. *Wonder if he's broke down? Better see if he needs help.*

Like a good mariner, he turned the *Gator Bait* toward the other boat.

Chapter Sixteen

Jack Watson recognized the boat immediately. He couldn't believe his eyes. The closer it came, the easier it was for him to see the two teens standing behind the wheel. *Now, what am I gonna do?* he thought. *Just sit here and pretend I don't know 'em? Actually, come to think of it, I don't know 'em. I just know who they are. Should I act like I've never seen 'em before?* His mind raced with questions. *I could pretend to be fishing and tell 'em everything's okay and just wave 'em on by, or I could let 'em tow me into Key West. Don't just sit here, you idiot! Think!*

At a hundred yards out, Jack stood up and with a smile on his face began waving his arms.

CJ opened the compartment door located below the wheel on the center console, reached in, and felt for the plastic bag holding the Colt automatic. Reassured, he closed the door, pulled back on the throttle, and eased the boat to a stop about twenty-five yards out from the skiff.

The stranger was shouting something at them, but they couldn't hear what he was saying. Skye reached for the ignition key and shut the engine off.

"What a sight for sore eyes," the guy was saying.

"What's going on? How can we help you?" CJ shouted back.

"I'm outta gas," the stranger answered. "Got any gas onboard you can spare?"

"Sorry, the only thing I can offer you is a tow. Where are you out of?"

"Key West. If you can tow me to the nearest marina, I'd be much obliged."

"Okay," CJ answered. "Sand by your bow line."

CJ turned to Skye. "Mind handing me that spring line in the anchor locker?" Skye moved forward, opened the compartment, and retrieved the spring line.

"Thanks," CJ smiled. "I've gotta rig a sling for his bow line."

Puzzled, Sky said, "How do you do that?"

Skye liked learning new things about boating from CJ. "Watch and I'll show you."

CJ went to the starboard side of the transom, bent down over the side, and began threading one end of the spring line through an eyebolt mounted on the outside of the boat. He expertly tied a bowline knot, pulled the line around the outside of the engine, and on the port side eyebolt, making sure there was ample line loose in the sling.

Satisfied, he called over to the stranger. "Tie your anchor line through your bow hook and give me about fifty feet of slack."

The stranger acknowledged CJ's request with a nod and began moving about the skiff.

Minutes later, he straightened up and gave CJ a thumbs-up.

Starting his engine, CJ slowly maneuvered his boat to within a few feet of the bonefish boat, taking the bow line from the stranger's hand. He then moved the *Gator Bait* about thirty feet in front of the skiff, put the engine in neutral, and then went to the stern.

Skye stood beside CJ, watching his every move.

Bending down, CJ reached for the sling line and began tying another loose bowline knot around the sling line, making sure the knot moved freely on the sling. Finished, he threw both lines into the water, stood, and then with both hands on his hips he observed his handy work.

Skye said, "Looks good."

CJ put the engine in gear and slowly began taking up the slack in the towline. He looked back at the stranger and gave him a thumb-up. He reached for the throttle and slowly began increasing speed.

As *Gator Bait's* speed increased, CJ watched the stern of the boat dig deeper into the water, creating a rooster-tail as it struggled to overcome the weight and drag of the skiff.

Skye reached over and took CJ's arm. "There's something freaky about that guy," she whispered above the noise of the engine. Her intuition told her he wasn't someone they could trust. She would be glad when their boat and his had disconnected.

Jack Watson sat behind the wheel of his boat trying to steer it with a dead engine. The propeller shaft made a poor rudder. The boat weaved back and forth, leaving a wake that looked like a prehistoric snake skimming the surface of the water. He forced himself to pay attention to the task at hand even though he had other thoughts in his head.

Boy, that tiny little thing sure is a baby doll. I saw her lookin' at me. I know she's interested. A guy like me can tell. Pete can have the gold. I'll take the girl. In Jack's mind, he actually thought Skye might be interested in him.

Chapter Seventeen

Detective Sean Callahan got the call at six thirty-three a.m. It had been almost one in the morning when he had finally gotten to sleep, and he was groggy as he swung his legs over the edge of the bed, picked up his phone and answered, "Hello."

The first words he heard were unintelligible. The connection sounded like a radio call patched in by the Key West marine operator. "Say again. I can't understand you." He listened to a Cuban male speaking in broken English and then switching to Spanish when he couldn't think of a word. His voice sounded excited, and he kept repeating himself. *What in the world is he trying to tell me?*

Finally, he understood. "Ok, I'll get someone over there as soon as I can."

Callahan was due to be off standby duty at eight o'clock that morning, but the call had come in an hour and twenty-two minutes before he got off. *Just my luck*, he thought. Now he had to get dressed and respond to the call. He picked up the phone again and dialed his office.

"Hey, Steve, this is Callahan. We've got a floater on the beach at Boca Grande Key. I need a lift over to the island. Have the pilot meet me at Marathon Airport in half an hour. Thanks."

He reluctantly lifted his body up from the bed and headed for the bathroom. After a quick shower, but passing on the shave due to time constraints, he pulled on a pair of green uniform shorts and a white Polo shirt. *I wonder who they found and what happened to him?*

Callahan hadn't personally investigated a suspicious death since last summer when CJ and Skye had found a man's body under a sunken hull. He still remembered the smell as the body escaped to the surface and exploded. Shivering involuntarily, he wasn't looking forward to seeing the next one.

Thirty-three minutes later, Callahan parked the patrol car at the FBO Building at the airport in Marathon. After locking it, he walked toward the Marine Patrol helicopter that was waiting for him. Instinctively, he hunched forward as he walked under the spinning rotors. *Don't know why I do that*, he thought. *The rotors are at least twelve feet above me.*

The twenty-minute ride to Boca Grande Key was uneventful. It gave Callahan time to gather his thoughts about the phone call he had received. From what little information he was able to understand from the caller, it seemed the body was in pretty bad shape. It was missing an arm and had been chewed up pretty badly.

Sounds like he had a run-in with a boat motor, he thought. Callahan knew he would just have to wait and see what it was all about when he got there.

As he gazed out the side window of the helicopter, there was one thing he was sure of. He did not like helicopters. They shook too much and made his stomach churn. *Give me a small plane anytime.*

In addition to his position as Detective Sergeant supervising the Monroe County Detectives, he and fourteen other sheriffs' officers had served on the Monroe County Dive Team. Until recently he had been their leader for two and a half years. Their primary mission was to search and rescue and to assist the US Coast Guard, Florida Marine Patrol, and Key West Police Department.

Those who were on this team were a special breed of men willing to spend time away from friends and family in the performance of this service. He had loved that part of his job; however, due to a recent back injury and imminent back surgery, Callahan had to resign from the dive team, which had left him feeling like a fish out of water. Of course, the upside was that he could spend more time with his family. Still, he missed the camaraderie of being a part of the team.

In the distance, Boca Grande Key came into view. He noticed two boats hauled up on the narrow beach. One was a Florida Marine Patrol boat, and the other was a private open fisherman craft. Five people stared up at the helicopter as the pilot checked the wind direction and prepared to land next to the mangroves.

Callahan recognized the man who was standing there waiting. *It's that idiot, Officer Daniel Rogers. That's just what I need right now.*

He remembered Rogers from the year before when he had been unnecessarily harassing CJ and Skye while they were diving on the sunken houseboat that had exploded. Callahan had not been impressed with the arrogant, young officer. *Oh, well, I guess I'll just have to deal with him.*

The other four people appeared to be Cuban. There were two females and two males who looked to be in their early twenties. They all looked pale and scared and like they would rather be anywhere but where they were. *I don't blame them. I don't want to be here either.* He loved being a detective, but these kinds of calls were not his favorite part of his job.

Officer Rogers had covered the body with a piece of plastic but to no avail. As the helicopter landed, its rotor wash blew the cover into the water, leaving the corpse exposed. Gasping in unison, everyone either covered their eyes or turned their heads from the blasting sand and the gruesome sight of the body.

Captain Hoppe did a great job landing the helicopter, and Callahan was out the door before the engines could be shut down. The rotors were still moving.

Officer Rogers met Callahan halfway between the body and the chopper. He reached out with his right hand and said something above the whine of the twin turbines. Callahan ignored his greeting and continued walking straight for the body. After the way he had treated CJ and Skye last year when they were diving on the sunken boat, the only thing he could think about when he saw Rogers was what a big jerk he had been.

Captain Hoppe finally shut down the engines. He decided to stay in the chopper. He loved flying one of the search and rescue helicopters, but he didn't like it when they found dead bodies.

Callahan reached the body. What he saw made him want to throw up. His stomach rolled, and he gagged. Nausea caused excess saliva to fill his mouth. He felt bile rise in his throat. *Here we go again.* Stopping two feet from the corpse, he put his hand over his mouth and nose. He was glad he had forfeited breakfast; otherwise, it would already be on the ground.

Looking down at the body, he shuddered. The nude, gray, chalky-looking corpse lay on its side. It had been in the water for at least a week, judging from its appearance. Callahan was no forensic expert, but he had seen enough floaters to know that this one had not recently died. Keeping his mouth and nose covered with his hand, he bent down to get a closer look.

What he saw shocked him. Large suction marks at least eight inches wide ran down from the shoulder and around the chest and stomach of the corpse. Peck marks resembling what a giant chicken would make covered the face and back of the dead man. There were empty sockets where the eyes had been, almost as if they had popped cleanly out of his head. *What kind of animal could have pecked the guy's eyes out?* Just the thought made Callahan shiver. *It certainly wasn't a boat motor.*

None of the bystanders wanted to come close to the body, not even Officer Rogers. *I don't blame them. If I didn't have to be here, I wouldn't be here either.* The scene was sickening, and the stench was overpowering.

Focusing on the job at hand, Callahan continued to squat over the body, his eyes taking in every detail. Remembering that he should take pictures for the medical examiner, he shook his head, upset with himself. *Crap! I forgot my camera.*

Looking closer, he saw that the corpse's right arm was missing at the shoulder. *What in the world could have happened to his arm?* He had no idea how it had gotten dismembered, but it had been severed cleanly. *The propeller of a boat motor, perhaps?* He stood up and walked around to the other side of the body.

Suction marks covered the corpse's back. Surprise covered Callahan's face. *What could have done that?* Callahan wondered. *The suction marks look like either a giant octopus or a giant squid, but surely not in these waters. The water in the Keys isn't cold or deep enough.* He could not think of anything else that could have made those round marks.

He was puzzled. He had never seen anything like this before. *There has to be another explanation*, he thought. *If word gets out that these marks are the work of a giant squid, it'll kill our fishing and tourist industry in a heartbeat, and right now I have no idea what it is.*

"Hey, Rogers," Callahan yelled over to Officer Rogers. "Get on your radio and get us a coroner and medical examiner out here. Pronto!"

Rogers jumped when Callahan yelled. His mind had been on the corpse and what could have caused his death. Shuddering at the memory, he grabbed his radio and called the medical examiner and the coroner. *Let them figure it out. That's not my job.* His stomach was queasy. Like Callahan, he remembered the previous year at the site of the houseboat explosion. When the corpse escaped the rescue diver's hand and rose to the surface, the remains had exploded and spewed everywhere, including on him. He had showered half a dozen times that day and thought he would never get the horrible odor off of him. He vowed never to get close to another body pulled from the water. But here he was again. *Lord, please don't let me throw up in front of Callahan*, he prayed. He knew the detective didn't like him, and throwing up would be the ultimate humiliation.

Chapter Eighteen

Captain Mark Anderson, known as Cap to his friends, stood on his aging sixty-five-foot shrimp boat waiting for the teens to arrive. Skye had called him late the night before to ask if he would help her and CJ with a diving project out at the Marquesas Keys. Of course, he had said yes immediately. He had been retired for five years, and he would do anything for those kids, especially Skye. Cap had often wished that she had been his granddaughter.

He and his deceased wife had been childless, and he had no other family. He thought the world of Skye's grandfather, George Hudson, who has been his friend for more years that he could count, but he felt a little tinge of jealousy that Skye was George's granddaughter instead of his.

His heart had ached last summer when Skye said goodbye before going back home to Connecticut. Spending time with the teens made him feel young and alive, and he was overjoyed at being able to see Skye and CJ again, and to help them in their adventures.

Cap had his boat tied to the dock at Garrison Bight Marina in Key West, and he had just finished topping off the fuel tanks. *Dadgummit, the price of diesel is going through the roof! Four dollars and thirty-five cents a gallon is ridiculous*! he thought, as he walked gingerly toward the bow. The arthritis in his back was getting worse the older he got. Doc said he could give him a prescription to help ease the pain, but he never had been one for taking pills, and he was too old to start now.

Cap stopped for a moment, turned, and looked admiringly at *Money in the Bank II*. Deep in thought, he remembered the day he decided that he wanted to spend the rest of his life on the water. He knew he couldn't live on his old lobster boat, *Money in Bank*. She was too small, so in the spring he donated her to the local Chamber of Commerce. He sold his small house too and bought a shrimp boat from an old friend of his who had decided to move to Alabama to be closer to his daughter and her family. The shrimp boat was quite a bit larger than *Money in the Bank* had been, and it had sleeping quarters for four people. He had spent the past few weeks sprucing up the old girl, knowing Skye would be arriving in three or four days. He wanted her to look good for his special friend.

He heard a distant rumble at the end of the dock. As he looked over his shoulder, he saw the yellow Volkswagen pull into a parking space and gently bump the curb. *Sounds like CJ still hasn't replaced that old muffler*, he thought. A smile crossed his face as he adjusted the greasy cap on his head. *One of these days, I might wash the darn thing again*, he thought. He had had it for more years than he cared to remember, and he hadn't washed it in at least three years.

CJ opened his door first, and Skye followed. *She looks even more beautiful than she did last summer,* Cap observed. Something about her reminded him so much of his deceased wife, who had been the love of his life. *I can certainly understand why CJ cares so much for her. They are such a cute couple.*

Skye walked past the gate and retrieved a two-wheel cart and then pushed it next to the car. CJ began loading the cart with enough supplies to last for a few days.

Skye heard Cap yell down from the boat. "Hey, little bit. Hey, CJ."

She turned, stood on her tiptoes, and seeing Cap she smiled and waved. "Hey, Cap. How are you doing?"

CJ straightened up and waved. "Hey, Cap! You got a new boat?"

"Well, she ain't exactly new, but she's new to me. I'm gonna live on her. Named her *Money in the Bank II*. Gonna call her *Money*, though. Sold my house too and donated my old boat to the Chamber of Commerce. They're gonna auction her off and donate the money to the Children's Shelter up in Tavernier."

"That's so cool," CJ said. CJ loved being on the water, and he understood why Cap wanted to make the water his home. He also admired Cap for donating to the Children's Shelter. *Sometimes he's a grumpy old guy, but he's got a heart of gold,* CJ thought.

"I sure am glad to see y'all. I'd give you a hand, but I been down in the back for the past few days," Cap mumbled.

"That's okay, Cap," CJ answered. "It'll only take us a few minutes."

Ten minutes later, CJ and Skye were rolling the dilapidated pushcart toward the boat. One wheel wanted to go its own way, and the other seemed set on following. It went sideways more than straight.

CJ and Skye struggled with the cart for a couple minutes. Finally, out of frustration, CJ dropped his side of the cart. "That's enough!" he groaned. "Let's carry this stuff the rest of the way. Otherwise, we'll be here all day."

Skye looked over at CJ with a smile on her face. "I'm glad you finally reached that conclusion, mister stubborn. All it wants to do is go in circles."

CJ reached into the cart, filled both hands with gear, and then began walking toward the *Money*. All of Cap's friends had called the old boat *Money*, and CJ figured this one would probably be called *Money* as well by everyone.

"Let me give you a hand, mate," Cap offered as he reached over the side of the boat to give CJ a hand.

"Thanks, Cap."

"I got y'all a nice air compressor to fill your tanks. We're loaded with lots of ice and enough supplies to last us four days."

Skye handed Cap more stuff from the cart. "Thanks, Cap. You're the best."

Cap beamed at the comment.

Twenty-three minutes later, Skye and CJ were on the boat taking a breather after all their exertion loading their supplies.

Cap handed them each an ice-cold Coke from deep inside the ice chest. "So, you guys know where the gold is, huh?"

"Yep, we're all gonna be rich," Skye smiled. "Squeaky showed us where it is."

"Well, have you seen it? You know the old saying; seeing is believing."

CJ looked Cap square in the eyes, knowing what was coming next. He wasn't going to let his old friend intimidate him or Skye. "No, Cap. We haven't seen it yet, but we will. It's in about a hundred fifty feet of water."

"What! A hundred fifty feet! Are you two crazy! You'll have the bends in no time."

Skye interrupted Cap's outburst. "Calm down, Cap. We'll be fine. We have all the dive charts and decompression tables if we need them. You're beginning to sound just like Poppy."

"Do your parents know about this, CJ? I'll bet they don't, especially about the depth. They'll have my hide if something goes wrong! So will your Poppy, Skye."

"Look, Cap," CJ soothed, "nothing's gonna go wrong. It'll be a piece of cake. A one tank dive will give us about ten minutes on the bottom without decompressing. It's standard procedure to stop at ten feet for three minutes regardless of the depth. The tables come into play with repetitive dives; that's all."

"Regardless," Cap grumbled. "I don't like this a bit." He was worried that something might happen to the kids, and there was no way at his age and physical condition that he could jump in and help them. *Maybe this wasn't such a good idea, after all,* he thought. His heart picked up a little speed as he thought of the dangers at that depth, especially for two youngsters that had never been that deep before. *What was I thinking?* he wondered.

Skye was excited and ready to go back down. She had decided that it had been the lack of oxygen that made her think she saw something below her on the first dive into the crevice. *This time CJ will be with me. He's bringing his big speargun just in case there is something down there.* Though she was excited about the dive, an unwelcome feeling kept nagging at her as Cap started the boat for the spot in the Marquesas Keys.

Chapter Nineteen

Detective Callahan looked down at his watch. Seven twenty-three p.m. His eyes were tired, and his shoulders ached from sitting at his desk for the past three hours. He glanced out his office window to see sunset shadows falling across the blinds. *Geez,* he thought. *I should have been home at five o'clock for dinner. Thank goodness Diane is used to this kind of life.*

His wife was happy that he was home more. He loved her and his son with all his heart, but he sure missed his dive crew and the rush he got every time they went out in the rescue boat. *I guess it'll just take time for me to adjust.* He felt certain that he would get used to not being with his guys, but he secretly wished he were still with them.

Rubbing his eyes with his right hand, he held the medical examiner's report with his left. He was not happy with the conclusion on the report. He had been afraid of what it would say, and unfortunately, this time his fears were justified.

The floater found on Boca Grade Key had positively been killed by a giant squid. He couldn't believe it when he read the report. Several questions rushed through his mind. *The water around the Keys isn't deep enough or cold enough for a giant squid, so what brought it here, and how is it surviving in the warm, shallow water? It has to be a rogue.*

Measurements from the squid's suction cups and bite marks on the body indicated that the squid had to be at least sixty feet long and weighed well over a ton. *Man, that's a big squid*, he thought. *I sure wouldn't want to run into it in a boat.*

Dr. Fernandez of the medical examiner's office had contacted the Miami Sea Aquarium, and their experts had confirmed his conclusions. Callahan knew one had been seen off the coast of Mexico but not in the Keys.

Now Callahan was confronted with the problem of how to tell the mayor of Key West that they had a major public relations issue on their hands.

Taking a deep breath, Callahan stood, stretched for a moment, then sat back down and reached for the telephone. He dialed the mayor's home number. Before the first ring, line two started blinking. Callahan instinctively pressed the other button and answered "Callahan."

Callahan sucked in a deep breath as he listened to the caller. Officer Morgan from the Key West Marine Patrol was on the other end. He and Morgan had partnered numerous times, and Callahan had a lot of respect for him.

"The craft was anchored in about twenty-five feet of water," Morgan was saying. "The marine patrol checked the registration number on it and then called the home number listed. They talked to the guy's wife, and she said her husband has been missing for three days. She said he goes fishing just about every other weekend, and she has no idea where he is now. Said she hasn't heard from him since he left on Friday afternoon. Name is…um, let me see, Rodriquez, Carlos Rodriquez."

"Where's the boat?" Callahan asked.

"Garrison Bite. The dockmaster can give you the slip number."

"Thanks, Morgan," Callahan said as he hung up the phone. *Crap, crap, double crap!* Callahan thought. *Another one!*

He shivered thinking about what that poor guy must have gone through before he died.

Callahan wasn't happy about having to make the call to Mayor Marco Morales. He and Morales had bumped heads a few times, and one time they had ended up in a shouting match.

Short, dumpy, and dark-skinned, the mayor had a bald head that always had drops of sweat standing on it. He was usually sarcastic and unreasonable every time Callahan called him on official business.

Not looking forward to the confrontation, he knew, nonetheless, he had to get the mayor up to date on the medical examiner's report on the first body. Dialing the number, Callahan waited for Morales to answer.

"Mayor Morales."

"Mr. Mayor, this is Detective Callahan. I think we may have two victims on our hands. I just got a call from the Key West Marine Patrol. They found an empty boat out by the Marquesas. The owner of the boat has been missing for three days."

The mayor was silent for several seconds. With sarcasm, he finally responded, "Well, Detective, what do you propose we do?"

Keep your cool, Sean, he told himself. Actually, Callahan hadn't given too much thought to what he was going to do until now, because he didn't want to believe it. He said the first thing that came to mind. "Well, sir, I guess the only thing we can do is try to catch it or kill it."

"Terrific! Just like that, huh?" Morales laughed. "I can just see a boat captain reeling in a giant squid on a Penn reel. You've got to do better than that, Detective. How big is it?"

"The ME figures it's about sixty feet long judging by the suction cups and bit marks." He couldn't stand Morales' attitude, but Callahan realized how ridiculous he sounded. There was no way anyone could catch a giant squid on a rod and reel.

Responding honestly, he said, "Well, sir, because this is almost unbelievable, I'm not exactly sure at this point what we'll do. It's a big sucker. I'll get together tomorrow with the wildlife officials to see what they can come up with."

"Keep me informed, Detective," the Mayor said as the line went dead.

———————

Skye looked to the west at the sunset. *What a beautiful sight,* she thought, as she placed her right foot on the piling and pushed the shrimp boat off as hard as she could. *The sun will be gone in less than an hour. I just hope we can make it to our anchorage before dark.*

Something was still nagging at her, giving her the creeps, but she pushed it aside. *I guess that dive scared me more than I thought, but I know everything will be okay when CJ and I dive in the morning.*

CJ let the stern line slide out and away from the cleat on the dock as Cap pushed the throttle forward, giving the old diesel engine a little fuel. The Money shuddered as the old boat moved forward.

She sure looks better than the old Money did, CJ thought. He had noticed the fresh coat of paint on her hull and wheelhouse. *Cap must have done it to impress Skye*, CJ thought with a smile. *Everybody loves Skye, me included. Whoa! I didn't just say that out loud, did I?* he wondered. *Lord, I hope not. I don't want Skye to think I'm an idiot.*

Chapter Twenty

Pete Samuels sat on his front porch. He sipped a cup of scalding black coffee as he leaned back on his decaying truck bench seat that served as a porch sofa. It swayed in the center like an overworked mule from his weight.

Jack Watson sat across from him in an aluminum chair that had some plastic straps missing. *Yeah, we sure are living the high life,* Jack thought, wondering if they would ever make any real money, instead of a few bucks here and there from breaking and entering jobs around Key West.

A cool morning breeze blew past, bringing fragrances of bougainvillea and honeysuckle. The fragrant scent collided with yesterday's sweat, permeating Pete Samuel's body. He didn't take a shower every day, and he never used deodorant or brushed his teeth.

Jack tried to avoid being too close to Pete. That's why he always sat on the front porch. Between Pete's body odor and rotten teeth, the smell was disgusting. Most days Jack wished he had someplace else go, but he had no family to speak of and no place to call home. *I guess I'm just stuck here,* he thought, at least until I get my share of the gold.

Pete crossed his hand over his face and rubbed a three-day stubble. "I got an idea," he said. "Those brats saw my face, but they ain't seen yours. Why don't you try and befriend 'em and see if you can get some information about the gold out of 'em.

Jack frowned. "Don't you think that's getting a little too close? What if they get suspicious? Then what'll we do?" *Pete thinks the kids have never seen me before. I can't tell him that they towed me in when I ran out of gas. He would kill me for sure if he knew that.*

Pete stared at Jack with contempt on his face. "You idiot! Just play your cards right, and they won't get suspicious!"

Jack lowered his head, embarrassed by Pete's outburst. He hated it when Pete blew up at him like that. *One of these days,* he thought, *I'm gonna kill the guy*, but to Pete's face, Jack said, "Okay boss, whatever you say." He stood up and walked down the steps. "I'll see what I can do." He had no intention of doing what Pete had asked, but he needed to get away from him for a while. I'll tell Pete that I couldn't find them, and that will satisfy him for today at least.

Cap, CJ, and Skye all awakened at about the same time. Skye took a towel to the stern where Cap had put up a temporary makeshift shower. The curtains were collapsible and could be easily stored during the day. He had secured a fifty-gallon plastic drum atop the wheelhouse. It was environmentally friendly. The sun's rays heated the water during the day. In fact, it was almost too hot in the evening to take a shower. Mornings were better because the water had time to cool.

Cap got busy frying bacon and eggs while CJ checked their dive gear. He placed a dive tank in a barrel of cold water that was used to keep the tank cool as the air compressor filled the tank. He pulled the starter handle on the engine. One easy pull and the Honda engine began purring like a cat. Then he connected the air hose to the dive tank, twisted the air intake knob and heard the hiss of compressed air entering the tank. The pressure gauge read six hundred psi. CJ knew he had to keep an eye on the gauge because when it reached twenty-two hundred PSI he had to close the valve; otherwise, the tank could blow up, and that would be a disaster.

The *Money* was anchored in about fifteen feet of water at Lakes Passage. Their anchorage was a little north of the Marquesas Keys. It was an ideal spot that put them on the lee side of the islands. The *Money* swayed in the cool morning breeze. She waited quietly as her sump pumps emptied the last few gallons of water from her bilge. Every morning, Cap turned on the bilge pumps to stave off the old leaks around the propeller packing that were in dire need of repair.

Skye came around the corner of the wheelhouse wearing a green and white two-piece bathing suit. CJ thought she looked beautiful as she leaned forward and toweled dried her wet hair. "Morning, CJ." Smiling as she straightened up, she said, "Ready for a big day?"

CJ returned her smile as he lugged the first tank up from the barrel. "Yep, just about. I'm ready for breakfast. How about you?"

"Sure, I'm famished," Skye said as she headed for the galley.

CJ set up the next tank before following Skye into the tiny dinette.

After breakfast, everyone got busy getting the Money ready for open water cruising. At six forty-four a.m., Cap started the engine, and CJ began working the anchor line, reeling it in as Cap maneuvered the boat forward. He soon had the anchor stowed in the chocks as Cap began cruising around the islands to open water. He had to avoid the coral heads close to the surface. If he ran into one, it would be a catastrophe. The boat would begin taking on water and could sink, and sinking certainly wasn't on their agenda today.

Chapter Twenty-One

Pete Samuels and Jack Watson sat in the front seat of Pete's old van counting their money. Their morning had been busy. Around four thirty a.m., they had broken into a beautiful house on Boulder Drive owned by two of the wealthiest people in the Keys, who happened to be up north for two weeks. With their ill-gotten gains, they had visited the shady pawnbroker in downtown Key West with whom they usually dealt. He never asked, but they both knew that the pawnbroker was aware that the merchandise was stolen.

Pete knew the area on Boulder Drive intimately. He had been checking out the vicinity for a few years. He knew which houses had burglar alarms and which ones had phony security system signs out front because the owners were too cheap to pay for the alarm service.

Statistics had shown that the best time to break into someone's house was around four o'clock in the morning. The bar hangers-on would be home by two o'clock, and the rest of the world would already be sound asleep at four.

Their bounty had been a fifty-two-inch HD Flat Screen Sony television, five speakers from a surround sound system, and a fine collection of high-grade costume jewelry. They had been in and out of the house within five minutes. The speed in which they committed their heists had saved them from being arrested. They never carried a weapon because neither of them ever wanted to go back to prison.

Jack sat holding out his hand as Pete counted out eight twenty-dollar bills. "That ain't a lot of money for the risks we have to take," Jack grumbled. "There's got to be a better way of making a living than this!"

"Yeah, what'd you have in mind, smart guy?" Pete admonished. "Neither of us ain't got any education, and besides, we both got a rap sheet two blocks long. We like to fish, but we cain't make a living doin' that. What else is there? Flippin' burgers at McDonald's? Washin' cars? If you got any suggestions, Einstein, I'd sure like to hear 'em."

Pete counted out three more twenties. "Here, take this for gas. I need you to go find those kids. The only way we're gonna git out of this rut is to get our hands on that gold they're after. Our gold. Don't you disappoint me, Jack," Pete said with a warning tone in his voice.

———————

Money in the Bank had taken her time getting out to the trench. As Cap eased back on the throttle, CJ looked down at his dive watch that showed eight fifty-five. *At this rate we'll never get in the water*, thought CJ. He walked into the wheelhouse and began watching the depth finder with Cap. Skye stood on the bow waiting for the signal to drop the anchor.

Cap maneuvered the boat along the edge of the trench, looking for a decent place to stop. "It's too deep in the trench to drop the anchor," Cap mumbled to himself. He looked over at CJ. "I'll pull up to the edge of the cliff in shallower water."

CJ nodded his head in agreement thinking, *Come on Cap. Let's get this show on the road.*

Moments later, Cap shouted to Skye. "Okay, let 'er rip."

The forty-pound anchor tested Skye's strength as she heaved it overboard.

"Give the line about three times the depth," Cap advised Skye as she nodded her head in understanding.

Jack Watson had the skiff going full bore. He had just passed Gull Key looking for the boy's boat when he spotted *Money in the Bank II.* He saw the girl throwing the anchor overboard. *There they are*, he said to himself. *Wonder whose boat that is?* He could tell that she was at anchor by the way boat rolled in the shallow swells. Jack eased back on his throttle. *Strange,* he thought. *There's an old man on board. I wonder who he is.*

Chapter Twenty-Two

At ten feet below the surface, CJ and Skye were on their way down into the trench when they heard the whine of an outboard motor. Instinctively, they both stopped and turned their bodies up facing the noise. A small boat had anchored about thirty feet from the *Money*. *Wonder who that is?* CJ, thought. He decided it was probably someone planning to fish. Skye looked over at CJ and pointed down. Forgetting the boat, CJ nodded his head as he bent forward to go deeper.

Occasionally, he would glance down at his depth gauge. Skye held on to his arm as they made their slow descent deeper and deeper into the fissure. She stopped periodically to clear her ears, quivering from the cold. The wetsuit she was wearing only helped a little against the cold water. As she and CJ went even deeper, her mind continually fought off the memory of her last dive. *Is it down there? No!* she told herself. *Stop thinking about it! You just imagined it.* Still, she couldn't get past that little niggling of fear that crawled into her blood just thinking about it.

At ninety-five feet, CJ switched on his dive light. Skye followed suit. Darkness began to surround them the deeper they went.

Both divers had been hugging the cliff wall as they made their way down. Suddenly, a ledge appeared below them. Skye shined her light around the rock projecting from the ledge. Her heart began racing with excitement at what slowly began to form in front of her. Rotten timber lay scattered about on the ledge. Sediment deposits from hundreds of years lay atop the wood. *It has to be part of a boat,* she thought excitedly. When she looked at CJ, he nodded to her that he saw it too.

CJ eased down to rest in the debris. Swirls of cloudy sediment oozed over the wreckage. He looked over and saw Skye staring at him. Her eyes were wide, and he could make out a faint smile on her face beneath her dive mask.

Skye checked her watch. Five minutes left until they had to head back up to the safety of the boat.

CJ swam slowly to the edge of the ridge. He pointed his light down, cringing at the blackness below. He suffered mild vertigo as he stared down into the abyss. Turning, he made his way back to Skye. She was poking around in the debris. All of a sudden, her hand touched something smooth and thick. She cleared away the debris and tried to pick it up. It was a gold bar. Trying to lift it, it was so heavy she could hardly hold on to it with both hands. CJ heard her scream through her facemask. Seeing what was in her hand, he thought, *Oh my Gosh! I can't believe it!* He kicked quickly to get to her side.

Struggling with the weight, Skye held the shining bar in the beam of her headlight. She handed it to CJ to hold. As he took the bar, Skye pointed to the surface. Four minutes and they would be out of air. *Time to head back to the boat.*

Both divers stopped at a depth of ten feet to decompress. They had agreed before the dive that they would use the ten-foot rule.

Four more minutes, Skye thought, as she looked up at the *Money.* She noticed that the skiff was gone.

As CJ and Skye surfaced, Cap was leaning over the side waiting for them. When Cap saw the gold bar that CJ was holding, he let out a whoop! "Dadgum, guys! That's unbelievable!" he shouted.

Skye was all smiles as she wiggled out of her tank straps. CJ was already handing his tank up to Cap.

"Hey, Cap! Who was in that boat?" Skye asked, out of breath.

Cap looked down at his sweet friend. "You don't want to know, little bit." Anxiety showed on his face.

"Yeah, we do, Cap," CJ prompted. "Who was it? What did they want?"

"Y'all come on up, and we'll talk about it," Cap muttered.

Skye handed Cap her tank and began making her way back to the dive ladder. CJ was already standing in the stern. He reached out his hand to Skye. They both looked into each other's eyes with questioning looks. CJ shrugged his shoulders, wondering what Cap was going to tell them.

Moving forward, they found him in the wheelhouse pouring a cup of coffee from the morning's brew. Skye took a seat on a bench on the port side while CJ leaned against the starboard bulkhead.

Cap turned and looked at Skye and CJ. "Guys, I think we got trouble brewing. Just after y'all entered the water, a guy in the bonefish skiff pulled up alongside our boat about thirty feet away."

"Yeah, we heard him as we were descending," Skye said with a smile. "We figured he must be fishing."

"This ain't no smiling matter, little bit. He wasn't fishing. This here is serious stuff that I'm fixin' to tell y'all."

Skye froze at what Cap had said. *What in the world is he going to tell us?*

"This mean-looking guy wanted to know what we were doin' here. I told him it was none of his business. Then he got agitated, swearing and stuff. He started movin' round in his boat like he was trying to figure out what to say. All of a sudden, he started yellin' at me, threatening me. Said this is his claim and nobody's got the right to dive here but him. He said if we don't stop and get the heck outta here he's gonna come back and kill us all."

Chapter Twenty-Three

CJ looked at Cap, "What kind of boat did the guy have?" he asked.

"Just an old skiff," Cap replied.

"What did he look like?"

"Aw, I don't know. I guess he was sorta young, 'bout six feet tall with greasy looking, long blond hair and bronze skin from the sun. Kinda looked shady if you know what I mean."

"Skye, I think we may know this guy. Remember the man we towed into Key West the other day? He was in a bonefish skiff."

"You mean the creepy guy?" Skye frowned.

"Yeah, the guy that was out of gas."

"Hey, Cap, was the guy about thirty years old?" CJ sounded excited.

"Yeah, I guess that's him," Cap said, still a little shook up from the confrontation.

"Wish I was a younger man. I'd have given that whipper snapper more than just a piece of my mind."

Skye looked over at CJ. "Since he's after the gold, I bet he's got something to do with that awful smelling guy that your dad got into the fight with the other night."

"Could be," CJ responded. "They both warned us about the gold. Maybe they're partners."

"Well, there ain't nothin' we can do about it now," Cap snorted. "Let's git on with our work 'fore they come back." Cap felt a little uneasy about the teens going back down in the water after the warning from the guy in the skiff, but he knew no matter what he said they were bound and determined to keep diving until they found more gold.

CJ looked at his dive watch. It was 1:33 p.m. Then he looked over at the islands a few miles in the distance. Small thunderheads were beginning to form off in the west. *They'll be here in a couple of hours,* he thought. *We better get moving.*

Earlier, Skye had prepared a small lunch for the three of them. She and CJ had to eat light so they could dive again. People had always been told to wait at least a half hour after eating before going back in the water. Skye read recently that that hypothesis had been disproved, but she decided she would rather be on the safe side. She didn't want to take any chances, especially not at the depth they were diving.

After lunch, Cap refilled their tanks, and CJ and Skye were preparing their equipment for another dive. CJ adjusted Skye's headlight, and they started working their way back to the stern. CJ looked at Skye and said, "Are you ready?" Skye nodded and stepped off the stern and into the water with CJ in tow. After the bubbles had cleared, CJ began making his way deeper, and Skye followed close behind.

At forty feet, they both flipped on their dive lights. Blackness loomed all around them. The temperature change became noticeable at sixty feet, giving Skye a chill, making her remember again her fear the first time she had free dived into the deep hole.

Skye did not like the feeling of diving in the dark. It was like slowly falling into an abyss. It made her feel out of control, and she was becoming disoriented. The deeper they went, the tighter she held to CJ's arm. Finally, the ledge came into view, giving

Skye a false sense of security. A hundred forty feet to the surface was a long way to swim.

As the two divers reached the ledge, their flippers and body movements stirred the bottom silt, causing it to rise up around their shoulders. CJ motioned to Skye to be still. He noticed a slight current and watched the silt slowly move away.

Skye began stirring her hands around in the muck, feeling for anything that resembled a coin or metal bar. CJ moved closer toward the ledge where the silt was not so deep.

Suddenly Skye's ears began to ring, quietly at first and then louder and louder. Then a massive jolt of pain shot up from the back of her neck into the back of her head. She became nauseated and dizzy. Her hands cupped her head as she tried to keep her balance. She remembered the first time it had happened to her. *Oh no, not now*, she thought. *Is it happening to me again? What could it be in this deep water?*

"Who are you?" she heard something in her head say. "I haven't seen you before." The voice was soothing and comforting, like none she had ever heard before.

Skye felt something weaving around her arm. Then she felt it gently wrap around her waist and her neck. In her panic, she twisted around to see what was holding her. As her headlight settled on the creature, shock filled her eyes, and a scream echoed in her mouthpiece when she saw two basketball size eyes staring back at her.

CJ heard Skye scream and twisted around to see what was happening.

"I'm not going to hurt you. I'm here to help you," it said soothingly. "Don't be afraid of me. It's the *other thing* that you have to be afraid of."

Chapter Twenty-Four

Jack had the bonefish skiff screaming across the water at breakneck speed. That is if you want to call thirty miles an hour breakneck speed. He had to get back to Key West to tell Pete what was going on with the teens who had found the gold necklace. He was sure they had found even more. If not, why would they be out diving on a larger boat? He had seen the air compressor and dive tanks lying on the deck. That meant they were making longer dives at deeper depths. His mind raced with thoughts of grabbing more gold. *I wish that old fisherman hadn't been on the boat. I coulda grabbed the gold when those kids came up, but the old codger could have had a gun onboard.* Just how he and Pete were going to go about it, he was not sure. He would just have to let Pete figure that one out.

CJ turned his head toward Skye. As his dive headlight fell on Skye, shock paralyzed his body. For a moment, his brain could not fathom what he was seeing. The debris he was holding slid from his hands. After what seemed like a long time but was only a few seconds, he wondered if he was suffering from nitrogen narcosis. *I have to be! That can't be an octopus wrapped around Skye, can it? Am I dreaming?* He blinked trying to shake off the vision, but it didn't work. He was still in the nightmare with a giant reddish-brown octopus holding Skye in its grips with all eight tentacles. He couldn't move. His feet felt like they were frozen to the ledge.

Skye's second scream a couple seconds later brought him back to reality as he quickly made his way toward her.

"I didn't mean to frighten you," the octopus said as it loosened its grip on Skye and began to back away.

Skye slowly recovered from her fright. "Oh, my gosh," she said, seeing that the octopus wasn't going to hurt her. "Where did you come from? I've never seen an octopus as big as you are."

CJ finally reached Skye and instinctively pulled her backward and away from the giant octopus. He could not take his eyes off the monster. *That thing is at least twenty feet across. I need to get Skye out of here.*

Skye resisted his tugging. She was becoming fascinated with what was happening. *I can communicate with this octopus,* she thought. *It can talk to me just like Flapper and Squeaky.*

"Of course, we can communicate," the octopus responded as it moved further away. "Why is that person pulling at you?"

"He's my friend, and he's afraid for me. He's afraid you'll hurt me."

The octopus continued to back away from Skye.

"No, don't go," Skye said to the octopus. "It's just that I've never seen anything like you before, and you startled me. I'm sorry I screamed."

CJ finally took his eyes off the octopus and looked at Skye. He became spellbound watching her and the octopus interact with each other. He knew she could communicate with Squeaky and Flapper, but an octopus? *This can't be happening,* he thought.

With all that was going on, CJ had forgotten about their dive time, and he glanced down at his watch. *Oh, my gosh, we're running out of air!* He reached over and shook Skye to get her attention.

Skye reluctantly turned her head toward CJ and saw him pointing up. He frantically put his index finger on his watch and then anxiously looked at her. When she didn't immediately respond, he reached over, grabbed her arm, and began pulling her up.

In her last moment on the bottom, she hurriedly communicated with the giant creature. "My name is Skye. I'll be back! Please don't go away."

She saw the octopus's eyes change color as she said to Skye, "I'll be here. Don't worry." Then realizing that she and Skye had telepathically spoken with each other, she thought, *I can communicate with a human girl.* Sadly, the octopus had no one to tell because octopuses are solitary creatures of the sea.

Chapter Twenty-Five

Detective Sean Callahan drove his Angler 230B open fisherman boat toward Lakes Passage at a moderate speed. He was in no hurry to get to Archer Key located about ten miles west of Key West. His dispatcher told him that a couple picnickers had found a body, or what was left of a body, on a small sandy beach at Archer Key. The dispatcher also said that the picnickers would be there waiting for him.

Callahan loved his job, but dead bodies with missing parts bothered him. He preferred working with the living. His mind drifted away from the task at hand as he made his way just south of Crawfish Key, looking for a small channel that would take him into Lakes passage and then on to Archer Key.

The water was very shallow around Crawfish Key. He strained his eyes against the glare of the western sun. He spotted a narrow channel leading into deeper water and maneuvered his boat along the edge of a sandbank. Moments later, he was clear of running aground. Up ahead, he saw Marker R8, and just beyond was his destination. Callahan increased his speed, but he felt like slowing it, dreading what lay ahead.

When he rounded the marker, he saw a small rental boat that had been hauled up on the beach. Two young people sat in the sand. Callahan supposed they were waiting for him. As he drew near the beach, the couple got up and waved at him, their hands urging him to hurry. Callahan waved back at them.

Taking a deep breath and dreading what he might find, Callahan beached the bow of the boat in the sand and revved his engine a little, which pushed the bow further up onto the beach.

"Hello, folks. My name is Detective Callahan," he said as he jumped from his boat onto the sand.

"We're sure glad to see you, officer," said the petite, red-haired girl, who was pale and a little breathless. Callahan noticed that her hands were trembling a little. She was wearing a colorful two-piece green bathing suit and no shoes. A young bare-footed man about her age followed behind. He looked like he would rather be anywhere but where he was at that moment.

"Hello, officer," the young man said, smiling wanly, showing three thousand dollars' worth of braces. "My name is Johnny, and my girlfriend's name is Shelby. The body is over there," pointing up the beach toward the mangroves.

"Are you the folks that found the body?"

"Yes, sir, about an hour ago. At first, we didn't realize what it was until we got a closer look. It sure doesn't look like a body, though. It, uh, well, part of it is missing."

"It's really disgusting," the girl said and kept swallowing with a sick look on her face as if she were trying to keep from throwing up.

"You folks stay here while I go take a look, okay?"

Callahan walked toward an unrecognizable lump in the sand. As he slowly approached the corpse, the stench got stronger and stronger. Flies were buzzing all around, and sand crabs began scrambling away at Callahan's approach. What looked like hundreds of them went in different directions. The detective started breathing through his mouth to keep from vomiting. Like the young man Johnny, he too would rather be anywhere but here right now.

There wasn't much left of the body. A head covered with sand was attached to the torso, but it was missing an arm and two legs. Small fish and sand crabs had devoured most of the carcass. *It* m*ust have been in the water six or seven days,* Callahan thought.

He bent down for a closer look. He was surprised to see two large suction cup marks near the back of the shoulders. *A novice investigator would probably have missed them*, he thought.

CJ and Skye had pushed the envelope on this dive. Skye was sucking hard on her mouthpiece as her head broke through the surface. CJ had been holding his breath the last eight feet before gasping for breath as he shot up and hungrily breathed in fresh air. They both clung to the dive ladder waiting to regain their strength. Neither spoke as they looked into each other's eyes. Nor did they mention what they had seen in the depths. Each was thinking about the events that had just occurred. One thing they were certain of was that one more minute on the bottom and they would probably be dead.

Chapter Twenty-Six

Jack Watson made a beeline for Pete Samuels' house. He had barely stopped long enough to tie up the skiff before jumping into Pete's van. He had heard the term, Don't kill the messenger, and now he was afraid of what Pete's reaction would be when he told Pete that he had followed the teens to a different spot, and they had an old man with them. He didn't even know if they were diving for gold or spear fishing or what. *Why couldn't they have been at the spot where they found the necklace?* Regardless, he had no choice but to give Pete the news.

———————

Pete was sitting on his front porch bench seat when Jack arrived. He was holding a cigarette in his left hand and a Miller Lite in his right. Pete reminded Jack of a beached walrus, sitting there with his stomach fat hanging in a blob below his belt. Each time he moved, he wheezed. Jack thought he was disgusting.

Sitting down on the front porch step, Jack leaned against the railing and looked up at Pete. "Don't know if I got good news or bad," he said.

"Don't tell me those kids are at it again."

"I found them just out of sight of Mooney Harbor Key. This time they're using an old shrimp boat. When I got there, this old man was fillin' dive tanks with a new air compressor. That means they're diving deeper and longer. I'm pretty sure they found something."

"It ain't at our site, is it?"

"Nope, not even close. I ain't even sure they're diving' for gold. They could be spear fishing or something."

"Nah, no doubt 'bout it. They're divin' for gold. I'd bet my life on it. Wonder why they picked a different spot? I say we just keep watching 'em and let 'em do all the hard work. When they start to come in, we'll just have to pay 'em a little visit."

Jack sat still, thinking about what Pete had said. He knew what paying 'em a little visit meant. His hands involuntarily curled into fists. "Look, Pete, I don't want nothin to do with killin' kids. It ain't my style. Breaking into houses is one thing, but killin'? I ain't doin' it."

"Look, you little soft-bellied jerk, you'll do what I tell you to do," Pete bellowed, raising his bulk from his bench. He stopped a moment to catch his breath. "Now, get on out there and keep an eye on 'em, or they won't be the only ones I'm gonna take care of, ya hear me?"

Cap had helped CJ and Skye remove their tanks and climb aboard the *Money*. He instinctively knew that something had happened because they were quiet as they went about removing their wetsuits. Their usual exuberance was absent.

"Okay, who's gonna tell me what happened down there?" Cap asked.

CJ went over to the cooler and withdrew two Cokes. "Want a Coke, Cap?"

"Nope, had one earlier." He patiently waited for one of them to start talking.

Skye sat down on a stool, put her elbows on her knees, and

placed her chin in her hand. "You're not going to believe this Cap, but we came across a giant octopus."

Cap just sat there with his mouth hanging open, stunned.

After thinking about what had happened, CJ couldn't hold back his excitement. "The thing was at least twenty feet wide, Cap, and it had tentacles as big as your thighs. It scared the dickens out of me. I thought I was seeing things. When I realized it was real, the octopus had wrapped its tentacles around Skye. I thought she was a goner. I started pulling her away, but she just stood there, and the octopus slowly let her go and backed away."

"A little shy," Skye said, "but you know the best part, Cap? I was able to communicate with it."

Cap looked a little skeptical. "You mean like you talk to that annoying bird and dolphin?"

"Yep."

"What did it say?" Cap asked quizzically.

"It was so gentle that I got a strong feeling it was a female octopus. We were running out of air, and it happened fast, but she told me she wasn't the one to be afraid of. She said it was the other thing I should be afraid of. I don't know what that meant."

Cap sat back on his stool. "Other thing, huh? Wonder what other thing she could have been talking about?" he questioned.

"Don't know Cap, but whatever it is can't be good."

Chapter Twenty-Seven

Grabbing the mike, CJ said, *"Lady Maria,* this is *Money in the Bank*; over." *Lady Maria* was the name of CJ's dad's boat, and CJ knew that Michael monitored all the local VHF channels used in the area from his home office.

"Money in the Bank, this is Lady Maria. Go ahead, Son," Michael responded. Michael was glad to hear his son's voice over the radio. He always worried about CJ and Skye when they were out in the water. Of course, he trusted Cap to look after them, but some strange things had been going on lately.

"Hey, Dad. How are you and mom doing?"

"We're fine, Son. The question is how are y'all doing?" "Oh, we're doing great, Dad. Skye and I made two dives today and believe me they were very interesting."

"Did you find that big grouper you were hoping to find?" Michael and CJ had decided to use a code when speaking over the VHF since the line was not secure. Grouper was the code for gold.

"Yep, we sure did. You won't believe how much it weighs." Michael smiled to himself. "That's great! And how are Cap and Skye?"

"Me and little bit are doin' just fine," Cap replied, taking the mike from CJ's hand. "Had a little visit from the partner of the guy that you put in the hospital, that's all."

"Really?" Michael questioned. "What was he doing out there?"

"Checking us out, I guess. Said we was in his spot, and if we're still here when he comes back, he's gonna kill us all."

Michael voiced his concern. "Ask CJ if he has that present that I gave him for his boat."

CJ took the mike back from Cap. "Yeah Dad, I have it."

"Well, keep it handy. I think I'll take a ride out tomorrow and give you all a hand."

"That's okay, dad. We'll be fine. There's no way he can board the *Money* from his little skiff without us hearing him. Cap and I can take care of him if he tries to come onboard."

"Hey Cap, maybe you should post watches tonight."

Cap got back on the radio. "Good idea, Michael. We'll do that."

"We'll chat tomorrow; over and out."

Michael sat at his radio thinking about the conversation. He did not like CJ's report. The more he thought about it, the more uneasy he became. After several moment's pause, he decided he needed to make two phone calls: one to his friend Sonny Mitchell with the NSA, and the other to Detective Sergeant Sean Callahan.

It was almost eight o'clock. After having finished their meal, the three of them sat watching a famous Key West sunset. Cap, CJ, and Skye were up on the bow, and Flapper was perched on top of the wheelhouse. A much needed northeasterly breeze blew in, cooling the wheelhouse and the interior of the boat. The dishes were put away, and everyone was trying to relax after a long day in the hot summer sun.

"I still can't believe you can talk to that dadgum bird," Cap grumbled, sipping on a cold Budweiser, his usual choice at the end of the day. His wife had not liked for him to drink, but they had compromised on one beer a day.

For some reason, Flapper didn't particularly care for Cap, and

Cap felt the same way about the pelican. *If that bird wasn't Skye's friend, he would have been on the supper table a long time ago,* thought Cap. If truth be told, they were both just old and grumpy.

Flapper sat watching them watch the sunset. He had seen thousands of sunsets, and this particular one was no different. *A sunset's a sunset.* He wished he could understand what the rest of them were saying, but Skye was the only one he could understand. It got tiring having Skye to translate what everybody else was saying, but he was happy that he had been included.

Cap was saying, "Skye, you take the watch from now till midnight, then I'll take it till four o'clock. CJ can have it the rest of the night. How does that sound to y'all?"

"Sounds fair to me," CJ answered.

"Me too," Skye responded. *At least I'll get some sleep after midnight. I'm exhausted.*

When Skye translated to Flapper, he stuck his beak out over the edge of the wheelhouse and said, "Why is everybody staying up all night? Pelicans don't have to stand guard over their roosts." *I guess they think somebody is going to steal their boat.*

Seeing the pelican nodding his head at Skye, Cap knew it was talking with her. "What's that ugly thing saying?" Cap asked.

Skye laughed. "He's just inquisitive," she said and smiled. "He wants to know what all the precautions are about. He thinks we're afraid somebody will steal the boat."

Responding to Flapper, Skye said, "It's okay, Flapper. Most sailors stand watch on their boats." She didn't want to have to explain the threat they had received from the guy in the bonefish skiff. She didn't think he would understand, and she was too tired to go into a long explanation.

"Oh, okay," Flapper replied. "In that case, I'll be heading back home before it gets dark. I'll probably see you tomorrow." That said, Flapper leaped from the wheelhouse and took flight toward Florida Bay.

All three sat contented after a hard day's work and watched the final minutes of the sunset.

"Well, kids, I guess it's time to get a little shuteye," Cap said and yawned, rising from his lawn chair and heading below.

Chapter Twenty-Eight

After finding out from Cap about the visit the foul smelling creep had made earlier, Michael Jansen decided he had had it with those two guys. The more he thought about it, the angrier he became. *If anyone so much as puts a finger on either one of those kids or Cap, I'll make sure they spend the rest of their lives in jail. That is if Callahan gets to them first.* Michael decided if he got hold of them first, anything might happen. He knew CJ felt safe in the old shrimp boat, especially with the gun Michael had given him, but with guys like those two felons, you never knew what might happen.

Maria, his gentle and beautiful wife, reached over and touched his arm. "What world are you in tonight, sweetheart?" she asked affectionately. "You've hardly said three words."

Michael leaned forward, stirred a fresh pitcher of vodka martinis, and then poured two drinks. He picked one up and handed Maria her first and only drink of the evening. Michael loved sitting out on their patio overlooking the pool. A cool breeze blowing across Florida Bay helped keep the bugs away. He enjoyed the patio even more when Maria joined him. Three evenings a week she was away with her meetings, raising money for various charities. She had not worked since their first son Jeffrey had been born, and Michael had not worked since he retired from the NSA. They were very financially secure. Michael sat back and tipped his glass to Maria's. "I spoke with CJ and Cap this afternoon. You remember the guy I put in the hospital? Well, his partner showed up at the dive site today and threatened Cap. The kids were diving, but the threat was meant for the three of them."

"What?" Maria said stunned. "Why on earth would they threaten Cap and the kids, Michael?"

"I guess they think it's their site. Why, I have no idea. Anyway, it's not their site. It's nobody's site. I've been checking with the State of Florida, and no one has ever staked a claim in that area. Those guys are just trying to intimidate the kids; that's all. I still think they may have seen CJ and Skye on the day they found the necklace. Those creeps were probably at the marina and decided to follow the kids to see if they found more gold and claim it for themselves."

"Honey, what are you going to do?" Maria asked with alarm in her voice.

"I called Sean Callahan and Sonny. They're going to find out as much as they can about the guys and get back with me. There's nothing else I can do for the moment."

Cap made it a point to relieve Skye fifteen minutes early. At eleven forty-five he found her sitting in the bow, covered with a small blanket. *She looks so tiny*, he thought. Dew had begun to fall, making the evening cool.

"Hey, little bit. You doin' okay?"

"Yeah, Cap, thanks. I'm just tired."

"I made some fresh coffee if you want some," he offered. "I'm sure going to need it."

"I think I'll pass on the coffee. I need sleep," Skye yawned. Being in the water was exhausting; especially at the depths she and CJ were diving. "See you in the morning, Cap."

"Okay, little bit." Cap watched her go below. *What a sweet young lady*, he thought, as he made his way to the wheelhouse. He took a seat in the only chair behind the wheel and tried to get comfortable. Every so often he would startle himself awake after nodding off for a few seconds. *This is not working,* he told himself. He raised his wrist to check the time. "Twelve fifty-eight," he said aloud, yawning. Sighing, he whispered to the darkness, "It's going to be a long night."

———————

The small prey that the predator had found during the night had not been enough for its voracious appetite. An encounter with a dolphin earlier in the evening had been futile. The dolphin's speed and agility were too much for the creature to overcome. Hunger was driving the monster to the surface in search of larger prey.

Chapter Twenty-Nine

It was three twenty-six a.m. Two dish size pitch-dark eyes broke the surface as its massive body turned, surveying its surroundings for unknown dangers. Its eyes instantly locked on a boat fifty yards ahead. One anchor light swaying in the night gave away its position. The predator was quiet and careful as it slowly made its way toward the light. Hunger was driving it forward.

Cap's head slipped from the palm of his hand as he nodded off into a shallow stupor. The sudden motion startled him awake. Slowly straightening his aching body, he glanced down at his watch. Three thirty-one. *It'll soon be time to wake CJ for his turn at sentry,* he thought as he staggered up from his chair.

When he reached the door of the wheelhouse, something slapped him so hard in the face it knocked his cap off his head. His ears were ringing. Blood gushed freely from his nose. His shaking hand reached up to touch his nose, and he could tell it was broken. The pain in his face and head was excruciating. *What the heck was that?* he thought, reeling in dizziness and temporarily blinded from the powerful blow. *How could anything but the kids and me be on this boat?*

Cap's heart began pounding so hard, he could barely catch his breath. Very unsteady, he lost his balance, fell backward into a chart table, and landed on the deck. He both felt and heard his ankle crack. Looking down, he saw it was lying at an odd angle, causing his stomach to churn with nausea.

In the semi-darkness, he was still wondering what had hit him. Suddenly his eyes focused, and he was horrified to see an enormous tentacle moving about the wheelhouse. *My God, What the heck is that thing? It's huge!* The tentacle continued slithering in the wheelhouse. *Sweet Jesus! It looks like it's searching for something. For me?* He knew he couldn't get up and run away from it, not with his broken ankle. Terrified, he let out a bloodcurdling scream that awakened CJ and Skye.

Simultaneously, they both jumped down from their bunks to investigate Cap's screaming. At the same instant, they felt the boat list heavily to port, knocking Skye off her feet. She grabbed the edge of her bunk to regain her balance. CJ fell against the bulkhead but was able to stay upright.

Cap saw another huge tentacle slide through the door, moving from side to side. His heart was racing like a freight train, and he knew he had to get away. Unable to stand, and ignoring the pain in his nose and foot, he crawled, dragging the leg with the broken ankle to the far corner to take refuge. His body was tightly curled like a frightened child's. *Dear God, don't let it find me. Don't let it get me.* Paralyzed at what he saw, he screamed again as it slithered closer.

As CJ and Skye hurriedly climbed the ladder leading to the deck, both stood immobilized in fear when they heard Cap scream again.

As CJ reached the hatch, he realized there were two massive tentacles moving around the outside of the wheelhouse as if searching for something. *What in God's name is that thing?* CJ had never seen anything that large before. His mind was racing. *Is it a giant octopus? No, it can't be. It's too big. Where is Cap? I've got to help him.* CJ looked to his right and saw that the monstrous thing, with two huge, glaring black eyes, was half in and half out of the boat. Its weight had the boat's gunwale almost lying in the water.

Seeing the sliding creature, Skye screamed and hesitated. "What is it, CJ? What is it?" Fear enveloped her, and she stood frozen on the steps.

Finally, the predator found purchase. Two giant tentacles encircled Cap's screaming body and pulled it from the wheelhouse. He grabbed the door and tried desperately to hold on to it with both hands. Some of his fingernails started tearing off, and his hands were becoming bloody, but the size and strength of the monster kept pulling him to the side of the boat. "No, no!" he screamed. "Somebody help me! Please help me!"

Seeing the huge tentacles wrapped around Cap, CJ was paralyzed for a moment. His fear was almost out of control, but he knew he had to do something, or the monster would pull Cap into the ocean. *I've got to help him. I can't let that thing take him.* "Hang on Cap!"

Quickly looking to his right, CJ's hand felt a fire extinguisher attached to the bulkhead. Blindly, he grabbed it with both hands and jerked it free. He looked out the hatch and saw Cap now desperately holding to a life ring attached to the outside bulkhead, blood covering his face, shirt, and hands, dripping down onto the deck. Cap kept screaming; "Help me, help me!" as the creature tugged at his bleeding body. The tentacles had wrapped completely around Cap's legs and mid-section, making it harder for him to draw breath. Bright red blood spurted from his nose and mouth. He saw CJ rushing to help him. *I can't give up. Please hurry, CJ.*

Weakening, he finally realized that no matter what CJ did, it would be too late for him. He was being squeezed so tightly, he couldn't even scream or utter a word, and blood gushed freely down the front of his shirt, turning it bright crimson. *Please God, don't let this thing hurt the kids*, he thought, slowly sliding into unconsciousness and then death. Cap's pain was finally over.

CJ turned the fire extinguisher toward the creature and pulled the pin. A freezing gush of CO_2 blasted against the body of the creature.

Unexpectedly, CJ saw Cap's body fly past him as he and the massive monster splashed into the sea, causing the boat to rock back and forth. "Cap! Cap!" he yelled, but he knew Cap was gone. Gone forever. He dropped to the deck, and with his head in his hands, he wept.

Chapter Thirty

CJ collapsed on the deck, his adrenalin pumping uncontrollably. Shaky and pale, Skye fell beside him, scream after scream rising from deep within her. Both were in shock from seeing Cap being pulled into the ocean by the massive creature.

Tears streamed down Skye's cheeks in rivulets of salt. "Oh, my God, oh, my God," she cried over and over. "Cap, I'm so sorry. Oh, God, please bring him back," she said, weeping hysterically.

CJ finally sat up, reached over and tried to hold Skye, but she pushed him away.

"No, no!" she cried. "I want Cap back. I want him back. He can't be gone. He can't be. Get him back, CJ, please get him back."

"He's not coming back, Skye," CJ cried, trying to console her, tears welling up anew and rushing down his cheeks. "Nothing we can do will bring him back! He's gone, sweetheart."

Over an hour passed, and finally both teens were silent. They lay on the deck, both dazed at the horror they had seen.

Occasionally, quiet whimpers welled up in Skye as she continued to sob softly.

"Why CJ, why did Cap have to die?" she moaned.

"I don't know, Skye." Fresh tears ran down CJ's cheeks as he thought of the horror and pain Cap must have felt just before he died. Slowly, CJ came back to reality. His mind began racing. *How am I going to tell mom and dad? What about Poppy? Should I call the Coast Guard or the sheriff's department? What are we going to do with the boat?* His mind refused to slow down. He knew that soon he would have to notify someone and take care of their immediate needs. He had to get both of them off the boat.

Darkness yielded slowly and quietly to daylight. Skye looked to the east and saw the beginnings of a gorgeous sunrise. *How can such beauty follow such a tragedy?* she thought in a daze. *It's not fair! Poor Cap will never see another sunrise.* Fresh tears ran down her face again, and a moan escaped her lips. She loved Cap like a second grandfather, and she knew no one could ever replace him. She lay on the deck, sniffing, as she remembered all the good times she had had with her old friend and how much she was going to miss him.

As the morning sun quickly breached the horizon, CJ sat up and looked at Skye. Her face was flushed, her eyes were swollen, and her hair was a mess. He scooted over and held her. She put her head on his shoulder and continued crying. "How are we going to tell Poppy? He and Cap have been so close for a long time. It will nearly kill him."

"It'll be okay, Skye," CJ said quietly. "Right now, we have to decide what we're going to do. We need to get off this boat."

Skye raised her head and looked at her closest friend. "Whatever you think we should do is okay," she softly sighed, unable to offer any suggestions. She felt lifeless. Drained.

"If my cell phone can get a signal, I guess we should call dad first. He'll know what to do, and he can call Detective Callahan and the Coast Guard for us."

"What was that thing, CJ?" Skye asked, not wanting to, but thinking again of the horrible monster that had taken Cap.

"I'm not sure" CJ said looking puzzled. "Maybe it was a giant octopus or a squid? No, it can't be an octopus. It was way too big to be an octopus. It had to be a giant squid."

Skye looked down at the deck. Sniffing, she said, "I've never heard of a giant squid being in these waters. They're always in cold, deep water. It just doesn't make sense."

"I know it doesn't, but whatever it is, it's a killer." CJ eased his arm from around Skye and stood to find his cell phone.

Skye stared out into the sunrise, her eyes not focusing on any one thing. Her heart was breaking from losing her dear old friend. *Life will never be the same without Cap*, she thought. *None of us will ever be the same.* She knew in her heart she would never forget that night.

CJ stood in the wheelhouse staring at his phone. *Two bars. Good*, he thought. He wondered what to say. How should he start the conversation? *Hey, Dad, Cap is dead. No, that's not the way to do it*, he thought. *Gosh, what if he doesn't believe me? No, once I explain what happened to him, I know he'll be here as soon as he can get here.*

Thinking ahead, he thought, *I guess this will probably be the end of our search for more gold.* He knew it would break Skye's heart if they couldn't come back out to the Marquesas Keys, but he also knew it was much too dangerous for them to be here.

Flashing back, he remembered again what had happened earlier. *It came up on the boat and looked around until it found Cap. If Skye or I had been on watch on the deck, it probably would have gotten one of us. I have to convince Skye that we need to stay out of the water for a while, at least until this thing is killed.*

Reluctantly, CJ pressed the speed dial number for his dad. He looked at his watch. *Six-thirty. Most likely he'll be up. He's an early riser. Please let him be the one to answer and not mom.*

Michael saw it was CJ and answered the phone on the third ring. "You're early this morning, Son," Michael teased.

"Dad, I've got some bad news." CJ waited for his dad's response. The line was silent.

"Dad, are you there?"

"Yes, Son, I'm here, and I'm waiting for you to tell me what's wrong." Michael's heart was racing. *Has something happened to Skye?* he wondered. *Please God, no.*

CJ wasn't sure how to tell his dad, but the words rushed out. "A giant squid came onboard the boat last night and killed Cap."

"What? You're kidding, right?"

"No, Dad, I'm serious. It came onboard and took Cap. He's gone, Dad. It was horrible. The squid hunted him down with his tentacles and squeezed him until he was bleeding everywhere. Then it pulled him into the sea. Cap was screaming. I couldn't get to my gun, so I sprayed it with the fire extinguisher, but it took him, Dad; it took him." Having to relive the nightmare made CJ's heart begin ache at the loss of their friend, and his eyes watered.

"Oh, my God!" Michael couldn't believe what he was hearing. "Are you and Skye okay?"

"We're both still shocked, especially Skye. She can't stop crying, Dad. Can you come?"

"You guys stay right where you are. Keep your pistol handy, okay? Text me your GPS coordinates, Son. I'll call Callahan and the Coast Guard, and we'll be right there. Stay safe until I get there, okay?"

Chapter Thirty-One

Maria Jansen stood in her kitchen crying. Michael had just given her the terrible news about the loss of Cap. She was also crying for CJ and Skye. *It must have been a horrifying night for the kids,* she thought. She began moving about the house the way most mothers do when something terrible happens, just trying to keep busy to keep from falling apart.

Michael finished making his calls to Detective Callahan and the U.S. Coast Guard. He agreed to pick up Callahan on the boat dock next to the Pier House at the southern tip of Key West. The Coast Guard said that they had no boats available, and that the sheriff's department had jurisdiction.

Next, Michael called Poppy and gave him the bad news. "Poppy, I wanted to let you know that Cap died last night."

Poppy had just turned on his coffee maker and wasn't completely awake. "What? What did you say? Cap is dead?"

"I don't have much time to talk right now because I'm heading out to the *Money* to see about the kids. They are very upset, especially Skye. I'll explain everything later."

"Michael Jansen, you just slow down a minute. Cap was my oldest friend. How did he die?"

Michael knew how determined Poppy could be at times, so he had to give him an answer.

"I don't know how to say this, Poppy, but CJ and Skye said a giant squid pulled him off the boat and into the water." Michael didn't want to give Skye's grandfather the gory details because he was afraid Poppy might not be able to handle it. After all, he was getting on up in age, and anything could happen to him from the shock. "I'll come by after I'm sure that CJ and Skye are okay, and the *Money* is docked."

"Do you want me to go with you? Maybe I can help, and I want to make sure Skye is okay. I know how much she loved Cap. She must be devastated."

"No, I think it would better if you're home when I bring Skye back to the house. She'll feel better seeing you in her safe environment. I'm supposed to meet Callahan at the Pier House, and I'm already running late."

"Okay, Michael," Poppy softly said as he hung up the phone. Then he sat down at the kitchen island, put his face in his hands, and cried like a baby.

As Michael headed for his boat, he asked Maria to check with some local funeral homes and decide on a memorial service for Cap. He had never heard Cap mention any relatives but would check with Cap's neighbors to see if there was anyone else they should contact.

Slamming the back door as he ran down the dock, Michael rushed to get his thirty-foot Wellcraft Scarab back in the water. He hurried over to the davits holding his boat, pressed the down button controlling the electric winch, and commenced untying the canvas covering the boat. By the time the boat was floating, Michael already had the twin Yamaha 250 horsepower xca's lowered and running. He quickly checked his instruments; everything was in the green. Then he expertly moved the boat from its davits, powered the boat out into the channel, and with throttles full forward he headed out into Florida Bay. Last, Michael pressed the saved button for Key West on his GPS. *Eighty-one miles.* He pointed his boat toward the Intracoastal.

In the confusion after CJ's phone call, Michael had pushed his emotions aside to deal with all the practical issues at hand. Now that he was alone and moving through the various mangroves, shooting past them at over sixty-five miles an hour, he began gathering his thoughts.

Poor Cap! What an awful way to die. No wonder the kids are in shock. I have to get there as fast as I can. Crap! Why did I agree to pick up Callahan at the Pier House?

An hour and twelve minutes later, Michael pulled the *Lady Maria* up to the dock next to the Pier House. *This place has many fond memories*, he thought, remembering several days that he and Maria had spent there on their honeymoon. *Wonderful days*, he recalled.

Detective Sean Callahan stood next to a piling waiting for Michael to nose the boat into the dock. He was wearing a sheriff's summer uniform of green shorts and a white short-sleeve Polo shirt. Sperry boat shoes completed his uniform.

In one fluid motion, Callahan stepped from the dock onto the boat. Michael eased back in reverse, careful not to throw the detective off balance. He waited a moment for him to work his way aft to the cockpit.

"Hey, Sean," Michael said, matter-of-factly.

"Hey, Michael, I'm so sorry to hear about Cap and the kids. If there's anything my office or I can help you with, just let us know."

Michael looked directly at Callahan. "I appreciate it. Let's just get this over with, okay? I have to get to the kids."

"Before we get underway and can't talk because of the noise, there's something I need to tell you."

"What's that?" Michael said, impatient to get to the *Money* and see about the teens.

"Well, you mentioned something about a giant squid. I wanted to tell you that we've had a few incidences in the past few weeks where we've lost some fishermen to a giant squid. We've tried to keep it quiet, hoping not to scare off the tourists. I didn't believe it at first. I couldn't see how it could be possible in these warm waters, but we finally got the autopsy results back from the medical examiner in Miami, and he verified it was a giant squid."

"You mean to tell me that this has happened before?"

"That's exactly what I'm telling you, Michael. Cap makes the third victim that we know of." Callahan had liked the old man and hated that he had died in such a horrible way, especially in front of CJ and Skye. *I have to figure out a way to kill that thing before it kills someone else*, he thought.

Michael shook his head. "Oh, my God!" It terrified him to think that the giant predator could have gotten one of the kids.

Chapter Thirty-Two

Jack Watson drove the skiff while Pete Samuels sat in the front. It was a beautiful day. A light breeze blew in from the north directly in front of the boat. Pete was lucky. The bow spray flew out from both sides of the boat giving him protection from the drenching water. With his wide girth, Pete wasn't always so lucky. Usually, he would be soaking wet by now.

Jack maneuvered the boat around some mangroves and then through a few narrow channels leading north toward West Harbor Key. It was probably the hundredth trip they had made to the island. During the past year and a half, the two had been building a makeshift shack on the lonely little key. With each trip, the bonefish boat had been filled with junk boards, rusted sheets of tin that had been salvaged from the beach, and whatever else they could scrounge up or steal from construction sites around the Key West area.

Today was no exception. The shallow draft boat filled with supplies plowed through the water making their ride unsafe. Pete was exceptionally happy because today they were putting the final touches on the shack. Their intention was to use the shack for storage of stolen goods that they had been having trouble getting rid of lately. Pete knew that keeping stolen goods in his house was taking a big risk, since he and Jack were both convicted felons. He did not intend to go back to jail. The ten years he had served was more than enough.

The tiny key was a nondescript island mostly consisting of mangroves. A four-foot-wide sandy beach not more than fifteen feet long was a welcome carpet as they slowed the boat.

Jack had planted a large stake at the edge of the water, mainly to identify where the path was located and something to which he could tie the boat. An overgrown path leading into the mangroves camouflaged the shack.

At the far end of the beach, an official looking State of Florida sign in bold red letters at the top said, "Danger" and below that "Florida Crocodile Habitat – Keep Out."

"Pete, where'd you get that sign?"

"I made it, you idiot."

"There ain't no crocodiles in Florida," said Jack. "Why'd you waste your time on that?"

Pete looked at Jack with contempt. "To scare people away, you imbecile. We don't want 'em stealing our stash".

Neither Pete nor Jack was aware that Florida Keys crocodiles made their home in the area around the mangroves, and they were slowly moving toward their shack.

Jack hated it when Pete talked to him that way. *You'll get yours one of these days, you slob.*

Jack made his way through the shallow water and eventually came alongside the stake. He powered the boat up onto the beach and then reached over the side and tied a stern line to the stake.

Pete hefted his bulk up from his seat and stumbled toward the bow. Jack remained in his seat, watching and shaking his head while Pete almost fell from the bow of the boat onto the sand. Jack resented the fact that Pete always bragged to his friends that he was building a secret hideout when in reality Jack had done all the work. Pete just sat on his butt, drinking beer and yelling instructions to Jack.

Grabbing his beer cooler, Pete headed for the path. Jack grabbed some supplies and followed.

Five minutes later, the mosquitoes began singing their usual buzzing songs. In the past, Jack had learned to cover himself with a liberal dose of repellent, but today, unfortunately, was one of those days he had forgotten. He regretted his mistake. He dropped his supplies and began cursing, not so much at the mosquitoes but himself. About fifty bites later, his body reeked of insect repellent. For an unknown reason, Pete seemed to be immune to the pests. Jack figured it was probably because of his reeking body odor. Even the mosquitoes couldn't stand his smell.

Jack walked another ten feet, and the shack came into view. *Not bad,* Jack thought, *even if I say so myself.* He stopped for a moment to admire his handiwork. The word cozy came to mind.

The shack was nothing more than a box; twelve by fourteen feet at the most. No porch, just three wooden steps leading up to a screen door with a solid wood door behind it. One window was on each side, and each window had a screen covering it and wooden shutters framing it.

The interior was sparse. Two aluminum folding chairs were the only creature comforts. Three homemade shelves lined the back wall, with each holding a hurricane lantern and a can of fuel.

This shack looks almost as good as the inside of Pete's house, Jack thought.

The trip out to *the Money* was uneventful. Michael and Callahan had strapped themselves into their seats to keep from being accidentally thrown overboard in case the boat hit an unexpected rogue swell. A conversation between the two was impossible because of the wind and engine noise. Callahan was impressed with the way the boat handled. He had decided this was the machine he would buy if he ever won the lottery. *Fat chance,* he thought, *but a guy can dream.*

Michael looked down at the GPS coordinates CJ had given him.

Perfect, he thought, as he saw the shrimp boat on the horizon. He had been concerned about the kid's state of mind as well as their safety. The sooner he could get them back home, the better off they would be. He was sure that Maria and Poppy were wringing their hands, anxious to see them.

Now all he had to do was get Callahan to release the boat since it would automatically be deemed a crime scene. *The first thing I have to do is to make sure the kids are okay.*

Chapter Thirty-Three

As soon as Detective Callahan threw CJ the bow line aboard the *Money*, Skye started climbing into the Scarab. Callahan could see that her eyes were swollen and bloodshot. *Poor thing*, he thought. *She's terrified.* Callahan could see it in her eyes. *What she had seen must have been horrible. She's still in shock.* He glanced up at CJ for a closer look. *Looks like he's doing better than Skye, not much, but a little better.*

The moment Skye's feet hit the deck of *Lady Maria*; she was in Michael's arms. "Oh, Mr. Jansen, I'm so sorry," she sobbed. "There was nothing we could do. It took Cap. It just took him!"

"It's okay, honey. I know you and CJ did everything you could to save Cap," Michael consoled, rubbing Skye's tangled hair away from her face. He looked up to see CJ coming aboard. Callahan moved aside for CJ to pass.

"Hi Dad," he said, as he moved over and began hugging his father and Skye. Both teens started crying, and Michael's eyes moistened.

The three just stood there with their arms wrapped around each other for the longest time. *These poor kids have gone through hell*, Michael thought.

Finally, Callahan cleared his throat. "Why don't we all go up and have some coffee?" he said. For the moment, at least, it seemed to break the ice, though the teens seemed reluctant to get back on the shrimp boat.

Skye wiped away her tears. Finally, taking a deep breath to get herself under control, she said, "Okay, I'll fix it," and she moved toward the larger boat. Callahan gave her a lift up to the deck.

———————

Maria sat at the island counter in Poppy's house joining him in a cup of espresso.

After Michael had left, Maria had headed straight for Poppy's house. She knew he would be worried out of his mind. Surprisingly though, when she got there, Poppy was cool, calm and collected. *He's stronger than I figured he would be, having just lost his longtime friend.*

The first thing he said as he sat down at the counter with Maria was, "Those kids are going to be the death of us yet, aren't they?" He quickly realized his mistake. "Oh, you know what I mean. I didn't mean any disrespect to Cap. All I have been able to think about since getting the news of Cap's death is what the kids must have gone through on that boat. I imagine they were terrified, and seeing Cap being killed by the squid probably put both of them into shock."

"It's okay, Poppy. I know what you meant. I can't even begin to imagine what they experienced. I shudder just thinking about it."

"I guess the old coot didn't have any family," Poppy offered, rubbing his chin, a sad look crossing his wrinkled face. "At least I never heard him say anything about any relatives."

Maria sat listening to Poppy ramble about how good a friend Cap had been to Skye and CJ. *He needs someone to talk to about it,* she thought.

"I wonder if he has a will?" Poppy asked, not expecting an answer. "Far as I know, all he has is that old shrimp boat. He sold his house in the spring, and I think he put that money into buying the larger boat. I guess we'll have to do a search for relatives that might want the boat unless he already has a will leaving it to one of 'em. For all we know, he could have a ton of money stashed under his mattress."

"Well, Poppy, I think maybe you're pushing it a little bit too far," Maria said and smiled. "Of course, he did live simply and was a very frugal guy, so you never know."

"Yeah, after his wife passed, he never went anywhere 'cept out on that boat. He was always happy when I invited him to eat with me. Said all he ever ate was bacon and eggs and baloney sandwiches. He was always so happy when he was with Skye and CJ too, 'cause she fixed her delicious sandwiches and chocolate walnut brownies. He loved her food." A feeling of fresh sadness threatened to overwhelm Poppy again as his eyes began to tear up.

Seeing the tears in Poppy's eyes, Maria put down her espresso cup and rose to leave. "I guess I'd better get back to the house. Michael asked me to make arrangements for Cap's memorial service, so I'd better get busy."

———————

"I know you guys probably think this is a bad time to talk about what happened, but it's my job, so the sooner we get it over with the better," Callahan said softly.

All four sat at the small built-in dinette table that hinged from the wall. Everyone was having coffee except Skye. She was nursing a cold Dr. Pepper.

"CJ, why don't you tell me what happened and the order in which it happened."

CJ looked over at his Dad and then down at the table. "I'm not really sure, Detective Callahan; it all happened so fast. One minute we were sleeping in our bunks, and then the next minute Cap woke us up screaming. It was terrible. I've never heard anything like it." His eyes stared at the floor, remembering.

"So, you jumped out of your bunks and did what?"

"Well, it was dark, except for the anchor light high up on the mast. It was really hard to see anything, but when we started up to the deck, that's when we saw it. I've never seen anything so terrifying. It stopped me in my tracks. I felt like I was frozen to the steps, and I couldn't move. It was all so unbelievable. These huge tentacles were everywhere, moving about the boat as if hunting for something. Cap kept on screaming, and then I felt the boat list to port. When I looked out the hatch to see what was causing the boat to move, I saw this enormous thing. It was big and heavy, and the rail was almost underwater." CJ's voice broke, and he had to stop a moment to gather his self-control.

"It's okay," Callahan said. "Just take your time, son."

Michael was watching CJ telling Callahan about the events. He was proud of his son, particularly about how he was managing his emotions. He could see that CJ was choked up a bit. He had always been so tenderhearted. Michael knew it must have been awful for him to see Cap killed that way.

Regaining her composure, Skye motioned to Callahan. "Yes, Skye," Callahan said, touching her arm.

Skye looked at CJ, who nodded to her, unable to continue. "That's when the thing drug Cap out of the wheelhouse. Poor Cap didn't have a chance. Anyway, CJ pulled a fire extinguisher from the wall, and he blasted the thing really good. That's when it slid back over the side with Cap. He was all bloody, and his eyes were closed. He wasn't screaming anymore." Skye tried but couldn't hold back another rush of tears.

Chapter Thirty-Four

Twenty minutes later, Callahan had finished talking with CJ and Skye. His conclusion was the kids had done all that they could have done to save Cap. He wasn't quite sure how to rule the situation. Was it considered an accident or homicide? Cap was murdered, but he couldn't charge a giant squid with murder. He would let the county prosecutors figure it out.

He motioned Michael out on the deck. They moved to the bow so they would be out of earshot of the teens.

"Tell you what, Michael. I know CJ and Skye are exhausted, so I'll take the *Money* back to Garrison Bight while you take the kids home. You'll have them there in no time flat. I'm sure Maria and Poppy will be relieved to see them."

"That's very nice of you, Sean. I really appreciate it."

"Before you cast off, give me a hand with this anchor line, will you? I've never driven a boat this big before. Hope I can handle it."

Michael smiled and nodded his head as he began lifting the anchor.

It was just before noon when Michael pulled the *Lady Maria* up to Poppy's dock. When Maria and Poppy heard the deep rumble of the boat, they ran out of the house and down to the dock.

Skye was the first off the boat, and she flew into Poppy's arms.

He held his granddaughter in a vice grip, so thankful that she was okay. *Thank you, Lord*, he said in a silent prayer.

CJ was next off the boat, and he headed straight into his mother's arms. "Oh honey, I'm so glad you're home and safe," she said. "You and Skye come on inside. Poppy's got lunch ready."

CJ said, "That sounds good to me." He was hungry, but the thought of eating after what he and Skye had gone through made his stomach a little queasy.

Michael secured the boat and headed for the back door. He, too, was feeling relieved and very famished. CJ had called early about Cap, and in his haste to get out to the *Money* he had skipped breakfast.

Pete Samuels and Jack Watson were making their way back from the shack to Garrison Bite Marina when Jack noticed the old shrimp boat tied to the dock.

Jack was in a foul mood. Pete had been ridiculing him all morning. "You're just a low life and you'll never amount to nothin! Hell, you cain't even swim. At least I kin tread water!" Pete had continued his tirade until Jack put his hand up, causing Pete to stop mid-sentence.

"Hey, that's the boat those kids were on out at the Marquesas," Jack said.

Pete looked over at the boat with his one good eye. He noticed a deputy sheriff moving around on the boat. *What in the world is a cop doin' on the boat?* he wondered.

Pete eased off the gas as the skiff slowly passed the *Money in the Bank*. They watched the cop jump down from the boat onto the dock. To their amazement, the cop began stretching out a roll of yellow tape, roping off the boat.

"I wonder what happened, Pete. Think those kids drowned

while they were diving," Jack whispered.

Pete snapped, "Crap, Jack, you'd better hope they didn't drown, or we'll never find the gold."

Jack just shrugged his shoulders.

———————

With lunch finished, CJ and Skye walked down to the end of Poppy's dock. They had left the three adults to clean the kitchen. They needed time alone away from the bad day they had had, especially seeing the monstrous squid kill Cap.

Skye sat down at the edge of the dock and dangled her legs over the side. CJ followed. Both were quiet. Skye looked out on Florida Bay and saw Flapper coasting in for a landing. *My old buddy*, she thought. *Just when I need him.*

Skye pointed her index finger in the air. "There's Flapper," she said.

CJ looked out over the water, and a smile crossed his face.

Flapper swooped in and landed on a piling next to the two teens.

"Hey, guys, where have you been hiding? I've been looking all over for you. Oh, and tell CJ that Squeaky was really ticked off at him the other day."

"Hey, Flapper. Yeah, we know, but it was an accident. CJ didn't mean to nearly run over him."

All three sat in silence for a moment. Skye looked over at Flapper.

"I've got some bad news, Flapper." Taking a deep breath, she said, "A giant squid pulled Cap over the side of the boat, and he's gone."

"What do you mean he's gone?" Flapper looked puzzled.

"By gone, I mean he's dead. The thing killed him."

"Oh, my goodness!" Flapper said, shaking his beak back and forth. "Oh, my goodness!" he repeated. He felt bad that he hadn't especially liked Cap, and he knew the feeling had been mutual, but he certainly hadn't wanted anything to happen to him. Flapper knew how much Skye cared about him.

Tears filled Skye's eyes for the umpteenth time that day. "Oh, Flapper, we're gonna miss him so much. He was such a good friend to CJ and me, almost like another grandfather."

Flapper could see the pain and tears in Skye's eyes, and he jumped down from the piling and wrapped his wings around his sad friend.

Chapter Thirty-Five

CJ leaned back to lie flat on the dock. He was staring off in the distance. Skye leaned over and placed her hand on his chest, wondering what he was thinking.

"I'm going to kill that dadgum thing if it's the last thing I ever do!" CJ said angrily.

Skye looked down at CJ with fear in her eyes. "No, CJ, don't talk that way. It's too dangerous to even think about it. Let Detective Callahan take care of it."

"Something has to be done, Skye. It'll kill again. I overheard dad the other day when he was on the phone with Detective Callahan. I didn't fully understand what they were talking about then, but now I do. That monster has already killed a couple of fishermen. Besides, Cap's death has to be avenged!"

Skye didn't know what more to say to CJ. She looked over at him and then up at Flapper.

Flapper was confused at what Skye was saying to CJ. "What's too dangerous?" he asked.

"Us going back into the water," she answered. "That giant squid is probably in the trench out at the Marquesas Keys." Tears quickly filled her eyes again as they did almost every time she thought about what had happened to Cap.

"Oh," Flapper said, "I think I need to go find Squeaky." It was the last thing he said before lifting off from the piling. *I'll get Squeaky. He'll know what to do to help Skye and CJ.*

Maria looked over at Michael and Poppy. "I forbid CJ from ever going back to those Keys. Do you agree with me, Poppy?"

"Yep, I agree with you, Maria, but you know your son like I know my granddaughter. They ain't gonna like it one bit!"

"Michael, do I have your support on this?"

Michael lowered his head and stared down at his espresso. He thought a moment before answering. "I agree with you one hundred percent, sweetheart, but it's like Poppy said, regardless of what we say, those two have a mind of their own. If we forbid them from going out there, they'll go behind our backs. Look what happened at Indian Key. Skye bailed out of the hospital just to go back and rescue CJ. Those two are bullheaded, and you know it. Telling them they can't go back to the Marquesas is like giving them the green flag to go ahead."

"I wonder where CJ got that from?" Poppy laughed.

Michael looked over at Poppy and laughed. "Yeah, that goes for you too, you know."

"This is no laughing matter," Maria admonished them both. "You both know I'm right."

"Yeah," Michael said, "but being right isn't all that matters." *I'll have to come up with a way to keep Maria happy and keep the kids safe,* he decided.

The ringing of Poppy's telephone halted the direction in which Maria's conversation was going. He looked down at the caller ID and said, "It's Callahan."

"Hello, Detective," Poppy answered while switching the speaker button on.

"Hey, Mr. Hudson. I'm in the neighborhood, and if it's not a bad time I'd like to stop by for a few minutes. I have something for the kids."

Poppy looked over at Maria. She shrugged her shoulders and nodded her head.

"That'll be fine, Detective. We'll be here."

About five minutes later, Skye heard the gravel crunching in the driveway. When she looked back, she saw a sheriff's car come to a stop.

"Hmmm," she said, looking down at CJ, "Looks like Detective Callahan. Wonder what he wants."

CJ rose up to a sitting position, turned around and saw Detective Callahan shutting the front door of his cruiser. In his right hand, he was holding a brown paper bag.

CJ and Skye got up and started walking up the dock to greet the detective.

"You guys are looking a lot better than you did this morning," Callahan said and smiled.

CJ smiled back. "Yep, nothing like a fast boat ride at seventy miles an hour and a good homemade lunch to perk us up."

Callahan could tell that CJ was putting on a front and wasn't as happy as he seemed. He could only imagine what the poor kids had gone through, and he knew how much Cap had meant to both of them.

Callahan eased over and gave Skye a light hug. "How's our little princess doing?" he asked, looking down into her tear-filled, blood-shot eyes.

"Could be better, but I'm okay, Detective." With her usual curiosity, she asked, "What's in the bag?"

"Oh, you guys left this onboard the boat," Callahan replied, reaching down into the bag.

Skye's eyes lit up when she saw the contents of the bag. Callahan was holding a ten-inch gold bar. He reached over and handed it to her. "Congratulations on your find. Just be careful who you tell about this, okay?" Sky's hand dropped to her side from the weight of the gold.

CJ reached over and shook the detective's hand. "Thank you, sir. We'll be careful."

"Are your parents inside?"

"Yes, sir," Skye answered, with a questioning look on her face.
"Do you want us to come inside with you?"
"If you don't mind, I'd like to speak to them alone."

Chapter Thirty-Six

It's sure not a good day for a memorial service. *I guess if I think about it, no day is a good day for a funeral.* Walking from where he had parked the car after dropping off Maria, CJ, Poppy and Skye, Michael braced against the strong wind.

As the locals always said, *It's a squally day!* Dark scattered rain clouds blew in from the northeast with winds gusting up to thirty-five miles an hour. Occasionally, brief thunderstorms would rumble through with just enough rain to mess up one's hair and clothing.

Other locals walked in front and behind Michael as they all trekked to the tiny chapel for Cap's memorial service. Michael pulled his foul weather jacket up over his head to keep from looking like a drowned rat as he walked through the entrance to the small building.

The San Pedro Catholic Church parking lot was full, and so was the church. People were beginning to line up at the back of the sanctuary.

Because of the long walk and the weather, more profanity was spread over the limestone parking lot than the blacktop covering the tarmac at the local high school. The overflow crowd had to walk down from Coral Shores High School, along the Overseas Highway, for four-tenths of a mile to the chapel. Needless to say, the guests were all grumbling and wet.

Maria, CJ, Skye, and Poppy sat on the front row waiting for

Michael. Maria's intuition told her to turn just as Michael entered the building. Her intuition never failed her. She watched Detective Callahan follow behind Michael as they walked down the aisle. Callahan stopped at the third row and quietly took a seat. Michael continued to the first row to join Maria, Poppy, and the teens.

Taking his seat, Michael whispered to Maria, "There must be at least a hundred fifty people here, maybe more."

Maria put her finger to her lips, which Michael knew was her way of telling him to zip it.

Looking down the row at Poppy, he noticed that his face was pale and drawn. He and Cap had been friends for about fifty years, and in spite of the way they argued with each other, Michael knew they both had cared about each other very much. He knew that Poppy probably would miss Cap more than any of them.

He glanced at Skye and CJ sitting on Poppy's left, closer to Maria. He noticed that Skye had worn a long skirt with tiny pastel flowers instead of her usual shorts. A simple pink summer shirt and pale pink lip gloss completed her outfit, except for the tiny pearl earrings her Poppy had given her for her sixteenth birthday. Skye never wore much jewelry, and Michael had rarely seen her dressed up. *She's a beautiful young lady. No wonder CJ is so crazy about her.* She was crying softly. CJ looked sad and had his arm around Skye, offering her what comfort he could. Michael thought CJ looked handsome in his navy cotton slacks and light blue, short-sleeved denim shirt, open at the neck.

It was a sad day for all of them. The kids had both thought the world of Cap and felt responsible for his death. Though Michael and Maria both had told them that they had no control over the monster that had killed Cap, CJ told his dad that Cap would still be alive if they hadn't asked him to go with them on the diving trip to find more gold.

After everyone was seated, and the priest, Father Joseph, began the service, the buzzing of conversation stopped abruptly. Hearing the sound of sniffing close by, Skye glanced around and noticed that she wasn't the only person that was crying. Most were women, and she wondered who they all were and how they had known Cap. Skye didn't know it, but Cap had touched so many people in his own gruff way.

The chapel was full, and the latecomers had to stand against the back wall. The priest said some very nice things about Cap. He told the congregation that he had known Captain Mark Anderson since he had taken over the parish many years ago. Neither CJ nor Skye had known Cap's real name. To CJ and Skye's surprise, Cap and his wife had attended the chapel until his wife had died. After that, Cap only attended the funerals of friends and acquaintances. He hadn't felt comfortable at the service without his wife at his side.

As the priest closed the service, Skye realized that she would never see Cap again. He was gone from her life forever. Tears poured from her eyes, and she sobbed openly. CJ's eyes filled with tears too, partly because Skye was crying, and partly because he felt Cap's loss as much as Skye did.

As the group stood to leave, CJ noticed the grubby-looking man who had confronted him and Skye in the restaurant. He was standing against the back wall, staring at him. CJ's heart skipped a beat as he turned to tell his dad. When they looked back, the man was gone. *What was he doing here at Cap's funeral? Had he known Cap?*

Chapter Thirty-Seven

Attorney Bill Marr sat at his desk waiting for CJ and Skye to arrive for the reading of Cap's will. Since they were both underage, a parent or guardian was required to be with them. In Skye's case, George Hudson, her Poppy, had a power of attorney over her and would be present with Skye. He understood from Michael Jansen, CJ's father, he would be coming with CJ.

Marr could not shake the terrible headache caused from a night of too much drinking and too much powder up his nose. It felt as if his head was going to explode. He had taken eight aspirin with no relief. On mornings like this, he would promise himself he would never do it again, but the moment he ran into his buddies down at the Plantation Yacht Harbor, the vicious cycle would repeat itself over and over.

Marr's bank account was shrinking. He knew he would have to come up with a money-making scheme fast, or his whole life would go down the tubes. His house was paid off, and he had seriously considered taking out a second mortgage on it, but his wife had to sign on the loan, and he knew she never would.

Frivolous spending of his money had even put his office space in jeopardy. He couldn't afford to get evicted from there. It was only three rooms, and it wasn't much to look at, but he needed it. It had one small room, which housed his desk and chairs. An even smaller room with a tiny sofa served as his reception area., an undersized kitchen, and a small bathroom. When he got loaded, he slept at the office because there was no way his wife would let him in the house in his condition.

His business at Mile Marker 86 was in a good location. With all the tourists around, he managed to get a credible amount of customers. Someone was always suing someone else. He also took care of some personal injury cases, and that made him more money than anything else. He made a pretty good living, but the problem was he spent more than he made. Thinking again of his dwindling bank account, he decided maybe he should call Pete Samuels, a former drinking buddy of his. Pete always had a money-making scheme going, and Bill Marr sure needed one now.

As the bells on the front door dinged, Marr opened his office door and welcomed Poppy and Skye, who were the first to arrive. He offered them the sofa in the eight by ten matchbox reception area, which he failed to admit to anyone, also served as his bedroom on the nights he enjoyed himself a little too much. It was painted a drab green, and the squeaky window air conditioner drowned out the phone calls in his office that was adjacent to the waiting room. Marr quietly left his guests and went back to his office to nurse his headache.

I wonder what's going on? Poppy thought. *Far as I know, Cap didn't have anything 'cept that old boat.* He had received a call from the attorney late the day before asking him and Skye to be at his office today at eleven o'clock for the reading of Cap's will. Poppy surveyed his surroundings and decided that this office reminded him of Cap's house. It was small, and all the rooms were painted the same dull green.

Skye sat in an old straight back chair with her hands folded in her lap. Every so often she would look over at Poppy, and then up at the streaked ceiling, and then back down at the dingy carpet, all the while wishing she was out on CJ's boat. Still, she was very curious about the appointment and sat impatiently, wondering what was going on.

She heard the bells ding on the front door and saw Michael and

CJ walking in. The two were surprised to see Skye and Poppy. Skye jumped up and hugged CJ.

"Fancy meeting you two here," Michael said and smiled. "Have any idea what this is about? The attorney said something about reading Captain Anderson's will. Did you know Cap had a will?"

Poppy stood and shook both their hands. "Morning, fellas. I reckon you're just as surprised as we are. No, I didn't know Cap had a will. Far as I know he didn't have much."

At that moment, Bill Marr pulled his door open, surveyed the room and then motioned everyone into his cubbyhole of an office. Three small, cushioned guest chairs sat in front of his massive mahogany desk with an expensive, dark blue leather chair behind it, both purchased before he had succumbed to all his money-draining habits. Because the room was so small, and his desk was so large, it almost sat against the back wall to enable his clients to sit in the chairs in front of his desk. Marr had to squeeze tightly behind it to get to his chair, which barely gave him enough room to sit down.

Without fanfare, Marr sat down and opened a manila file folder with one piece of paper inside. With his reading glasses perched on the bridge of his nose, he looked up and gazed around the room. Since there were only three chairs, CJ stood behind Skye, leaning against the back of her chair with his hands on her shoulders.

"Would each of you please introduce yourselves for the record?" Marr forced a smile. His head was pounding, and he just wanted to get the reading over with so he could go lie down on the sofa his guests had just vacated.

When the introductions were over, Marr said, "This is a simple will and won't take long to read. As we go along, if anyone has a question just let me know." Marr began reading Cap's will.

"Being of sound body and mind, I, Captain Mark Anderson, do hereby bequeath the following assets: To CJ Jansen and Skye Somers, jointly, I give my old reliable shrimp boat, *Money in the Bank II*, and all the equipment onboard, to do with as they see fit.

The boat and equipment are insured for $100,000, and the premiums are prepaid for five years. The rent on the boat slip at Garrison Bight Marina, if that is where they choose to moor the boat, is also prepaid for five years.

To CJ Jansen and Skye Somers, I also give ten thousand dollars each from my safe deposit box for which my attorney holds the key. The remainder of monies in my checking, savings, and safe deposit box, I bequeath to the Salvation Army."

Signed: Captain *Mark Anderson*

"And that's all there is," Marr said as he looked around and smiled. "Like I said, the will wasn't very long. Cap was a simple man, and he wanted a simple will. From what he told me, Skye and CJ were very special to him, and since he had no family, he thought of them as family and wanted to give them most of what he had. There was a total of about a thousand dollars left over, which will go to the Salvation Army as Cap requested. Over the years, he was always helping someone out with money or food. I met Cap about ten years ago, and he was one of the most generous and kind-hearted men I've ever known." The eyes of everyone in the room were moist.

CJ and Skye left the attorney's office in disbelief. Both had tears in their eyes, remembering how Cap had always been there for them, no matter what escapade they asked him to participate in with them. Knowing that he cared enough about them to leave them the majority of his estate made the teens miss him all the more.

Poppy and Michael were both touched that Cap had remembered CJ and Skye in his will. "The old bird's feelings had been closed off since his wife died, but these two kids helped open up his heart again. He really had lots of fun helping them out on their adventures. They were like grandkids to him. I'll sure miss him too. He was always a good friend, and he had a heart of gold."

Michael nodded in agreement, and glancing at CJ and Skye he said, "Well, let's go celebrate your good fortune over lunch at the

Green Turtle. That was Cap's favorite place to eat. We can also talk about the boat and what the two of you want to do with it."

"Do with it?" CJ and Skye said in unison and laughed. "We're going to keep it, of course."

Chapter Thirty-Eight

Divorced, and out for Sunday breakfast, Mayor Marco Morales absentmindedly dropped four quarters into a newspaper vending machine outside Denny's restaurant on Duval Street in Key West.

The mayor was short, stout, and nearly bald. What little hair he had was black sprinkled with gray and made a narrow ruffle around his head just above his ears. His belt wasn't quite long enough to fit comfortably around his thick waist, giving him a puffy roll of flab over his belt. Since it was a weekend, he was casually dressed in lightweight beige cotton slacks and a light blue short-sleeve oxford shirt, which stretched tightly across his wide girth. His busy schedule, and too many business lunches, had added twenty-five pounds to his previously average size body.

Without looking at the front page of the Sunday edition of *The Key West Citizen*, he folded the paper in half, tucked it under his arm, and then opened the glass door into the restaurant. He paused for a moment, surveyed the room full of early morning patrons, and then opted for the counter. *There are too darn many tourists and Cubans,* Morales thought. *Just like Miami, they're taking over.* It didn't seem to occur to him that he too, was Cuban. He didn't think of himself as Cuban. He thought of himself as American. That's why he could relate so well with the locals. He spoke perfect English, unlike his relatives who spoke with heavy accents. Morales sat down on a stool, placed his folded paper on the counter, ordered a cup of espresso, picked up the menu standing between the metal napkin holder and the salt and pepper shakers. Savoring the thick, strong taste of the dark brew, he thought, *I'll bet this is the only Denny's in the country that has an espresso machine. No, I think maybe Miami has one too.*

After the server brought him his coffee and took his order, he unfolded the paper. The Sunday headline, in bold thirty-six-point font, glared at him from the front page.

GIANT KILLER SQUID OFF KEY WEST COAST KILLS LOCAL MAN!

He sat in disbelief. As he began reading the article, his heart began racing, and his blood pressure began to rise, along with his anger. He looked around the room and realized that almost every table had a paper on it, and nearly all the customers were staring at the headline. A loud buzz around the room sounded like bees around honey. *Oh, my God, they are all talking about it. Everybody knows. It had to be Callahan! I'll ring his neck when I see him.* It had never occurred to Morales that it might have been someone other than Callahan who had spoken to the press. He and Callahan had never particularly liked each other, and both kept their distance unless they had to discuss city business.

———————

CJ and Skye arrived at Garrison Bite Marina at nine forty-five that morning. To their surprise, they found at least a hundred people milling around the dock next to *Money in the Bank II*. Two television vans waited with long arms attached to satellite dishes extending high into the air, pointing toward Miami. CJ parked his Volkswagen next to the dockmaster's shack and shut off the engine. He figured most of the group were media.

"What in the world is going on?" Skye muttered.

"Looks like somebody's put out the word about Cap, and the media is here," CJ answered. "I know Detective Callahan was trying to keep this thing quiet, but you know how that goes," he said, rolling down his window. The sun was already hot, and the VW would be like a furnace if he left the window up.

"I'm sure Detective Callahan doesn't want us talking to the press," Skye said. "Maybe you should call him. He'll know what to do."

"Yeah, I think you're right. I sure don't want to get on his bad side," CJ frowned, shaking his head.

He made the call to Callahan, but he was out of the office, and CJ was put through to his voicemail. He left a message explaining what was happening at the dock and assuring him that they would say nothing to the press.

After making the unsuccessful call to Callahan, the teens decided to go aboard the *Money* as previously planned prior to their arrival. CJ had left his gun in the wheelhouse, and they had clothing and supplies to pack up and take back home.

As they walked toward the old shrimp boat, television and newspaper reporters saw the two getting ready to board the craft. With lights, cameras, and microphones stuck in their faces, CJ and Skye were swamped with questions.

"Did you know the man who was killed by the giant squid?"

"Why are you going on the boat?"

"Was the deceased a relative?"

"Were you with him when he died?"

"How did that make you feel?"

"Were you afraid?"

"Just one more question, please!"

With his arm around Skye, CJ pushed through the throng of reporters, and they rushed aboard the *Money*. They immediately went below to gather their belongings, out of sight of the media.

"Wow! I didn't think we'd ever get through that crowd, did you?" CJ asked.

"No, and I was a little afraid, the way they rushed at us. It was scary. I wonder how they knew about Cap and the squid. I know Callahan didn't tell them."

"It was probably someone from the medical examiner's office."

"I'll bet Detective Callahan is furious," CJ said.

"Yeah, probably," Skye responded. "I can't imagine who else it could have been. Well, let's get our things together and try to escape the crowd again."

Neither looked over at the wheelhouse, both vividly remembering how the creature had pulled Cap, bloody and screaming, into the sea. CJ knew he had to get his gun, but he would wait until everything else was done to do that. *If only my gun had been closer, maybe Cap would still be alive.*

Mayor Morales was not a happy camper. "What do you mean, you don't know who leaked the story?" he screamed into the phone at Callahan. "Do you have any idea what this is going to do to our tourist and fishing industry? I can just see the city council members biting at the bit, waiting to stab me in the back! This is just what they need to get rid of me. Now I'm probably finished, thanks to you!"

Detective Callahan stared down at the floor. He had no idea how to respond to the Mayor's ranting. The only consolation was that he knew for sure that the leak had not come from his office. He was, however, fairly confident that someone in the Miami Medical Examiner's Office had let the cat out of the bag. After all, a giant squid in the warm South Florida waters was big news.

"Mr. Mayor, if I may suggest, perhaps you should call a press conference and do some damage control. Our public relations department can put something together for you if you'd like them to do that."

"Look, Callahan, I don't need you telling me how to run my office! You just do your job and find out who let this thing leak!"

Jerk! Callahan thought as if he hung up the phone. *Okay, Mr. Mayor, if you don't want our help, you're on your own. Good luck! The press will eat you alive.*

Chapter Thirty Nine

Nearly ready to vacate the *Money*, CJ decided to give his dad a call. "Hey, Dad, you should see all the people gathered here on the dock waiting to interview us. There must be at least a hundred journalists and media people out here. There are even two TV trucks. When we got out of the car, they swarmed around us asking us all kinds of questions. We didn't answer them, though. We just got on the boat as quickly as we could and went below to pack up our things."

"Son, you and Skye hang tight, okay? You did the right thing by not talking to them because Detective Callahan nixed all media coverage. I'll be down in the Scarab to pick you all up in about an hour. I'll come alongside the boat and y'all can jump onboard. We can come back later and pick up the VW after everybody leaves."

"Thanks, Dad," CJ said, pressing the disconnect button on his iPhone.

Skye had put all hers and CJ's belongings in a duffle bag and had set it down on the deck, all except CJ's pistol. She was leaving that for him to retrieve and store. There was no way she was going in the wheelhouse to get it, not after what she'd seen the night Cap died. She shivered again as she remembered the terror. Skye's tee shirt was sticking to her from the heat, and her cheeks were flushed. She was ready to go, and her patience with the crowd had run out. She and CJ were being held captive on the boat as they waited to be rescued by Michael. She had never realized that notoriety could be such a pain. She quickly decided she wanted nothing to do with it.

Already feeling the sun's blazing heat, Pete and Jack sat on the front porch discussing the morning's newspaper article about the giant squid. A stock photo of one that was reddish brown was next to the article. "Man, that's one heck of a big squid," Jack was saying. "Wonder how much it weighs?"

"I ain't got no idea, but I'd hate to have a run-in with somethin' like that, Pete mumbled. "I bet you anything that's what got Joe!"

"Yeah, you're probably right. Now I'm thankful I cain't swim." Said Pete.

"You idiot, that guy wadn't swimming. He was in that shrimp boat!"

After a couple minutes of silence, Pete looked over at Jack as if he had a secret and didn't know if he wanted to let Jack in on it.

Finally, he decided to say what was on his mind. He figured he might need Jack to help him. *Jack's not too smart, but he's too afraid of me not to do what I say.* "I gotta call this morning from that shady lawyer up in Islamorada. What's his name?" Pete paused, rubbing his chin, trying to recollect the attorney's name. Before Jack could answer, Pete remembered. "Marr, that's it! Bill Marr. Seems he's interested in puttin' somethin' together for a few easy bucks. Says he needs money fast. That guy's always lookin' to make a fast dollar, but I ain't sure if I trust him."

Jack leaned back against the railing. "Any idea what he's got in mind?"

"Knowin' him, it's probably got somethin' to do with drugs. The word's out he's been doin' a lot of blow. If we do somethin' with him, we gotta be really careful. Those white-collar guys cave easily if the law gits involved."

CJ and Skye sat on the opposite side of the boat from where the media was camped out on the dock. Both were leaning against the bulkhead of the wheelhouse. Skye nursed a Dr. Pepper, and CJ held a cold Coke can to his forehead, rolling it back and forth to cool his face a little. "It's going to be a scorching summer," he mused. Both were in shorts. Skye's were white, making her slim, tanned legs look even darker. Her baby blue tank top matched her eyes perfectly. As always, a light blue scrunchie held her hair in a perfect blonde ponytail, with wispy tendrils hanging in front of her ears.

CJ's tan cargo shorts did nothing to shorten his long legs, always dark from the summer sun. He had worn a baggy white University of Florida tee shirt but had taken it off because of the heat. He took the Coke down from his forehead, popped the top, and took a swig. He kept wiping away the sweat that had popped out on his upper lip and forehead.

Skye stretched her legs out and gave a little sigh. "I sure miss Cap," she said softly. "Every time I come on this boat, I feel guilty because we couldn't save him." Thinking again of how horribly he had died brought tears to her eyes for the umpteenth time.

"I feel the same way," CJ said, his face flushed bright pink from the heat. "We just have to get past it, Skye. I know that's what Cap would want us to do. He wouldn't want us to be sad all the time."

Brushing tears away with the back of her hand, Skye looked back over at CJ with a little smile. "You're right. That's what Cap would want. From now on, we have to stay positive. It's just so hard to let him go, CJ. I still have trouble believing it. I loved the old guy. He was always there for us. He even dressed up for my going away party last summer. That's the only time I've seen him without that old cap he always wore."

"Yeah, I know. I miss him too."

CJ's ringing cell phone, held loosely in his hand, startled him, causing him to drop it on the deck. Picking it up, he glanced over at Skye and said, "It's dad."

Pressing the speaker button so Skye could hear, he answered, "Hi, Dad, where are you? Are you close already?"

"No, I'm not close. I got to thinking about those reporters. You can handle the *Money*, right?"

"Sure, Dad, she's a piece of cake to operate. Cap let me drive her a couple times."

"Maybe you should drive her up to Tavernier Creek Marina. That way you'll lose the reporters, and we can do whatever maintenance is necessary up here. What do you think?"

CJ's mind raced. *It'll take about three or four hours to get to Islamorada in this old boat, and that'll give me more time with Skye.* He liked being with Skye as much as he could.

Michael continued, "Hey, I'll invite Poppy over this evening, and we can grill some steaks. How's that sound?"

"Sounds like a plan, Dad. I'm hungry already."

Skye jumped up from the deck and took a cheerleader pose, bending down, jumping up, and clapping her hands. "Yay, steaks for dinner!" After the excitement, Skye suddenly sobered. "You can drive this thing, can't you?"

Chapter Forty

Pete Samuels and Jack Watson waited at the end of the dock at the Mile Marker 88 Restaurant in Islamorada. Twenty minutes had passed since their arrival, and still there was no sign of the shyster attorney, Bill Marr. Pete was seriously thinking about leaving. *Where the heck is he?* Marr had called Pete earlier in the day, asking him to meet at the restaurant at seven o'clock, and it was now twenty minutes after. Their conversation had been short and cryptic, just in case the phones weren't safe.

Both men nursed a can of beer that had grown warm as they waited. Pete had taken a seat on a weather-beaten wooden bench to relieve his aching feet from the heavy bulk they supported. He always wore sandals or flip flops, and the rubber soles were worn down from age and from his weight. His feet were black with ground in dirt. The rest of his body wasn't much cleaner, and he kept scratching himself below his belt.

He oughta take a bath once in a while, Jack thought, covering his nose and discretely wrinkling it in disgust as he nervously paced back and forth. He kept gnawing on his dirty nails that were already bitten down to the quick. He was cleaner than Pete, but that wasn't saying much. *C'mon, Marr. Where the heck are you?* Jack was not good at waiting. Waiting reminded him of his confinement in a prison cell for ten years, waiting to be released. *Never again*, he vowed.

Still scratching and deep in thought, Pete glanced up and saw

Marr, red-faced and drunk, with half of his shirttail hanging out of his rumpled-looking black dress pants. He was staggering down the dock toward them. A drunken smile curled up one side of his face as he approached the two men. As he moved forward, a pink rum runner sloshed in a clear plastic cup, defying gravity.

"Hey, dogs!" Marr laughed, as he nearly fell onto the bench next to Pete.

"Who're you callin' dogs?" Pete snapped. "Ain't no dogs here!"

"Aw, come on. I'm just teasing you all. You know you're my main men."

Jack looked at Marr with disgust. "Whacha' doin' showin' up here all messed up?"

"Messed up? What do you mean? I'm not drunk. I just got a little buzz," Marr replied, swaying in his seat, trying but failing to look sober. "Hey, guys, why don't we go inside, get us a table, and have a little supper? I guess I probably could use something to eat." While trying to get up from his seat, a little of his pink drink sloshed on Pete's ragged plaid shirt.

Not even noticing the wetness, Pete pushed his heavy body to a standing position. "We can talk here! What's on your mind Marr? Let's hear it."

Bill Marr kept his seat, looking up at Jack and Pete with heavy-lidded eyes. "Look, guys, I'm running short on cash, and I was just wondering if you fellows had something going on that I could help you out with? I need money, and I need it quick," he said, unable to keep from rocking back and forth.

"Like what?" Jack asked. "Whatcha think we got goin'?"

"Hell, I don't know. Maybe I could help you move some pot or something."

"Nah, pickings are pretty slim right now. Ain't nobody moving nothin'," Pete said. "Besides, if we had somethin' goin' on, we'd take care of it ourselves. Why would we need you?"

Desperate, Marr said, "Look, guys, the other day I did a will reading for the old man killed by the giant squid on his shrimp boat a couple weeks ago. The old man left everything to two kids, including twenty grand in cash. They were with him when he died. I thought maybe we could snatch one of the kids and demand the twenty grand they got. That would give us close to seven thousand apiece."

Pete looked over at Jack, and Jack stared back at Pete. Both men had question marks in their eyes. Both realized it had to be the same two kids that had found the necklace, the two they had been following.

"So, you say these kids have some cash?" Pete asked.

"Yeah, that's what I'm saying. Twenty big ones. Ten grand each."

Pete rubbed his soft, flabby belly, scratched again, and took the last swig of his hot beer. *Crap*, he thought, *if we don't team up with this guy, he might go to someone else and make 'em the same offer. This way, we can force the kids to tell us where the gold is. Marr don't even know bout the gold. We'll git money on both ends of the deal. Almost seven grand each.*

Pete quickly made his decision, a decision that would change his life forever.

Chapter Forty-One

CJ groaned, "Are you crazy?" He was trying to convince Skye to forget what she was thinking. He had been listening to her for the past hour, trying to convince him to go back out to the trench and dive for more gold. "What if that thing is still out there? Then what? I don't know about you, but I don't want to be squid food. Have you forgotten about Cap?"

Becoming exasperated with CJ's negativity, she said, "Look CJ, it could be anywhere by now. It's been over two weeks, and no one else has been killed, and no one's even reported seeing it. It could be in the middle of the Gulf of Mexico now for all we know. Besides, I told myself at Cap's memorial that I'd go back out there even if it kills me, and that's what I'm going to do, whether you go with me or not."

CJ just sat there, a little pale and shocked, speechless at her words. His mouth hung open, and it felt like a searing knife had pierced his chest. For a moment, he couldn't respond because he was too stunned. *I can't believe what Skye just said. Surely, she can't be serious.*

Looking her straight in the eyes, he realized she was dead serious, and he answered a little sharply, "You are the most stubborn person I have ever met, Skye Somers! It's too crazy to even think about." The thought of Skye going alone frightened the dickens out of him. *Wait, how can she go alone? She doesn't even have a boat, and she sure can't handle the Money.* He realized that

Skye was pressuring him into taking her back out to the dive site, knowing he would never let her go alone.

Leaving the wheelhouse, she walked up to the bow, took a seat on the gunwale and folded her arms, her pretty pink lips in a pout. She knew that CJ couldn't stand to see her upset. He always gave in, and she knew he would this time.

CJ followed close behind, trying once more to convince Skye it was a bad idea. When he saw her sitting on the gunwale sulking, he knew he had already lost the argument. He also knew there was no changing her mind. She had always been that way. Once she made up her mind to something that was it.

"You know you're going to get us both killed, don't you?"

Skye sat in silence, contemplating his words. Finally, she looked over and saw the hurt and fear in his dark eyes. "I'm sorry, CJ," she whispered. "I really am. It's just that I need your help. We've always done everything together. We're a team, and a darn good one. You know I can't do this without you, and I don't want to."

"What about my parents and Poppy, Skye? You know what they said about us going back to the Marquesas. They'll have our hides if we go out there behind their backs. Dad might even take the Mako back for all I know."

"Oh, don't be so dramatic! You know your dad won't do that. He's no Indian giver."

"I wouldn't be so sure about that." *Would he take back my boat?* CJ decided he didn't want to bet on it.

"Look," Skye smiled, taking CJ's hands, "let's take the shrimper back down to Garrison Bight. Cap paid the dockage for the next five years. We can moor it there for a few days, and then we'll talk about it again, okay? Besides, by then maybe someone will have figured out a way to kill that thing if it's still around. It scares me too, CJ, but we both want to find more gold. And besides, I want to talk with that octopus again. What do you say?"

After CJ had dropped Skye off at Poppy's, she checked in with her grandfather and then walked down to the dock, finding Flapper relaxing on a piling. Squeaky was lazing in the water next to the dock. Skye's mood perked up when she saw her two friends.

"Hey, Flapper, fancy meeting you here," she said, and smiled as she walked over and gave Flapper a kiss on his beak. "Oh, and I see your best buddy is here too."

"Maybe in your mind he is, but not in mine," Flapper said grumpily. Though he and Squeaky had had more interaction with each other this summer than ever before, he certainly did not consider him a buddy. He put up with Squeaky because of Skye.

"Hey, Skye," Squeaky said, jumping in the air. He swam over to the dock and waited for Skye to rub his sleek silver-gray snout and give him his usual pat.

"Hi, Squeaky, how have you been?" She sat down on the edge of the dock, bent forward, tickled the top of his head, and rubbed her soft hand down his snout. "Boy, I've sure missed you two."

"Where has everybody been hiding?" Flapper asked. "We haven't seen you or CJ around."

"Yeah, we've both been down to the dock a few times, and you and CJ haven't been here. Flapper thought we should check on you. What's been going on?" Squeaky asked.

Skye just realized that Squeaky didn't know what had happened to Cap.

"Oh, I'm sorry guys. Squeaky, I don't know if Flapper told you or not, but a giant squid came on the boat when we were out at the Marquesas Keys, and it killed Cap." Even now, tears filled her eyes, causing her to sniff a little.

"Yes, Flapper told me. I'm so sorry, Skye. What a horrible thing to happen!" Squeaky said. "I know how much both of you thought of him."

"Have you ever seen a giant squid?" Skye asked Squeaky.

"I've heard of some squid being almost that big, but I've never seen one," Squeaky was saying, "and I don't want to. The only thing that can kill them are Sperm whales. That's the only thing big enough."

"Really?" Skye questioned.

"Yep, that's right. Sperm whales are the answer if you want to kill this one."

"Are you sure?" Flapper asked. "You're not making that up, are you? I've never heard that." He had never trusted the no-it-all dolphin, and he wasn't about to start now.

"No, I'm serious. This is too important to lie about, and besides, I would never lie to Skye. Maybe to you, but not to her." Squeaky loved to irritate the pelican. If truth be told, he actually liked the pelican, but he had lots of fun teasing him.

Skye sat in silence, thinking about the new revelation. *A sperm whale*, she thought. *How do you get a sperm whale to kill a squid, much less get one out to the trench at the Marquesas?* "Squeaky, do you think you and your pod could find a sperm whale and get him to go out to the trench?" Skye asked, hesitantly. "It's important. CJ or I might get hurt or killed if that thing is still in the water, and we want to go back out there to find more gold."

Squeaky was silent for a moment. He sure didn't want anything to happen to either her or CJ, but he wasn't sure if he could even find a sperm whale. "I don't know," he finally answered. "You know they are few and far between, especially out here in these waters. Finding one might be a problem, but I'll ask around and see what I can do. As soon as I find out something, I'll let you know."

Chapter Forty-Two

Jack Watson looked around the shack with satisfaction. Glancing out the window, he noticed the small white flowers on the thick mangroves rising from the edge of the salty water that helped to hide the building. *The only way anyone could find this place would be from the air, and they would have to look hard.*

His hair was wet, and beads of sweat trickled down his face like tiny rivers. He had spent half the morning getting things ready for their planned event. *Not bad*, he thought, rubbing his hands together. *We'll teach those kids that they can't steal our gold, and we'll get lots of cash to boot. Plus, I get to be alone with that pretty little blonde. I know she likes me.* Puffing out his chest, he thought Skye might find him appealing. What a joke! With his homely face, greasy blond hair, scars from teenage acne, and rail-thin body, he hadn't had a girlfriend since being released from prison.

A small Porta Potty was wedged in the far corner of the room, and an ancient army cot with a soiled mattress lined the back wall. In the center of the room was a card table topped with an old, rusty kerosene lantern. Four new Walmart lawn chairs were placed strategically around the table to give the space a welcoming appearance. There was little room to move around in the small space.

"Oh, I almost forgot! I need to cover the windows with pillowcases," Jack mumbled to himself, trying to make sure he did not forget something and give Pete another reason to yell at him.

He reached into a cardboard box and withdrew three threadbare, yellowed pillowcases. He grabbed his filet knife and slit two sides of each pillowcase, which made three curtains. *I'll wait until she gets here to cover the windows.*

Cans of provisions were stacked neatly under a window on makeshift shelves that Pete had salvaged from a dumpster at a local renovation site.

All we need now is our guest. Jack was already making a mental list of how he was going to spend his seven thousand dollars.

Like Jack, Pete Samuels had been busy all morning. He soon realized that following someone around all day without being detected was far more difficult than he had imagined. Sweat from the blistering sun poured down his face and neck, soaking his tattered and soiled tee shirt. It was his job to figure out the easiest and safest way to grab the girl without being seen. At his last meeting with Bill Marr and Jack, they had unanimously decided to kidnap only the girl. She would be easier to snatch. She was tiny and didn't weigh much, plus girls were easier to intimidate than boys, and they had less body strength.

Pete would handle the logistics of the pick-up. He and Jack would grab her, and Marr would be the liaison with the family, arranging the money drop. The rest of the operation seemed pretty much cut and dry.

The real issue had not been discussed. What to do with the girl after the drop. She would see both Pete and Jack at the shack, and she could identify them to that nosy detective who had been cruising by their house like they were criminals or something. In Pete's opinion, they had no choice. He knew what he had to do with her, but he wasn't going to say anything to Jack or Marr.

CJ was in the wheelhouse of the *Money* entering Bowlegs Cut at Peterson Key Bank, just north of Indian Key Channel. The old shrimp boat moved along at a brisk twenty-one knots on glassy, smooth water. Coming up on Green Marker 93 on the right, he looked south to Indian Key Channel.

CJ flashed back to the terrifying incident last year on Indian Key. He had been bound to a chair, hands and feet, by a Russian smuggler, in a flooding cave where he had nearly drowned in the rising water. A miracle had prevented his death that day. His memory of the Indian spirit that had saved him was as clear today as it had been then. In that miraculous moment, his life had changed forever. His thoughts drifted over the events of the past year. *Pay attention or you'll run aground*, he told himself.

CJ felt truly happy. Being on the water with the wind blowing through my hair on a clear day like today makes me feel euphoric. *I just wish Skye was here!*

Skye had persuaded him to take the boat back down to Garrison Bight Marina, and she would take the VW and pick him up there. He couldn't shake the conversation they had had yesterday. He realized that he was in love with her, but he couldn't let his emotions dictate her flawed logic. His only hope was for Squeaky to locate a sperm whale, so that it would rid them and the local fishermen of the nightmare that had plagued them for the past few weeks.

When Skye picked him up at the marina, they would have some time together on the ride back to Islamorada to discuss going back out to the Marquesas. *I just hope she listens to reason this time.*

Chapter Forty-Three

As CJ pulled up to the dock at Garrison Bight Marina, Skye was waiting for him in his yellow VW Thing. *It's hot today*, she thought. *Yuk!*

Earlier, when she had left Islamorada to drive down to the marina, she had the windows down. It had helped hold the heat at bay a little. But sitting in the hot car for the past fifteen minutes waiting on CJ had caused tiny beads of sweat to pop out on her forehead and her upper lip. Her shirt was already sticking to her back. Blotting her face with a Kleenex she had retrieved from her purse, she jumped from the car, looked up at the boat, and gave CJ a big smile. *I'm so glad to see him again. I miss him when we're not together.*

Her beaming face was a welcoming sight to CJ, particularly after the three-hour shrimp boat trip up the Intracoastal. Skye waved and then stepped back to receive the bow line. CJ tossed her the rope, and minutes later the boat was secure.

"How was your trip?" CJ asked, stepping down onto the dock.

"Oh, it was uneventful. Just hot! Maybe you should consider buying a car with air conditioning," she joked.

CJ laughed, "Maybe next year. A few more gold bars and maybe I'll get that Corvette I've had my eye on."

Skye thought about his remark for a moment and then looked over at him. "More gold bars? Is that a yes to our conversation yesterday?"

"I gave it lots of thought on the way up, Skye. You're right about doing it for Cap, and I still think it's dangerous, but if we make it a quick dive, I guess we have a deal!"

Skye leaped into CJ's arms. "Thank you, thank you, thank you," she squealed in delight.

It was all CJ could do to refrain from kissing her.

They held each other for a long moment, smiling and looking into the other's eyes, first in close friendship, and then in something deeper. Realizing he had held Skye much longer than usual, CJ slowly lowered his arms. His face red with embarrassment, he noticed that Skye's face was flushed as well, and she had a strange, questioning look on her face. *Wonder what that means? Did she like the hug, or is she mad?* CJ stood there not knowing what to say.

Finally, Skye cleared her throat and spoke, "We'd better hit the road, or we'll be late getting home. We can plan our next dive on the drive home. Does that sound okay to you?"

Bill Marr walked out of Wal-Mart Super Center on South Dixie Highway in Florida City. He had just spent the past hour shopping for disposable phones, the ones that needed no contract and didn't have GPS. He had settled for three TracFone's. He had to pay extra for the new unused numbers, but that was okay with him. *The harder they are to be tracked the better.* He hoped that the antiquated cell phone system in the Keys would work to his benefit.

Throwing his packages in the back seat of his blue, late model BMW M4, he slammed the door, turned up the air conditioning, and began driving south toward Mile Marker 88 to meet Pete and Jack. He was anxious to get the show on the road. He needed money, and he needed it fast. He had just put his last twenty dollars into his fuel tank. Last night's binge had cost him over two hundred dollars. *I gotta quit that crap*, he decided. Of course, he told himself that every week when he realized he was broke.

———————————

Skye looked to the west and saw the brightest red sunset she had seen in years. It reminded her of the old sailor's tale; Red sky in the morning, sailors take warning, red sky at night, sailor's delight. *That means tomorrow will be a beautiful day*, she thought as she slammed the door to Poppy's Cadillac. She was in a hurry. CJ and his family were on their way over for dinner. At the last minute, Poppy had asked her to run over to the Winn-Dixie to get a bottle of cayenne pepper for the fish he was preparing. Her stomach growling, she thought, *I can't wait to eat. Poppy cooks the best fish in the world.*

In her rush to turn into the parking lot, she didn't see the white van following behind the Caddy. Finding a parking spot two rows from the entrance to the store, Skye rushed up the stairs and through the automatic sliding glass door.

Chapter Forty-Four

Almost stumbling in her haste, Skye rushed down the six steps leading from the grocery store to the parking lot. As she reached the driver's side of the Cadillac, she heard the metallic sound of a sliding door. Through her peripheral vision, she saw two men step down from a white van parked very close to the Caddy. Turning, she recognized both of them. *What the heck?* She was so shocked she couldn't speak. Her white plastic grocery bag dropped from her grasp. Before she could react, one man had grabbed her by the arm, covered her mouth with a foul smelling hand, and was pulling her toward the cargo opening. The other grabbed her free arm, almost dragging her toward the van. Unable to scream, she instinctively began kicking, hitting one hard on his shin and hearing an expletive. Jack was glad that Pete had decided to come along. Neither had realized how spunky the tiny, blonde girl was. Pete kept his clamped hand over her mouth, while Jack jumped into the van, trying to pull Skye inside by her arm.

With superhuman force, Skye jerked her right arm from away from Jack and reached back and grabbed the door handle on the Caddy. The door swung open about halfway.

"Crap!" she heard someone say as if she felt a hard blow at the back of her head. Her mind went blank, her knees buckled, and the two men lifted her inside the vehicle, sliding the door closed.

CJ looked at his watch. It was eight thirty-three. *Where is Skye? She should be here by now.*

Maria stood next to Poppy, observing his culinary skills. "That's going to be a great Caesar salad, Poppy." It took all of her willpower not to grab a pinch of it.

"Just for you, my dear," Poppy teased. "I know how much you like it. Hey, Michael, how are those Martini's coming along?"

Michael smiled. "Coming right up, Monsieur Chef."

Listening to the banter, CJ looked at his watch again. Eight forty-one. He fidgeted on the bar stool next to the center island. "What time did you say Skye left for the store, Poppy?"

Poppy turned to answer the question and looked at the wall clock. "I guess almost an hour ago. You're right, CJ, it seems like it's taking her a long time just to get cayenne pepper. The store is less than a mile away." Poppy suddenly got a strange feeling in the pit of his stomach. He thought about the threatening note taped to his door.

CJ was very concerned, almost to the point of panic. *It's not like Skye to do this. Something must have happened to her,* he thought. Trying not to visualize her being involved in a traffic accident, he stood up and grabbed his keys. "I'm going to go to the store and see what's holding her up."

Arriving about five minutes later, CJ saw Poppy's car parked in front of the Winn-Dixie. As he pulled around to the driver's side, what he saw made chills run up his spine. He braked to a halt, jumped out of the VW, and ran over to the Cadillac. The driver's door was half open. A plastic Winn-Dixie bag lay next to the car. CJ picked it up, looked inside, and saw a bottle of McCormick's Cayenne Pepper. His heart had begun beating so hard, he felt as if it would come out of his chest. A hundred thoughts flashed through his mind, none of them good.

Just to make sure he wasn't just panicking, he ran up the steps to the grocery store, went through the automatic doors, looked around and then yelled, "Skye!" Several shoppers turned to look at him, but there was no answer. Skye was not in the store.

Outside, CJ ran over to the Caddy, slammed the driver side door, and then jumped into his VW Thing. He had to get back to Poppy's and get help.

"This can't be happening. Why would anybody want to take Skye?" His mind was racing. "I have to find her. They'd better not hurt her, or I will hunt them down if it's the last thing I do."

"Now, slow down, Son," Michael said, gently shaking CJ's shoulders. "We'll find her, I promise."

Maria and Poppy had gathered around CJ, asking questions and giving each other what comfort they could. Poppy looked pale and became quiet as Michael grabbed his cell phone to call Detective Callahan.

"Have CJ meet me at the Winn-Dixie," Callahan commanded, quickly hanging up his phone.

It was difficult to tell who was the most upset, CJ, Poppy, Maria, or Michael. Maria turned off the stove, and they all followed CJ out to the yellow Thing and piled in. Even with all the weight, the little car burned rubber out of the driveway.

Chapter Forty-Five

With the car loaded, CJ drove at breakneck speed up the Overseas Highway. The Thing, which maxed out at a top speed of fifty-five miles an hour, groaned with every lane change as CJ zipped in and out of the heavy traffic. Up ahead, he saw flashing blue lights in the Winn-Dixie parking lot. He counted three police cars.

"Slow down, Son," Michael warned. "The rusted springs on this thing may not hold up, and then what would we do?"

CJ hit the brakes as he made a sharp left-hand turn and zoomed across two southbound lanes into the Winn-Dixie parking lot. Three police officers in uniform stood next to the Caddy. Detective Callahan was just getting out of his gray unmarked car.

CJ already had his door open as the vehicle ground to a stop next to Callahan. Within seconds, everybody was out of the VW. Poppy headed for the Caddy but was stopped by a police officer.

"Sorry, sir! We have to dust the car for fingerprints first. This is a crime scene."

"Oh, that's right," Poppy said, his face blushing in embarrassment. He turned and walked over to Michael and CJ, who were talking with Detective Callahan.

Callahan directed his attention to CJ. "Okay, Son, tell me exactly what you found when you got here."

"Well, Detective, there's not that much to tell. When I got here, the driver's side door was half open, and I found a plastic bag with a bottle of cayenne pepper lying on the ground next to it. Then I went inside the store and called for Skye, but she wasn't there. That's all I know, sir."

Not expecting an answer, Callahan asked the question, "Any of you know who might want to harm Skye?"

Poppy stepped forward. "The only person I can think of is the guy Michael put in the hospital."

"Yeah, that's right. I'd forgotten about him," Michael replied.

"Mr. Hudson, I think you should go home and wait by the phone. Whoever took Skye may demand a ransom. I'll send an officer with you, just in case."

Poppy nodded his head and headed to the police cruiser.

Skye's head was pounding from the blow to her head. It felt as if it would never ease up.

I'm in a boat, Skye thought, still a little groggy, her head reeling in dizziness. An outboard motor purred in the background. Now and then warm salt spray would blow over her when the boat hit a large wave, helping to make her a little more conscious of her surroundings.

A blindfold placed over her eyes earlier in the evening prevented her from seeing what was going on around her or where she was being taken. Her mouth was dry from a rag stuffed into it to keep her from talking or screaming. The feeling of wide tape stretched tightly across her mouth made her very uncomfortable. Her shoulders ached from her hands being bound tightly behind her back. As her head cleared a little more, panic welled up and she felt nauseated. She had to fight back the urge to vomit, knowing that if she did, she would surely drown from the bile produced in her empty stomach.

Oh, God, please don't let them hurt me, she prayed. Thoughts of CJ, Michael and Poppy doing everything in their power to find her gave her comfort, but she couldn't help shaking from fear. Her teeth began chattering. *Calm down,* she told herself. *Where are they taking me? And why? Must be to an island; otherwise, why would I be in a boat?* After being knocked out, she had no idea how long the boat had been traveling to its destination.

Skye noticed the waves had smoothed, and the outboard motor had decreased speed down to a few hundred rpm's. She felt the boat slowing, and then it came to a sudden halt as if the bow had been forced onto a beach. *Where in the world are we? Will CJ ever be able to find me? How will he know where I am?* Skye figured that they probably had taken her for ransom, but she wondered if it was for ransom and if the ransom was paid, would she ever be returned to Poppy's. She had seen their faces and knew who they were. How could they let her go when she could identify them? Fear clawed its way up her spine, and nausea climbed its way up her throat.

Chapter Forty-Six

A dark cloud of fear and helplessness hovered over the Hudson residence. CJ, Poppy, Michael, and Maria sat in silence around the center island in Poppy's kitchen. Forgotten empty coffee cups had been pushed to the side, with crumbs from a half-full package of Chips Ahoy scattered around them. Each was staring at the phone, and each was willing it to ring. There had been no calls for ransom, and that wasn't a good sign.

Detective Callahan and Manuel Lopez, a senior FBI agent, sat in the living room, discussing their game plan. *We've got to find Skye, and we've got to do it quick*, Callahan thought.

Earlier that evening, communication officers from the Monroe County Sheriff's Office had installed phone recorders and tracing equipment to Poppy's phone system. Now, all they could do was wait.

Michael looked over at Maria, who was holding her right hand against her chest, her face was flushed, her breathing shallow. "You okay, sweetheart?" Michael asked with concern.

"I'm feeling a little anxious," she whispered. Mental pictures she had not visited for years began pouring in from the past. Skye's kidnapping had sparked memories of a time, years ago, that Michael and Sonny Mitchell had rescued Maria from a boathouse where she was being held after being kidnapped by Cuban drug smugglers.

Michael and Sonny were both working for the National Security

Agency at the time. She could remember the sounds of the gunshots, and the blood that had splattered on her and the walls as the two rushed in to save her. She remembered the bloody bodies lying grotesquely on the floor. She had suppressed those memories for over twenty years, but now they were as vivid in her mind as if they had happened only yesterday.

Michael sensed her intense distress. "Let's go outside and take a walk, sweetheart." He got up from his stool, took Maria's hand, and led her outside.

They stood on the dock while Michael held her close. With her head resting on his shoulder, she began to sob, both for herself and for Skye.

"It almost feels like it happened yesterday, Michael. It all came back when I realized what Skye must be going through," she sobbed. Tears poured from her beautiful, dark eyes. "Poor Skye. Poor baby. Why her, Michael? Of all the people in the world, why did they choose her?"

"I don't know, honey, but it will be all right. We'll get her back safe and sound, I promise," Michael whispered softly.

Watching his mother nearly fall apart, CJ knew he had to stay strong for her and Poppy, but inside his emotions were a mess. *If anything happens to Skye, I will hunt her kidnappers down and kill every last one of them,* he told himself. Of course, his gentle nature made it impossible for him to kill even a fly, but he would see to it that they would spend the rest of their lives in prison. *Please, please be okay, Skye. I need you. I love you.*

Michael looked at his watch. Two forty-seven. Skye's kidnapping and all the raw emotions that followed had made him forget to call his best friend at the National Security Agency, Sonny Mitchell. Michael reached for his cell phone and left the kitchen. *If anyone can find Skye, it's Sonny.*

Walking outside and down to the dock, Michael placed his call.

"Hello," a sleepy masculine voice answered.

"Thought you'd be out partying, grumpy," Michael joked.

"Yeah, I was dreaming about the prettiest baby doll you've ever seen," Sonny said. "What's happened when I get a call from you at this hour?" Sonny asked.

"We got a big problem here, Bro. I need your help."

Sonny Mitchell sat up, turned, and placed his feet on the floor. "You've got my attention."

"You remember Skye, right?"

"CJ's cute little blonde girlfriend? Oh, yeah. If I were forty years younger, I would give CJ some competition."

"Yeah, well, somebody snatched her in a Winn-Dixie parking lot down in Tavernier last night."

Sonny sat in silence for a moment, picturing what Michael had just said. "What time did it happen?"

"Between 8:30 and 8:45."

"Okay, fill me in on the details." Grabbing the pad and pen on the nightstand, Sonny was instantly awake. Michael was the best friend he had ever had, and CJ was his godson. If anything ever happened to hurt Michael, Maria or CJ, Sonny would move heaven and earth for them. He had contacts in the NSA that would be able to help find Skye. He knew that after the first forty-eight hours, there wasn't much chance of her being returned to them. *I'd better get busy.* After asking Michael several questions, he immediately placed a call.

Skye would never be able to forget the odor, nor the wheezing. *Pete Samuels stinks*, she thought. Both men had hoisted her up from the bottom of the boat and were leading her down what seemed to be a path. To where, she had no idea. She could tell it was dark from the night sounds emanating all around her. As usual, the mosquitoes were intolerable. Momentarily, they stopped, and then she heard a screen door open.

"Watch your step, kid," Jack Watson ordered. "You gotta go up three steps."

Skye carefully felt her way up the steps, and Jack pushed her thru the door, none too gently.

Pete Samuels took her arm and led her to the center of the room. "You be nice, and we'll take the blindfold off. Otherwise, you'll stay just like you are. Understand?"

Skye nodded her head.

Moments later, she blinked from the bright light of the Coleman Lantern as Pete removed the blindfold. Next, the tape and gag were removed. "Go over there and take a seat on the cot," Pete commanded.

"Please, I need water," Skye whispered in a raspy voice. Her mouth was so dry she could hardly speak. It had been about midday since she had had anything to drink.

Jack walked over to an ice chest, withdrew a bottle of spring water, and twisted off the cap. He suddenly realized he'd have to hold the bottle so she could drink. Her bound hands were behind her back.

Skye took a small sip of the cold liquid, swished it around in her parched mouth, and spit it out on the floor.

"What the heck!" Jack shouted, offended that she had spit on the floor inside the shack. He raised his hand to strike her.

"Leave her be," Pete ordered. "If you'd had a rag stuffed in your mouth for six hours, you'd do the same thing," Pete said, looking at Jack with contempt.

Jack pushed Skye toward the bed. "What about my hands?" Skye whispered.

Pete turned her around and removed one side of the handcuffs. "Sit down on the bed."

Looking at the filthy cot, Skye sat down on the edge. Her stomach rolled just thinking about who had been on the bed before her. From the odor, she figured it must have been Pete. He leaned down and shackled her hand to the railing. She glanced up at Jack, who had a strange gleam in his eyes. Looking away, she shivered and then took another sip of water from the bottle he had handed her.

Chapter Forty-Seven

On vacation for the first time in years, Buddy Bryson stood on the dock, staring at the sign. It read *Lady Diane*. Having arrived late last evening, he hadn't seriously thought about how he might spend his time in the Florida Keys. He had visited Key West about ten years before with his wife and had loved the easy rhythm of the small island.

His job in New York was very stressful, and he needed time to unwind and enjoy life a bit. His time-consuming career had caused the end of his ten-year marriage, and this was his first trip alone to the Keys.

Making a quick decision to reserve his place on the fishing charter boat, he walked over to a ticket booth that was about the size of a Porta-Potty. Pressing two fifty-dollar bills through the window, he waited for his ticket and thirty-five dollars in change. Satisfied that he had made the first fun decision of his newly single life, he headed back to his car.

Turning the key in the ignition, Mark remembered that Duval Street had a few bars. He figured he could use a couple beers to unwind before he departed for three hours of bottom fishing off the Marquesas Keys. The sign had given the hours of seven p.m. to ten p.m. for the fishing trip. Seeing Sloppy Joe's Bar ahead, he decided the cold beer would taste good in this heat, and he could relax until it was time to return to the boarding dock.

Sitting at his desk, Detective Callahan's cell phone rang. Rubbing his eyes, he answered on the first ring and was told that there still had been no call for ransom at the Hudson residence. *I sure wish the call would come so Poppy could make the payment, and Skye could be returned home to her grandfather.* He didn't want to think about what might have already happened to Skye if they had not taken her for ransom, or if the ransom wasn't paid.

He thought about dropping by Mr. Hudson's house on his way home, but he knew he had to finish up a bit of paperwork on the case. Then he decided he was going to head on home because he was dead tired. It had been a long day.

His office phone rang. "Callahan." *I sure hope this is good news about Skye*, he thought. *I'm so groggy I can't think straight. I need to get home and get a few hours' sleep.* He had only slept a total of about four hours in the past two days.

"Detective Callahan, this is Boatswain Mate Richardson at the Islamorada Coast Guard Station. We just got a call from the ticket booth where the *Lady Diane* docks at Garrison Bight Marina. Seems the owner is worried sick. The *Lady Diane* didn't make it back in last night."

"So why are you calling me? That's a Coast Guard issue."
"Well, sir, all of our equipment is tied up, and I have nothing available to send out to look for her. I was hoping your department could send out a chopper and search the area."

Callahan slumped back in his chair. *Oh, no! It's going to be another long day.*

"Where did you say she went?"

"Marquesas Keys, sir."

Callahan stood and looked at his watch. *Only eight twenty-eight a.m.?* "All right, I'll get somebody on it right away. I'll keep you posted."

The shack was getting hot, even in the early morning sun. The makeshift tin roof did nothing to help cool the building. In a couple more hours, it would feel like an oven inside. With no air conditioning, three small windows, and a screen door, and only humid air outside, the temperature had begun to rise inside the small room.

Due to the heat, Skye had slept fitfully, her face to the wall to avoid looking at her captors. It was bad enough having to look at Pete's disgusting face during the day, but Jack's menacing eyes were even more frightening. He kept looking at her with that strange gleam in his eyes, which scared her. The old cot didn't exactly smell like clean sheets either.

Having held her bladder as long as she could, she dreaded the embarrassing task of asking one of them to let her go to the bathroom. She felt like she was about to burst. Twelve hours was a long time to wait to pee.

With effort, Skye managed to turn over. Glancing around, she saw Pete lying on the chaise lounge chair, with drool escaping down one side of his wide-open mouth. He was making a noise somewhere between a muffled wheeze and the most awful snore she had ever heard. Just looking at him made her shiver in disgust. Jack was nowhere in sight.

"Please, I need to go to the bathroom." Her voice sounded raspy, and her throat was still dry.

His snoring momentarily interrupted, Pete stirred and finally moved his massive body from the chair. A big roll of sweaty blubber hung over his dirty, faded, and torn shorts. In a fog, he walked over and picked up a gallon plastic bucket, put it down next to the cot, turned, and walked out the screen door, letting it slam as he headed down the steps to relieve himself at the edge of the mangroves. *Where the heck is Jack?* he wondered. *He should be back by now.*

First, checking in with Agent Lopez at Mr. Hudson's, and then making some other calls, Callahan headed home for a few hours of badly needed rest. As he pulled into his driveway, his cell phone rang. *Not now, please*, he thought.

He looked down and saw that it was his office calling. "Callahan," he said with fatigue in his voice.

"Detective, this is Morgan. I just got a call from our helicopter. "They've located the *Lady Diane* off the Marquesas Keys."

"That's good news."

"Not exactly, it's run aground, and it seems there's no one onboard. The call also said that they located several people stranded in the mangroves."

"Okay, Morgan, get one of our boats out there right away. Those poor people are probably being eaten alive by mosquitoes."

Morgan hesitated for a moment, knowing Callahan wouldn't like what he was about to say. "Boss, I'm sorry, but your boat is the only one available right now."

Callahan groaned, almost in pain. It was as if everything was against him, keeping him from his much-needed rest. First, it was the Coast Guard, and now his own department was coming up empty-handed. Having no choice, he said, "Okay, Morgan, it looks like it's just you and me. Where's my boat docked?"

"Last I heard, she was at the Islamorada Coast Guard Station."

Sighing, he said, "Okay, meet me there in twenty minutes."

Maybe I can rest when I'm dead, he thought morbidly, his brain almost to the point of non-functioning.

Chapter Forty-Eight

When the phone rang, everybody jumped. Agent Manuel Lopez rose from his chair and headed to the kitchen, holding one finger to his lips, indicating that everyone should remain quiet. By the second ring, he had two fingers pointing at Poppy as if counting down, and on the third ring he pointed three fingers and nodded his head, motioning for him to pick up the phone.

For George Hudson, it was a relief to hear the ringing. He felt as if he had been in limbo, not hearing anything about Skye, and the ringing phone brought him back into the real world again. With this call, he could open communications with Skye's captor and get his precious little granddaughter back.

Taking a deep breath, he said, "Hello."

"Is this Mr. Hudson?" a deep voice asked. It sounded as if the voice was coming from deep within a tunnel, like the automated voices in the suspense thriller movies when the bad guys were trying to disguise their voices. *Lord, I wish this was just a movie and Skye was home safe with me.*

Immediately realizing that it was Skye's captor, he said, "Yes, this is Mr. Hudson. Who is this? What in the heck have you done with my granddaughter?" His anger was rising at the caller who had taken Skye.

"Hold on Mr. Hudson, not so fast," the voice soothed. "We can do this without either of us getting upset. In fact, it would be to your advantage to remain calm and listen to what I have to say.

I'm only going to say it once."

"What do you want?" Poppy demanded. His heart was pounding, both in anger at the caller and fear for Skye. "Just give me back my granddaughter!"

"It's simple, Mr. Hudson. Just do as I say, and I will return her to you unharmed; otherwise, you'll be very sorry. Get my drift?"

Agent Lopez looked at Poppy. He motioned with his palms pressing down, trying to get Poppy to remain calm. Lopez was a sharp, level-headed agent with a kind nature, and Callahan had immediately approved his assignment to stay at the Hudson residence.

Poppy took a deep breath. His throat felt dry as if it had a wad of cotton in it. Finally, he responded to the strange voice on the other end of the phone, "Yes, I get your drift."

"Now, Mr. Hudson, I know you have money. I want you to go to the bank and withdraw twenty-thousand dollars and have it available to me by tomorrow at noon, and not a minute later. I will call back at that time and give you instructions as to where to deliver the money. Understood?"

Poppy's irritation with the caller was obvious, but he was afraid for Skye. "Look, whoever you are, be reasonable. Today is Saturday. It's impossible for me to come up with the money by Sunday noon. Don't you know the banks are closed today and tomorrow?"

"Mr. Hudson, I suggest you get in touch with your banker and have him meet you at the bank today. Remember, no later than noon tomorrow." The line went dead.

Poppy slammed the phone down onto the receiver. "Ain't no way I can get the money by noon tomorrow!" he shouted in frustration.

Callahan parked his car at the Coast Guard station, got out, locked his doors, and walked toward his boat. Officer Courtney Morgan already had the engines idling and the boat ready to go. He waved Callahan aboard. Morgan was the officer who had been with Callahan the year before on Indian Key during the storm when CJ Jansen had almost drowned. He was a good man and a good police officer, and Callahan liked and trusted him.

"I called Key West EMT's and Sea Tow and have them both on standby," Morgan was saying, as he untied the mooring lines.

Callahan put on his old dive team cap and eased the boat out of the marina.

Poppy, Michael, Maria, CJ, and Agent Lopez sat in silence around the island table in Poppy's kitchen for almost a minute. They looked as if they had just arrived at a wake. Agent Lopez was the first to speak after the phone call.

"Please be assured that our technicians are trying to trace the call at this very moment. I should have some information shortly," he said, hoping to reassure the group.

Michael looked over at Agent Lopez and then at Poppy. "Wonder why this guy decided on twenty thousand dollars? He said he knows you have money. Why not ask for fifty or a hundred thousand?" Michael asked, wrinkling his brow in thought. "That seems strange, doesn't it? Twenty thousand dollars isn't all that much for a kidnapping."

"That's a good question, Dad," CJ said thoughtfully. "It does seem strange because that's the exact amount that Skye and I inherited from Cap. Do you think it has anything to do with our inheritance?"

His curiosity piqued, Poppy said, "Good thinking guys," and he looked over at the agent. "What do you think, Agent Lopez?"

"Who knew about the inheritance?" Lopez questioned the group.

Everyone looked around the kitchen island to see who would

be first to speak.

Maria responded, "It was just the five of us, and Cap's attorney, Bill Marr."

"That's it! The only person outside of us is the attorney. It has to be him!" CJ answered with excitement in his voice.

"Don't convict him yet, CJ. Twenty thousand dollars might just be a number the kidnapper grabbed out of the air, but we certainly should give him a good look. What do you know about him?" Agent Lopez asked, looking over at Poppy.

"Not much. After Cap's memorial service, I got a call from Mr. Marr, saying that we were to come to his office for the reading of Cap's will. That's all I can tell you. I had never heard of him until he called."

Agent Lopez scratched his chin, which was in dire need of a shave. They had all been up most of the night, and his morning had been busy with calls from Callahan and the FBI office. "I'll have an agent go by his house and interview him, but don't get too excited. I can't imagine an attorney getting involved in a kidnapping like this. It's probably the work of more than one person, though. Kidnappers don't usually work alone."

"What about those two bozos who wanted CJ and Skye's gold?" Michael questioned. "Maybe someone should pay them a visit."

"That's being taken care of as we speak," answered Agent Lopez. "Detective Callahan let me know earlier this morning that he was sending an officer to see them. What we need to do now is locate the president of your bank, Mr. Hudson. In kidnap cases like your granddaughter's, you want to have the money ready to go when the next call comes in. You might not get a second chance."

Chapter Forty-Nine

Callahan and Morgan arrived in the area where several people had been seen earlier by the helicopter. The first task for the officers was to locate and pick up all the stranded passengers of the *Lady Diane* from the mangroves. At least they assumed they were from the *Lady Diane*.

Their search began on the southeast side of the evergreens and shrubs at the Marquesas Keys. The first survivor was spotted a few minutes before noon. Callahan could tell he was a tall man who looked to be in his early sixties, sitting in about two feet of water with his arms folded around his shoulders. His gray hair was plastered to his head. As Callahan slowly moved the bow of the boat in closer, the man just sat there staring out into space, seemingly oblivious to their boat. He didn't even look up. Although he wouldn't be able to fully comprehend or accept what had happened to him until much later, Buddy Bryson of New York was a very lucky man. He was one of the few who had survived the night.

"Hello, there" Callahan called out. "Are you okay? Where are the others?" The man finally turned his head to face them, but his light blue eyes were not focusing. He did not make a move to get up. *What's going on with this guy*? Callahan wondered.

Morgan walked to the bow. When the boat was within four feet of the man, Callahan put the engine in reverse, bringing it to a stop. "Looks like he's in shock," Morgan responded. He lowered himself over the side and into the water and then moved over a few feet to stand beside the man. "Sir, are you all right?"

The man slowly looked up at Morgan but said nothing. When Morgan reached over and touched him, the man flinched.

"Now what do we do?" Morgan asked Callahan.

"Looks like we need a medic. I don't want to get into a tussle with him. Can you tell if he's injured?"

Morgan visually examined the man as best he could without touching him. "No, I don't think he's hurt. He just seems to be in shock. What the heck happened here, Callahan?"

"You know as much as I do. Hop back in the boat. We'll leave him here until we can get him medical attention. We'll go check to see if we can find the others. Whatever happened here last night must have been pretty bad."

———————

Jack made it back to the shack at about ten-thirty that morning. By then, the temperature in the building was nearly ninety degrees. With luck, they'd have a typical afternoon shower that would temporarily cool things down. In the summertime in Florida, it usually rained for about twenty minutes almost every afternoon, and then the sun reappeared. There were also occasional thunderstorms that lasted for hours. Either would have been a welcome change to cool the tin-roofed structure. Until then, they would have to suffer.

Skye lay in a bed of sweat as Jack opened the screen door and walked into the sweltering room. Her face looked flushed from the heat, and she was dehydrated and listless. The last drink of water offered to her had been the night before when they had arrived. She had begged Pete for water all morning, but he just ignored her. Her mouth was dry, and her throat felt so parched she could hardly produce enough saliva to swallow.

Pete heaved himself up from the chaise lounge, farted loudly, and then headed for the ice chest for his first beer of the day. He had made sure to stock the cabin with several twelve packs of his favorite brew.

"Hey Pete, the cops are swarming 'round your house like bees," Jack said with excitement. "I rode by Marr's place, too. I could swear there was an unmarked cop car there."

"Did you see Marr's car?" Pete growled.

"Nope," Jack said.

"He musta made the ransom call to the ol' man." Sweating profusely, Pete wheezed his way back to his chair. The hot, humid air inside the shack covered its occupants like a heavy shroud.

"Ya know," Pete groaned as he sat down, "this may notta' been as good an idea as we thought."

"Too late now, buddy," Jack said with sarcasm. "You know the old saying, "Be careful what you wish for, you just might git it. We might git more than we bargained for this time."

"Yeah, well, soon as I get my money, I'm outta here."

Skye looked over at the two dirty, pathetic men. In a raspy voice, she said, "If you guys let me go, I promise I won't say anything to the police."

Jack turned to look at Skye, his face red with anger. "You 'spect us to believe you won't say nothin? Girl, I didn't get off no turnip truck yesterday. You'd be making a beeline for the cops before me and Pete could get outta town. Besides, I got plans for you, little lady."

That same gleam that Skye had seen the night before flashed across Jack's face, and her bowels started to loosen a little in fear. Holding her breath, she held herself in check as she managed to keep from being embarrassed in front of the two creeps. Having looked around earlier as she lay in bed, she had noticed that the haphazard structure was only one large room. There was no bathroom.

Chapter Fifty

Callahan had just got off the phone with the Monroe County Sheriff's Department as he turned his boat toward the mangroves to pick up the others. He had requested a helicopter with medical assistance and transportation for the all the survivors and a Sea Tow for the *Lady Diane.*

Pulling the boat in closer to the shrubs, Callahan saw a disheveled-looking, middle-aged man and woman sitting in the shallow water. Both looked to be in pretty bad shape. The instant the man saw the boat, he started waving his hands and shouting at the top of his lungs. "Help us! Help us, please!"

As Callahan and Morgan drew closer, they could tell from the condition of the couple that they were suffering from exposure. They were both covered in mosquito bites. The woman's face was red and swollen, her lips were puffy, and large welts covered her body. She appeared to be having trouble breathing.

Must be an allergy, Morgan thought. He quickly looked under the seat for the first aid kit. There was usually a box of Benadryl inside, and from the looks of the woman, he knew she needed something fast, or she might not make it.

"Thank God you're here," the man moaned. "Oh, my God, thank you. Hurry, please, my wife needs help. She has an allergy to mosquito bites."

Morgan shouted out, "Hang on folks, we'll be right there! Just hang on."

Callahan eased the boat forward, and the man grabbed hold of the bow.

Morgan jumped into the water, and with a little help from the trembling man they pulled the woman along the gunwale to the rear of the boat where a swim ladder waited. In her condition, she could offer no help, but she was petite, and both men were able to lift her up into the boat.

Morgan took the lid off a bottle of cold water and gently coached the woman into trying to swallow two of the tiny antihistamines. Her throat was nearly closed. Weak from lack of oxygen, she tried to lie down on the deck, but Morgan kept talking to her. She finally opened her mouth and with effort swallowed the pills with a sip of water, though not easily. Morgan hoped she would last until the rescue helicopter made it out to their location. With a bottle of water in his hand, the man, visibly shaken and upset, sat down on the deck and held his wife's head in his lap as she fell asleep.

Callahan steered the boat out from the mangroves and slowly began maneuvering it around the brush to pick up the next group. Glancing at the survivors, he asked, "What happened, folks?"

"Oh, my God, it was horrible," the man sobbed. "I've never seen such an awful thing in my life. I thought we would all die. It was terrifying! It killed them!" he said.

Moments later, his wife stirred. Able to breathe a little better, she began crying along with her husband. Neither was making any sense.

They said it killed them. What killed them? wondered Morgan.

Callahan and Morgan could only stare down at the couple. "I can't wait to get onboard the boat and see what happened," Callahan whispered under his breath to Morgan.

Their search continued. As Callahan rounded the last mangrove, they heard a young male voice yelling. "Over here, over here. Help me, please. Oh, God, somebody please help me!"

Moments later, they saw a young teen standing alone. He

looked to be in a little better shape than the others. He had a few mosquito bites, but he seemed a little more alert and able to communicate. Morgan waved as the teen began climbing down from the bushes into the water. "Need any help?"

"No, I can make it okay. Have you seen my dad? I have to find him." The next instant he was in the water swimming toward the boat.

Callahan put the engine in neutral and waited while the boy swam around to the dive ladder. Morgan stood to help him up into the boat. Finally, he raised his hand for assistance. Morgan noticed the teen had suffered fewer insect bites than the others. *Lucky kid*, he thought, *in more ways than one.* "Are there any other survivors around here?" Morgan asked.

"I haven't seen anyone else," the boy responded, taking a big gulp of water. "We need to find my dad. Please help me find my dad."

"We'll try our best to find him. What happened on the boat last night?"

With an unexpected stricken look on his face, and not willing to talk further, he curled up on the deck and closed his eyes.

Callahan turned the boat around and headed back to pick up their first survivor. After a bit of difficulty, he and Morgan managed to get him onboard. He was still in shock and unable to speak.

Callahan decided not to go on the *Lady Diane* until the rescue helicopter had removed the survivors from the boat. *They've been through enough*, he thought.

As they made their way around the eastern side of the mangroves, they heard the sound of the helicopter. Callahan looked up and saw it approaching. It was a Sikorsky S-76A Trauma Star, the same one used last year to pull Skye out of the old cistern on Indian Key. Hanging out the door, rescue diver Curt Shields stood ready to go into the water.

Chapter Fifty-One

Agent Lopez sent a car to the large, Italian style home of Bruce McConnell, President of Capital Bank in Islamorada, Florida.

Before stepping out of his car, Agent Johnny Jackson checked his watch, 12:47p.m. He walked up the concrete pathway, stepped up on the portico, and pressed the doorbell. Easy listening music flowed softly through the glass and screen door. While waiting for a response, he glanced around the yard and noticed that the lawn was a beautifully manicured, rich green color. Bright flowers bordered the walkway. Agent Jackson wondered if the banker and his wife employed a full-time gardener. Turning back to the door, he saw a shadow pass through the living room, and a moment later a white-haired, matronly looking woman came to the door.

"Yes, may I help you?"

"Mrs. McConnell?"

"Yes."

"Ma'am, my name is Agent Jackson with the FBI," he said, through the screen door, holding out his FBI identification.

"Is something wrong, young man?" she asked.

Before Agent Jackson could answer, she pushed the door open and stepped out onto the porch.

"Mrs. McConnell, it's critical that we get in touch with your husband as soon as possible. We need to ask him to make an emergency withdrawal from his bank. Someone's life depends upon it."

"Oh, my goodness, I wish I could help you, but my husband is in the Bahamas and won't be back until Sunday evening," she said, wringing her hands. Remembering her manners, she offered an Adirondack chair to the handsome, young agent.

"No, thank you. Do you know where in the Bahamas your husband might be?"

After thinking for a moment, she responded, "Bimini, I believe. The Bimini Big Game and Fish Club. Yes, I'm sure that's it."

Agent Lopez hung up the phone with Agent Jackson, who was heading back to the Hudson residence. Lopez gave Skye's grandfather the news, and he was devastated. His face looked flushed as he paced back and forth in the kitchen. Under more stress than his already high blood pressure could manage, Poppy was gently led to a recliner by Agent Lopez.

Not to be deterred, Poppy looked up at Lopez and said, "Even if we find him, how on earth are we going to get him back here before noon tomorrow?"

Trying to keep him from getting too upset, Agent Lopez slowly sipped his espresso before calmly responding. "We've got a call in to the Bimini Big Game and Fish Club as we speak. The banker's wife claims that he is there. If he is, we'll let him know how critical it is that he flies home immediately. Seeing the look on Poppy's face, he said, "Don't worry, Mr. Hudson, we'll find him, and we'll get the ransom money by the deadline."

The front doorbell chimed. "I'll get it," Maria offered.

When Maria reached the front door, she paused a moment and looked through the peephole. Sonny Mitchell stood on the opposite side. She took a deep breath and stood tall, at least as tall as a small, five-foot-three-inch woman could be, and then she quickly opened the door. *Thank goodness he's here. He'll help us get Skye back.*

"Sonny," she sighed, her eyes glistening at seeing hers and Michael's old friend, "what a sight for sore eyes you are."

"Hey, girl. You're more beautiful than ever. How about a big hug?"

Maria jumped into his arms. "Michael will be so happy to see you. Thank God you're here!"

Pouring a cup of espresso in the kitchen, Michael heard the commotion at the front door and headed that way.

"Hey, Bro," Michael beamed. "Come on in. CJ and Poppy sure will be glad to see you."

Sonny wasted no time in getting down to business. "Any new developments?"

"Just trying to find the banker so we can pay the ransom money," Maria interjected, ushering Sonny toward the kitchen.

CJ jumped to his feet when he saw his godfather come through the door. He ran to greet Sonny and gave him a big hug. Sonny was not a relative, but CJ had always called him Uncle Sonny. Next to his dad, Sonny had been his mentor, and besides that, he always had great stories to tell CJ about all the women he had had fun with over the years. Of course, his dad had no idea, and CJ wasn't about to tell him.

"Uncle Sonny! I'm so glad you're here," CJ said and smiled. He had heard stories about Sonny's and his dad's escapades, and with Sonny's presence, he felt so much better about finding Skye. *If anyone can find her, Uncle Sonny and the NSA can.*

Sonny greeted Poppy, who shook his hand. Next, he was introduced to Agent Lopez. Lopez filled Sonny in on the progress of the investigation, which so far had not produced much information to help in finding the kidnappers. Lopez was happy for the extra help, especially when that help was one of its toughest and most famous agents at the NSA.

"There are so many places down here to hide someone," Sonny was saying. "There are tons of islands, and thousands of boats, houses, condos, and God only knows what else. I called my friends in DC, and they've aimed a satellite with night vision in this direction. Maybe with a little luck, they'll turn up something."

"Agent Lopez, maybe you should consider placing a helicopter in Bimini, just in case we locate the banker. Time is of the essence, as I'm sure you know."

"Thanks, I'll get right on it."

Chapter Fifty-Two

It took well over an hour to locate and retrieve the survivors from the mangroves, among those the father of the young boy who had asked Callahan for help in finding him. He was in bad shape, but he would live. After the last person had been put onboard the helicopter, Callahan turned the boat toward the *Lady Diane*. She was a real beauty and easily accommodated fifty people.

Callahan was anxious to see firsthand what had happened onboard the boat the night before. With the survivors in shock, neither he nor Morgan had gotten much information from them. No one wanted to talk about it.

When the large boat came within view, Callahan noticed the Sea Tow anchored off her port side. As they drew closer, he heard Morgan say something about windows being broken out.

With a sinking feeling, Callahan looked up at the larger boat. *Yep, he's right.*

"How are we going to get onboard?" Morgan asked. "The rail must be at least six feet high."

Callahan thought about it for a moment. "Guess we can throw a line over a cleat and shimmy up to the rail."

"Yeah, well, I'm not a spring chicken like I used to be," Morgan complained.

Since Callahan had known and worked with Morgan, Morgan had been overweight. However, he had shocked Callahan last year when they had taken the boat in a heavy storm out to Indian Key to find CJ. His partner had been as nimble as a twenty-year-old. Heavy or not, Morgan had the strength and agility to get any job done, and Callahan had confidence in him. Of course, he did look a lot heavier than he had last year.

Considering Morgan's complaint, he laughed, "We'll sort it out."

Minutes later, the line was ready. Callahan eased his boat up next to the large drift boat. Two tries and the line was hooked to a stern cleat.

"Here, hold her off while I go up," Callahan said, handing Morgan the bitter end.

In less than a minute, he had shimmied up the line and crawled over the rail. As he stood, Morgan heard him say. "Good Lord, what a mess! You should see this!"

"What is it, Boss?"

Callahan was silent, surveying what must have been utter chaos. Not one window was intact. Glass was everywhere. Wide splatters of blood were on the bulkhead, deck, and inside the wheelhouse. Seat cushions and life jackets strewn about the deck had bright red stains on most of them. *All this blood,* Callahan thought and gagged at the putrid odor that emanated from the slime covering nearly all the flooring and walls.

Making his way across the slippery deck to the door of the main lounge, he gasped at what he saw. A blood-covered, crumpled body was half in and half out the door to the toilet, with mouth and eyes wide open as if screaming in horror at the time of death. Bile rose up in Callahan's throat, his stomach churned, and his heart began racing wildly, the way it always did before his stomach relieved itself of its contents. *Please don't let me throw up now.* Callahan looked over and saw Morgan coming onboard. With a heavy thud, his feet touched the deck.

"Oh, my gosh," Morgan said, as he struggled to draw a lung full of air. "I didn't think I was going to make it." Embarrassed, he said, "I've got to get some of this weight off."

Turning to look around, his face paled at the carnage. He had seen dead bodies before, but nothing like this. He stumbled to the side of the boat and vomited. Wiping his face with a handkerchief in his back pocket, he regained his composure and looked at Callahan.

"There's a body in the lounge," Callahan said woodenly. "It's not much to look at, so watch yourself. This thing wasn't just killing to eat; it was killing because it enjoys it!"

There was a total of eight bodies onboard the *Lady Diane,* and they had retrieved six from the water, totaling fourteen. *That's strange*, Callahan thought. The owner of the *Lady Diane* had told him twenty-four men and women were loaded on the boat when it left the dock. *What happened to the rest of them?*

"What in the world could do something like this" Morgan asked.

Callahan had told no one in his department about the autopsy of the dead man found by the Cuban couples.

Suddenly very tired, Callahan rubbed his hand across the stubble on his face, looked Morgan in the eyes, and answered truthfully, "It's a giant squid."

Chapter Fifty-Three

The aging 51 Bertram Convertible struggled against the tide as she made her way up the channel to the dock at the Big Game and Fish Club in the Bahamas.

Bruce McConnell, tall and silver-haired with a deep cleft in his chin, looked to the west and figured it was half an hour before dark. His day on the water had been a bust. A few strikes on his rod had produced absolutely nothing that was unusual in these waters. His forehead, forearms, the tops of his hands, and the back of his neck were sunburned, and he was dead tired. He stood on the bow, anxiously looking forward to something cold to drink. After such a brutal day in the heat, his mouth watered for some cool refreshment. A shower and a fine dinner would follow, or so he thought.

McConnell noticed a well-dressed stranger, about thirty years old, standing at the end of the dock. *Wonder who that is?* He briefly thought, not particularly interested as he wiped the sweat from his face with a small towel he had snagged from the hotel.

The Bahamian captain eased the boat up to the dock while two deckhands readied their lines. As the boat touched the dock, it resisted and bounced back as two spring lines held her tight. McConnell wasted no time disembarking. He turned toward the bar for his chilled drink as the young stranger took him by the arm. "Mr. McConnell?"

The banker turned to see why the stranger had his arm. "Yes?"

he said, annoyed.

"Mr. McConnell, my name is Agent Johnny Jackson with the FBI," he answered, showing his credentials and looking very serious. "I have to ask you to come with me, sir."

"Young man, what's this all about?" Bruce McConnell demanded, jerking his arm away.

"Mr. McConnell, we have a kidnapping in progress in the Keys, and I have been instructed to take you back to Islamorada immediately."

"Like hell you will!" McConnell pointed toward the bar. "I'm going over there, have a cold drink and dinner, and then I'm going to get a good night sleep. I'm beat, and I've been out in the heat all day. Besides that, I didn't catch even one fish, which didn't make me very happy, so don't tell me what I have to do."

"I'm sorry, Mr. McConnell, but if you resist, I'll have to arrest you for obstructing a federal investigation. One way or the other you're coming with me, sir. Your choice."

After having nothing to drink since the day before, Skye greedily drank a bottle of water.

Seeing that she was weakening, Pete had relented and decided to give her the water because he didn't want her to die before they got their ransom money. After he was sure the money had been picked up, he would decide how to get rid of her.

Sweat rolled down Skye's brow into her eyes and down the back of her neck. Her hair was soaking wet, turning it from blonde to a medium brown. Still dehydrated, she thought, *Man, it's like an oven in this dump.* She looked out the window and saw the clear sky as dusk readied to finish the hot day. Pete had allowed her to relieve herself once, and soon she would need to go again. The bottle of water was going straight through her.

Jack had adamantly refused to leave the room when she used the bucket, even after she screamed at him. She had to sit on it with the worn sheet covering her from the waist down. The jerk just leaned back in his chair, crossed his arms, and stared with a nasty smile and that frightening gleam on his face. *I'm going to get this guy if it's the last thing I do. Pete is a stinking, fat slob, but he doesn't give me the creeps nearly as bad as Jack does.*

Earlier in the day, her handcuffed wrist had become raw and began bleeding when she moved it around, but Jack refused to do anything about it. Pete had left earlier, about five o'clock, to get some food. Skye had heard the engine on the skiff fade away, leaving her alone with Jack.

Feeling the urge to relieve himself, Jack rose from his chair and headed for the door. He wore a smirk on his face. "Don't go away little girl, ya hear?"

Skye quickly grabbed the bucket and relieved herself again before he returned. *I guess I'm not the only one who has to go.*

Placing the bucket back on the floor, she lay in silence, listening to the rustle of the bushes through the open window as Jack walked around to the back of the shack.

Finding his favorite spot to pee, Jack stood at the edge of the water where the mangroves were thinner, unzipped his shorts, and began taking care of business. Thinking of the money that would soon be split three ways, and the fun that he was going to have with the girl before Pete got back, he stared out at the slowly fading sun.

Suddenly, out of the corner of his eyes, something large rushed at him from his right rear, grabbing his leg and causing excruciating pain. "What the...?" A loud hissing noise followed.

Instantly realizing what it was, Jack let out a blood-curdling scream. His heart raced in fear, and the pounding felt as if it would split his chest wide open. He looked down and saw bright red liquid from a severed artery squirting high in the air and then splattering to the ground.

Unable to keep his balance, Jack fell to the grass on his back, paling at the sight of his blood pooling beneath his leg. *Oh, my God, I've got to get away from this monster. I don't want to die,* he thought, as he tried unsuccessfully to pull his leg loose. The pain was unbearable. In a panic, he kicked at the face of his captor with his free foot, causing his worn tennis shoe to fall to the grass beside him. His sock was turning red from the arterial spray. The monster momentarily loosened its grip, opened its mouth wide, and then bit down hard. "Ahhhhh! Oh, God, no!" Jack felt his leg bones snap several times. Furious, the creature twisted Jack's body around, causing his back to break in three places. In shock and fading to an unconsciousness from which he would never awaken, Jack did not feel the sixteen-foot creature pulling him into the salty water.

Skye had heard Jack's screams and then what sounded like hissing and rolling noises and finally snapping noises as if heavy twigs were breaking. Unable to see out the window, she couldn't control her imagination. Her heart began pounding in terror. *What in the world is happening out there? Who is Jack fighting with out there? Are they going to come into the shack?* The salty perspiration from the hot, humid temperature in the shack dripped down her face, causing her eyes to burn. *What were those snapping noises?* She wondered.

Skye had no idea that it had been Jack's bones shattering. Finally, there was silence. She no longer heard the hissing and rolling noises, and Jack had stopped screaming. Skye lay there on the damp cot, wondering what had just happened as she waited for Jack to come back into the shack, mad and probably bloody. She cowered on the cot, waiting for the screen door to open. Skye didn't realize it then, but Jack would never return. The Florida Keys Crocodile had slashed him with long, razor sharp teeth and had broken nearly every bone in his body before dragging him to his death.

Chapter Fifty-Four

Having no choice, the annoyed banker quickly grabbed his belongings from his room and followed the federal agent down to the dock where the twenty-four-foot ferry would take them about two hundred yards to the airport.

McConnell glanced over at the agent. Stoic, with thick blond hair, green eyes, a square jaw and a ruggedly handsome, determined-looking face, Johnny Jackson reminded the banker of a football player friend of his from college at the University of Florida, with whom he had lost touch.

Nearing dusk, the FBI agent and Bruce McConnell arrived at their destination. Both walked briskly from the small concrete building at the Bimini International Airport to the waiting helicopter for the hundred-mile flight back to Islamorada.

An avid angler, McConnell used every opportunity he had to fly to Bimini for fishing and relaxation. He loved the Bimini Big Game Club Resort and Marina. The sport fishing was usually excellent, though not today. The resort was unique, the staff friendly, and the restaurant superb.

His position as Bank of America president on Islamorada afforded him little time to get away, and this was his first trip in over six months. He had asked Agent Jackson who had been kidnapped, but had gotten no response, which ticked him off. He had a right to know who had taken him away from his weeklong getaway. He had no idea it was George Hudson's granddaughter who had been kidnapped. George had been his friend and a good customer for many years.

As they boarded the chopper, a chill slowly crept up McConnell's spine. With no explanation for his fear, he hesitated before climbing into the craft. *Hmmm. What's that about?* he wondered. The pilot, Jim Johnson, a handsome, prematurely gray, affable man in his early forties smiled at them as they seated themselves behind him. Jackson usually sat in the front seat next to the pilot, but McConnell looked scared to death, so he figured he had better sit with him to keep him calm. With rotors turning, the helicopter lifted off the ground for Islamorada.

Johnny Jackson wondered if the young girl would still be alive when the ransom was paid. So many times, the victim was killed. Lopez had told him that the girl was staying with her grandfather for the summer. Jackson and his wife had a two-year-old baby girl. He shivered to think that something like this could happen to his little daughter.

Fifteen minutes into the bumpy flight, Agent Jackson noticed the pilot weaving a little at the controls. Over the noise of the rotors, he yelled, "Hey, Jim, are you okay?" There was no response. Sitting behind the pilot, Jackson unfastened his seatbelt, turned, and touched the pilot's shoulder. "Jim, what's wrong?" Still no response. As Jackson eased out of his seat, Jim Johnson's head fell to his chest, his face ashen, and his eyes wide open. *Heart attack* flashed through Jackson's mind as the helicopter began spinning around. Having no time to react, both passengers saw the choppy ocean below rushing up to meet them.

———

Two hundred twenty-eight miles over Key West, Florida, a spy satellite, operated by the National Security Agency and stationed in geosynchronous orbit, began scanning high-resolution images down to the size of a tractor trailer. The scan, scheduled to cover fifty square miles and take less than eighteen minutes, would then be downloaded to the NSA in Washington, D.C. Preliminary results should be available within an hour.

During the satellite scanning, Pete was making his way back to the shack in the old skiff. His trip into town for supplies had been uneventful until he had found Bill Marr drunk at the Mile Marker 88 Tiki Bar. Walking up to him, Pete heard him bragging about some money he was going to make on a big deal he was working on with friends of his. Pete was furious, and a raging argument ensued.

Customers turned to look at the inebriated lawyer and the grimy, foul-smelling man. Pete grabbed Marr by the collar, pulling him up from his seat and pointing his finger in the drunken man's face. Staggering, Marr argued with Pete about letting him go. The manager intervened and asked both men to leave.

Out in the parking lot, the quarrel continued until Pete, disgusted with Marr, gave him an uppercut to his chin and knocked him out cold. Shaking the pain from his right hand, he left Marr on the pavement, got into his van, and drove away. *I'm through with him! The idiot's gonna get us all busted 'cause of his drinking. I shoulda known better than to get involved with him. He always runs his mouth when he's drunk.* Pete hoped that Marr hadn't boasted about any specifics to anyone before he had gotten there.

Still fuming, Pete picked up his spotlight before making his way back to the mangroves. Quickly tying up the skiff, he walked to the shack where the NSA satellite images tagged him.

Back at the shack, Pete, wheezing, opened the door, and Skye immediately sat up on the cot, looking bleary-eyed. He shined the light around and saw her, but he didn't see Jack. *Where is Jack?*

he wondered. Skye's blonde hair hung wet and stringy from the unbearable heat. Dark circles made rings around her eyes. Her lips looked parched, and her face had an unnatural pallor.

"Where's Jack?" Pete grumbled, looking over at Skye.

She lowered her head and whispered, "If there's anything left of him, I guess it's out back." She kept her head down, not looking Pete in the eye, wondering what he might find. She was glad she hadn't been able to see what had happened to Jack.

"Girl, what are you talking bout? Don't you give me no crap!"
"I'm serious. He went out back. I heard screaming, and I think a crocodile must have gotten him."

"Ain't no crocs 'round here."

Skye sighed, "Yes, there are. I read about them. Maybe you should go see for yourself. I heard a terrible noise back there. At first I thought Jack was fighting with someone, but when his screams got louder, and he didn't come back, I figured it must have been a crocodile."

Pete thought about it for a second, hesitated, and then with the spotlight still in his hand, he eased out the door. *Ain't no way no croc got him. That girl's just tryin to scare me.* And it was working.

Skye listened as Pete made all the noise he could, probably trying to frighten off any critters that might be outside. He made his way around back and stopped dead still.

What the…? Oh, my God! What's this bloody mess? It can't be Jack. Pieces of flesh, part of a leg, and Jack's tattered tennis shoe lay on the wet, bloody grass. The strong copper smell of blood permeated the air.

Skye heard Pete gag and then throw up.

Moments later, his heart pounding, he ran as fast as he could to get back inside the shack.

Chapter Fifty-Five

Agent Lopez had gotten a call from Bimini just after eight o'clock that evening. Agent Jackson had coerced an unwilling Mr. McConnell into the helicopter, and they were ready to head back to Islamorada.

Poppy breathed a deep sigh of relief at hearing the good news. *Now we can pay the ransom and get Skye back.* He felt like a forty-pound anvil had been lifted from his chest. Michael, Maria, and CJ gathered around Poppy and gave him a big hug. Everyone was celebrating. CJ was so happy to hear the good news that he was jumping up and down and clapping his hands together. He said, "She's coming home! She's coming home!" Everybody smiled at his antics.

The whole group had been concerned about Poppy because they could tell his nerves were about shot. The stress he had been under had made him look like he had aged ten years in the past twenty-four hours.

Still a little worried, Maria held Poppy at arm's length, and seeing the exhaustion on his face, she said, "Why don't you try and get a little shuteye? Everything's going to be all right now."

"I suppose you're right. It's been about thirty-six hours since I slept." Lifting his weary body off the stool at the island counter, he winced from the arthritis in his knees and hobbled up the stairs to his bedroom. Exhausted, he lay down on the bed, fully clothed, and instantly fell asleep. He dreamed, but his dream was settling.

He could see Skye in the distance, and she was calling to him, but he couldn't reach her. Something was holding him back.

Three unmarked FBI cars sat in the Winn-Dixie parking lot waiting for the helicopter, but it never arrived. The agent in charge placed a call to Bimini when the helicopter was an hour overdue and found that the helicopter had left as planned. The second call was to the U.S. Coast Guard. The third call was to Agent Lopez at Poppy's house.

At eleven p.m. the phone rang. An exhausted Agent Lopez was sitting in a recliner trying to keep his eyes open and wondering why Jackson hadn't called to say that they had landed.

Answering on the first ring, the caller told Lopez that the helicopter had left Bimini on time but had not arrived. Lopez was instantly wide awake. The U.S. Coast Guard had already been called, and a search had begun to cover the area between Bimini and Islamorada. Lopez's heart felt like it had dropped into his stomach. *How am I going to tell them?* he wondered.

Earlier, feeling confident that the ransom would be paid on time, Michael, Maria, and Sonny had gone to the Jansen's house to get a few hours of shut eye. It had been a long day and night. Maria's eyes had dark shadows around them, and her face looked drawn and tired. They all needed a shower and some rest.

CJ had refused to budge. He had been sound asleep on the sofa when he heard the ringing of the phone. Instantly alert, he looked at Lopez's shocked face as he placed his cell on the end table by the recliner.

CJ's heart picked up speed as he asked, "What's wrong, Agent

Lopez?"

Not wanting to verbalize the situation, and willing it not to be true, Lopez just looked down and shook his head.

"What?" CJ asked, becoming alarmed.

Sighing deeply, the agent looked into CJ's eyes and admitted, "The helicopter didn't make it to Islamorada. The Coast Guard is searching for it, but it will probably be hard to find anything until morning."

"You mean it crashed? Oh, my gosh. I hope they're okay." Then it hit him like a ton of bricks. *How are we going to pay the ransom if the banker is dead?* he wondered.

Unable to sleep anymore, Poppy had gotten out of bed, splashed water on his face and headed downstairs. Hearing the agent say something about crashing, he cried out in alarm as he held to the banister for support, "What crashed?"

"They think the chopper went down somewhere between Bimini and Islamorada, sir."

"Oh, no! Those poor people. What are they doing to rescue them?" Poppy was still half asleep and hadn't considered that without the banker, there would be no withdrawal from the bank, and there would be no rescue for Skye.

"What about the ransom money?" CJ said shakily, knowing without the ransom money Skye would likely die. "What do we do now?"

"I'm not sure, CJ. Maybe you'd better call your parents and Mr. Mitchell."

After receiving the call from CJ, Michael, Maria, and Sonny had rushed back to Poppy's. When they arrived, Poppy was shaking like a leaf, CJ was on the verge of tears, and Agent Lopez sat quietly, staring at the floor.

Maria went to her son first while Michael headed to Poppy, who looked as if he was on the border of collapsing. Sonny walked up to Lopez and said, "Snap out of it, man, and help us figure out what we're going to do." Gathering their strength, the six of them talked well into the wee hours of the morning, but the solution evaded them.

About three a.m. Sonny asked Michael to walk outside with him. Once they were on the dock and clear of the open glass sliding door, Sonny said, "Michael, how much cash do you have?"

"Cash? I guess I've got about three grand in the safe. I stopped keeping so much at the house after I resigned from the NSA. Half of what we have is offshore, and the rest is here in a local bank. Like Poppy, I can't get my hands on it until Monday. Maria and I had already thought about that. Why?"

"I was hoping between you, me, and Poppy, we might be able to come up with the ransom money, but I guess that's not an option. I've got five grand on me. I didn't know what I might need while I was here. Poppy probably doesn't keep very much cash at the house."

Noon Sunday wasn't too many hours away, and they had to figure out what they were going to do fast, or Skye Somers would be dead.

Attorney Bill Marr awoke on the sofa in his office, fully dressed, with the mother of all hangovers. As he slowly walked to the bathroom to grab a handful of aspirin to ease the pain, Marr felt a tinge of nausea in the pit of his stomach. He ached all over and felt like he could swallow a gallon of water with no effort. The day-old alcohol in the attorney's system made his mouth feel so dry he couldn't even lick his lips. Squinting from the brightness of the light as he flipped it on, his head began to spin. Looking into the mirror, he was shocked to see his swollen jaw, discolored to the shade of pale eggplant with a little blue and green mixed in for good measure. *What the heck happened to me last night?* Unable to concentrate clearly, he grabbed the aspirin and swallowed them with a Bud Light that was in the tiny refrigerator in his office.

Wanting nothing more than to go back to sleep on the sofa, he noticed the time. It was nine o'clock on Sunday morning. *Three more hours and we'll have our pockets full of the ransom money.* He had no idea that the FBI would be knocking on his door in exactly twenty-eight minutes.

Chapter Fifty-Six

Pete had tossed and turned all night with visions of the gruesome mess out by the water that had once been various parts of Jack.

As he slowly awakened to the bright sunlight, he remembered knocking the crap out of Bill Marr at the Tiki Bar the night before. *I hope he kept his big trap shut about the kidnapping. I knew better than to involve him because he gets loaded every night and starts running his mouth. What if he told someone who might have called the police? They could be headed to the shack right now.*

Calming his rising hysteria, he realized that Marr had never been to the shack, so even if the police questioned him, he couldn't tell them where it was.

Wondering what he should do, he glanced over at Skye. She was awake and staring at him with wary eyes. *Maybe I should just cut my losses and get rid of her. I can take the skiff back to the van and haul butt out of town.* Remembering that he had less than twenty-five dollars on him, he knew that he wouldn't get very far. He was afraid to go back to his house where he had a couple hundred dollars hidden in a shoe in his closet. If Marr had talked, they could be watching the house. *Just keep calm*, he told himself. *The only way out of this mess is to get rid of the girl, pick up the ransom money at noon, and get out of town. The Marr can do whatever he wants to do.* Pete Samuels had no idea that the NSA satellite had picked up his image and were at that moment in the process of trying to identify him.

———————

At exactly nine twenty-eight that morning, the FBI opened the unlocked door to Attorney Bill Marr's office, after repeatedly ringing the doorbell and getting no response. The dinging bells attached to the door let Marr know when he had a visitor.

Marr was sleeping deeply on the sofa, the aspirin fast at work on the pain in his head. Finally hearing the bells on the door, he groggily looked up and saw two FBI agents standing in the doorway to his reception room. They didn't look like they had come to shoot the bull with him. He knew immediately what their visit was about this early Saturday morning. *I've been caught,* he thought, but his dazed mind didn't have time to concoct a believable lie.

"Mr. Marr, we are here to talk with you about the kidnapping of Skye Somers."

Swallowing his fear, Marr responded with what he thought resembled surprise. "Who is Skye Somers? I have no idea what you're talking about."

"Mr. Marr, we believe you and two of your friends, Pete Samuels and Jack Watson, conspired to kidnap Skye Somers for a ransom of twenty thousand dollars."

"That's ridiculous! I don't even know any men with those names."

"Mr. Marr, we have witnesses who saw the three of you on the dock at Mile Marker 88 Restaurant in deep conversation several nights ago. We also have a witness who saw you get punched in the jaw by Pete Samuels at the Tiki Bar last night. From the looks of you, I'd say that eyewitness account is accurate."

Stuttering and not able to think of a good defense, Marr hurriedly said, "Look, it was their idea. I tried to talk 'em out of it."

"Mr. Marr, we want to know where the girl is right now. If you tell us, we promise you a lighter sentence, but you will have to serve some time. Do we have a deal?"

Marr's face drained of color. "Agent, I would tell you where she is if I knew. All I know is they are holding her in a makeshift shack out in the mangroves."

"Where in the mangroves?"

"I don't know. I promise you. I don't know. The only thing I did was make the call to her grandfather demanding the ransom at noon today. Pete and Jack kidnapped her and took her to their shack, wherever it is. Pete was supposed to pick up the ransom, and the three of us were going to split it."

"What about Miss Somers? Were they going to let her go when they got the ransom?"

Shrugging his shoulders, he answered, "I guess so. We never talked about it. Pete Samuels was in charge."

"Mr. Marr, you are under arrest for conspiracy to kidnap a minor for ransom. Please place your hands behind your back."

Marr placed his hands behind his back. The FBI agent quickly handcuffed him and led him to the door.

Lopez hung up the phone after being advised of the arrest of Bill Marr. Looking at Sonny Mitchell, he said, "The attorney has been arrested. He claims he doesn't know where Skye is. He said Samuels and Watson took her to a shack they built in the mangroves."

Sonny quickly dialed the NSA to see if they had identified the locations of either of the other two suspects. "Hey, Brian, this is Sonny. Any luck finding Samuels or Watson?"

"Not sure. We think we may have found Samuels. Nothing yet

on Watson."

"Text me his coordinates as soon as you have them and keep looking for Watson. Thanks, Brian."

Looking at Michael and CJ, Sonny said, "C'mon guys, let's get ready to go. They think they found Samuels, and they're going to text me his location. I'll bet a thousand dollars that's where they're holding Skye." He looked over at Poppy. "Don't worry Poppy, we'll find her."

An hour and a half later, Pete Samuels was still trying to decide what to do. It was almost noon. He paced back and forth, glancing at Skye every time he made a turn around the floor. *Has Marr made the call and given the kid's grandfather the location to drop the money?*

After having had nothing to eat since a granola bar for breakfast two mornings before, and nothing to drink since before Jack's untimely death, Skye was severely dehydrated and felt so weak she could barely lift her head.

Please CJ, you can find me. Just go with your instincts. You know these waters. Get in the Gator Bait and find this shack. She kept repeating it over and over in her mind. Because of their close connection, she desperately hoped she could will him to the shack in the mangroves to rescue her before she died from dehydration and hunger, or until Pete decided to get rid of her. He had been mumbling to himself all morning about "gittin' rid of the girl and hauling butt." Her only hope was that she would be saved before anything happened to her.

Flying over Poppy's house for the past couple days, Flapper had noticed that there were strangers going in and out of the house at odd hours. Skye was nowhere in sight. Always curious, he wondered where she was and who those people were. He recognized CJ and his family. He had seen them last summer at Skye's going away party, but there were two and sometimes three strangers that he had never seen before. *What's going on and where is Skye?* he wondered, becoming concerned about her. The last time they talked, she had been so excited about diving for more gold, but he hadn't seen her, CJ, or his boat anywhere near where they had found the last gold bar, and that was before Cap, had died. *Maybe I'd better see if I can find Squeaky and see if he knows where she is.*

Chapter Fifty-Seven

After receiving the coordinates for Pete Samuel's last location, Sonny, Michael and CJ quickly left Poppy's just after noon in Sonny's brand new, black Chevy Tahoe four-wheel drive heading for the Jansen's.

Sitting in the front passenger seat, Michael looked out the window and noticed the darkening sky and a stiff wind beginning to blow. Lightning was flashing in the distance. The weather forecast earlier had warned of a storm.

Pulling into Michael's driveway, they jumped out of the Tahoe and headed for the dock where CJ's boat was tied. Grabbing three yellow rain slickers and snatching the keys off a nail from the back of a piling, all three jumped into the Gator Bait. They had decided to use the Gator Bait because it had a shallow draft.

Michael took the wheel. Worried about their safety, he said, "A storm is coming, guys. I hope we can make it to our destination before it hits. This weather sure isn't looking very good."

CJ said, almost begging, "Please, Dad, let's try. We've got to find Skye."

At the wheel of the nineteen-foot Mako boat, Michael again looked up at the darkening sky and felt the strengthening wind begin to blow harder, making the waves choppy and the boat a little more difficult to maneuver. Lightning flashed angrily in the east, and then the dark sky opened up, pouring blinding rain on them. Michael could barely see.

Yelling over the roaring noise, Michael said, "We're going to have to head back until this rain stops. We can't see where we're going. As soon as the rain slows, we'll try again."

CJ and Sonny sat with their arms curled around with their heads down to keep the stinging rain from hitting their faces. Though they wanted to continue, all three knew it wouldn't be safe, and if something happened to them, Skye might never be found.

Returning to Michael's, they pulled the boat up to the dock and tied it off. "Let's go in, get dried off, and change clothes. These summer storms don't usually last too long." Michael was wrong. The thunder and the downpour raged in fury outside, and bright flashes of lightning hit the water in jagged lines.

Flapper was heading for cover in his tree in the mangroves. As he flapped his wings harder to shorten the distance, he looked below and saw CJ and his dad and another man in a boat. He looked closely to see if Skye was with them because CJ and Skye were always together, but he only saw the three men. *It looks like they're heading for the distant mangroves. Why would they be going to the mangroves in this storm?*

Earlier, he had found Squeaky, and he hadn't seen Skye lately either. Flapper told him about all the strangers at Poppy's and asked if he knew who they were. Squeaky said he had been up to the dock for the past two or three days and had noticed strange cars in the driveway, but he hadn't seen anybody. Both realizing that something might have happened to Skye, they became worried. Flapper decided to turn around and find Squeaky again to tell him what he had just seen.

On her cot in the shack, Skye heard the driving rain. Lightning flashed across the windows, almost as if it were going to strike inside the makeshift cabin. The wind was blowing the tin roof so hard that she was afraid it might blow off. She saw water on the floor where it had started to leak under the tin. *Please, Lord, don't let the roof blow off.* The ramshackle place afforded little protection from the elements, and Skye was more afraid of the storm now than she was of Pete, even though he had been looking at her with a strange, questioning look in his eyes. *What's going on in his mind?* She wondered if maybe he was thinking about killing her. She didn't like that look he kept giving her. Even in the hot, humid air, Skye shivered in fear.

Pete didn't like storms, and he especially didn't like this one because it meant he couldn't leave. He had been thinking seriously about leaving Skye handcuffed to the cot instead of just getting rid of her. He knew no one would ever find her in the heavy mangroves. When they had built their getaway, he and Jack had made sure it was well hidden.

With the raging storm outside, Pete knew he would just have to sit it out. The little skiff would never make it to shore where he had left his van, and he would never survive in the choppy water because he couldn't swim. Thinking about his escape, he wondered if Marr had picked up the money. Pete had no way of knowing that Marr was sitting in the Islamorada County Jail and singing like a bird to the feds.

––––––––––

Squeaky and his pod had taken refuge from the powerful storm under the long public dock when Flapper reappeared, landing in the water close to him.

"What happened? What are you doing here? I thought you were going out to the trees in the mangroves."

"I was, but I saw CJ and his dad and another man heading out to the distant mangroves. They had to turn around and go back to CJ's because the storm was getting so bad. I keep wondering exactly where they were going in this downpour. Do you think they might be looking for Skye?"

"In the mangroves? What would she be doing in the mangroves? The only things in the mangroves are trees and shrubs. Oh, yeah, and there's an old shack. I forgot about that. I saw it the other day when I was exploring." Always adventurous, Squeaky liked to be familiar with his pod's area and was constantly discovering new places.

"A shack?"

"Yeah, isn't that what I just said?" *Sometimes that bird is so dense,* he thought.

"If their boat was heading to a shack in the mangroves, do you think Skye might be there?"

"What would she be doing by herself in a shack in the mangroves? She would never go anyplace like that without CJ. Besides, how would they even know about it? I just discovered it myself."

"Did I say she's by herself?" Flapper snapped. *That show-off isn't as smart as he thinks he is.*

"Well, you just saw CJ, so he's not with her."

Getting nowhere in solving the mystery of Skye's disappearance, they were beginning to bicker, and the two were finally silent.

All of a sudden Flapper said, "What if someone took her there? Maybe that's why we haven't seen her in several days."

"Why would someone take her out there?"

"I don't know." *Am I supposed to know everything, you idiot?* "All I know is no one has seen her lately, and CJ and those other men were going fast heading that way until the rain made them turn around. As soon as the rain slows, we need to go to CJ's house. We have to figure out a way to let CJ know where we think she might be."

The sky cast a dark shroud around Islamorada. Sitting on the covered deck with his eyes closed, thinking of Skye, CJ kept trying to imagine that she was okay, willing her to be okay. He was anxious to get back in the boat to try to find her.

Michael and Sonny were in deep conversation on the sofa in the sunroom, trying to figure out where Pete could be hiding in the direction they had been going. There was nothing out there but mangroves.

Please CJ, you can find me. Just use your instincts. CJ's eyes popped open. "Skye?" Looking around, he saw that he was alone on the deck. *She's trying to communicate with me. That means she's still alive.* His eyes filled with tears, and sighing with relief he looked down and saw Flapper sitting on a piling in the rain with Squeaky furiously splashing in the water.

The wind was strong enough to blow Flapper off his perch, but with pure determination, he hung on. Somehow, they had to be able to communicate with CJ.

What are they doing here? he wondered. *It looks like they're trying to get my attention. Wonder what's going on?* Grabbing a rain slicker, he headed down the stairs, quickly making his way in the deluge to the dock.

Chapter Fifty-Eight

Sitting in the sunroom deep in conversation, Michael was telling Sonny that he wasn't aware of any buildings in the mangroves where the satellite coordinates were directing them. "I'm familiar with the area because CJ and I have been fishing out there lots of times."

Looking out through the glass doors to check the weather, he noticed CJ running down to the dock.

Pointing, Michael asked, "Where in the world is CJ going in this rain?"

His forehead furrowing in thought, Sonny was wondering the same thing. "I don't know, but I guess we'd better find out."

Throwing on their yellow rain gear, they headed down to the dock. Both noticed the bird sitting on the piling. CJ seemed to be talking to it, and then he looked down and seemed to be talking to something in the water. That's when Michael saw the dolphin.

"That looks like Skye's pelican and dolphin friends, Sonny."

"Her what?"

"We've both been so busy, and I haven't had time to tell you about Skye and the pelican she calls Flapper, and a dolphin she calls Squeaky. The two of them saved Skye and CJ's lives last summer."

"How in the world did they do that?"

"I know this is hard to believe, but Skye can communicate with them through telepathy."

"Get outta here," Sonny said, scoffing.

Walking up to where CJ was standing, Michael said, "I'll explain later, Bro."

"What's going on, CJ?"

"I don't know, Dad, but I think Flapper and Squeaky are trying to tell me something. The problem is I can't understand them. Skye's the only one who can tell us what they're saying."

Sonny just looked at CJ as if he had grown two heads.

Suddenly, Squeaky turned over in the water and headed out to sea, then stopped and looked back at CJ, squeaking. Flapper took to the air and followed Squeaky.

"Dad, I think they're trying to communicate with us. I've got a strong feeling it's got something to do with Skye. She's still alive, Dad. When I was on the deck with my eyes closed, I heard her calling to me, telling me to use my intuition and find her."

Michael and Sonny were both speechless. Neither of them knew how to respond.

The random lightning flashes had stopped, and the rain was beginning to lessen.

Flapper was slowly circling around Squeaky, who was doing his best to talk to CJ by squeaking and then swimming out a little further each time.

"I think they know where Skye is, and they're trying to take us to her. C'mon Dad! C'mon Uncle Sonny, let's get into the boat and go find Skye."

––––––––––

The raging storm was almost silent. Water was in puddles around the room, yet there was none to drink. After two days with only one bottle of water, and the unbearable heat in the shack, Skye was severely dehydrated. Her throat was so dry that she could barely swallow, and her mouth tasted like it was full of sand. She had begged Pete for a bottle of water several times, but he just ignored her. Trying again, weak and her scratchy voice barely above a whisper, she said, "Please, I need water."

Pete glanced down but ignored her pleas. She knew then he was going to kill her or leave her to die, handcuffed to the soiled army cot. Pete recognized the resignation in her eyes. *Time for me to git going*, he thought. With no concern for Skye, he began gathering up what few things he needed. Realizing that he was leaving, she began to cry, causing her already dry throat to close up. She felt like she was choking. Without even glancing at her, Pete walked to the door and closed it behind him.

Michael had the boat traveling at about twenty-five miles an hour as he followed Flapper and Squeaky. CJ's heart began to pound in anticipation of finding Skye. *Please, please let her be okay.* Sonny sat looking out toward the mangroves, astounded at what he was seeing. *That little bitty girl can actually talk with birds and dolphins.* As a former NSA undercover operative, he had seen many things, but never anything like this.

Getting closer to the mangrove location, they saw someone at a distance maneuvering a skiff toward them, but not on their same path.

"Dad, it looks like that creep, Pete Samuels! Is Skye with him?" CJ's rapid heartbeat increased even more when he didn't see anyone but Samuels in the boat. *Where is she? What has he done with her?*

Pete was close enough to see that it was three people; the boy, a stocky, serious-looking stranger, and the kid's father, the jerk who had sucker-punched him in the restaurant and put him in the hospital. *Do they know it was Jack and me that kidnapped the girl?* Realizing the direction they were heading, he figured they did. Turning the small skiff away from them, but still heading to his van, he increased it to top speed, which wasn't much compared to the speed of CJ's boat.

Michael began turning the Mako toward the flat bottom boat.

"No, Dad, forget about him! Let's find Skye first. Uncle Sonny, is your cell phone getting reception out here?"

"I'm already calling the FBI, CJ."

Satisfied that the thug would be taken care of, CJ began looking for any structure in the mangroves they passed. *"I wish we could hurry faster,"* he thought as they followed close behind Flapper and Squeaky.

Finally, seeing Flapper land in a tree and Squeaky turn around in circles as if giving them a signal that they had arrived at the right spot, Michael slowed the boat to a near stop. Patrolling around the mangroves, CJ shouted, "Dad, I see something through the trees!" Seeing what CJ was pointing to, Michael pulled closer and turned off the engines.

CJ jumped out into the water, clawing his way through the shrubs. Seeing the shanty, he said, "Dad! Uncle Sonny! She's here. I just know she is! She has to be."

Running toward the crudely built structure, CJ prayed that Skye was alive. As he came to the door, he took a deep breath before opening it. *Please, please, let her be alive.* Curling his right hand around the rusty doorknob, he pushed it open. A wave of oven-like heat and the smell of unwashed bodies assaulted him. As he glanced over at the cot, he saw Skye lying there, unmoving. Rushing over to her, dropping to his knees, and shaking her arm, he cried, "Skye, Skye, wake up!" There was no response.

Not far behind CJ, Michael and Sonny hurried through the doorway. Seeing Skye looking lifeless and CJ in tears, both rushed to the cot.

"Move over, Son," Michael said, gently nudging CJ out of the way. CJ stood. Tears filled his eyes and ran down his cheeks.

"She's dead, Dad," CJ sobbed as he hovered over his father, hoping that he could bring Skye back to life.

Sonny bent down to listen for a heartbeat while Michael felt for a pulse. "She's alive, Son, but she's in bad shape." Seeing her flushed face and feeling her dry skin, Sonny said, "She's badly dehydrated. We need to cool her off and get water in her right now!"

Michael looked around. There was no kitchen sink, which meant no running water. Noticing an old cooler on the floor by a beat-up chaise lounge, he said, "CJ, see if there's any water in that cooler. If there isn't, go out to the boat and get a bottle. Hurry!"

CJ hurried to the cooler and opened it, dreading that he would find it empty. Two unopened plastic bottles were lying in the tepid water, along with some small pieces of quickly melting ice. *Thank God!*

CJ handed a bottle to his dad and one to Sonny, who opened it and began rubbing Skye's face and arms.

Michael opened the other bottle, lifted Skye's head and gently poured a few drops on her lips. He repeated the process several times.

Feeling the moisture, Skye opened her eyes but couldn't keep them open. She didn't seem to recognize any of them. With effort, she managed to lick her lips with her parched tongue. Opening her eyes again, she whispered, "Water, please."

Michael gently lifted her head again, put the bottle to her mouth and allowed her small sips until a small part of the bottle was gone. He pulled it away then, knowing that drinking too much too fast could cause the level of sodium in her body to drop dangerously low. Breathing a sigh of relief that Skye was alive, Michael thought about what the poor girl had been through in the past days. Satisfied that she was going to be okay, Michael moved over, and CJ knelt on the floor beside the cot, picked up Skye's hand and gently kissed it. Looks passed between Michael and Sonny, and they smiled.

"Skye, it's me. Open your eyes and look at me."

With effort, Skye slowly lifted her eyes open. CJ could barely hear her when she softly whispered, "I knew you would find me. I willed you to come."

Chapter Fifty-Nine

The next day, after twenty-four hours of searching by the Coast
Guard, the FBI helicopter still had not been found, but
surprisingly, clinging to an inflatable life raft, were FBI agent
Johnny Jackson and banker, Bruce McConnell, dehydrated, a bit
battered, and covered in cuts and bruises, but very much alive.
Jackson had a broken wrist, and McConnell had a badly swollen
ankle. They were exhausted, thirsty, and hungry enough to eat a
two-pound steak with all the trimmings. With help, they climbed
aboard the rescue vessel. As Jackson explained, when they hit the
water, both were thrown out, and the helicopter sank, but the life
raft automatically inflated and popped up close to them. They had
seen sharks nearby, but they were both able to lift themselves up
into the raft, which saved their lives.

When Agent Lopez received the call, he was very happy that
they had been found alive. Johnny Jackson was a friend of his,
and their wives were friends as well. When he called Poppy to let
him know that his banker friend was alive, Poppy breathed a sigh
of relief. He and Bruce McConnell had been casual friends for
over forty years, long before McConnell had become president of
the local bank.

Ten days later, with Skye safe and feeling much better after
recuperating in the hospital, life was good for Poppy and the
Jansen's.

———————

Sitting quietly on Poppy's dock, CJ and Skye stared out at the horizon, both thinking about what had happened to Skye ten days before. Neither had openly broached the subject since Skye had been released from the hospital and was back at Poppy's. That would have made it too real, and neither wanted to relive it.

Just thinking about what had just happened, and all he and Skye had been through in the past couple of years, made CJ realize that there would never be anyone else for him, and he needed to gather the courage to tell Skye how he felt.

He also knew that Skye wouldn't be sitting here with him today if it hadn't been for Flapper and Squeaky. They owed both of them so much for saving Skye's life. CJ had given both of them a bucket of fish, but that was hardly enough for what they had done. *How can we ever repay them?* CJ wondered.

Skye was still a little weak but ready to start enjoying her summer in Islamorada again. She said, "In a few more days when I've completely recovered, how about we load up *Money in the Bank*, head out to the Marquesas Keys and look for some more gold? It's time we had a little fun, don't you think?"

CJ just smiled and shook his head. *She sure has a one-track mind.* But he was so happy that she was safe he would do anything she asked. *It will be nice to be alone with her again,* he thought. Since Skye had been so close to dying, CJ didn't want to leave her side.

Skye heard a soft flapping noise, looked up at the closest piling and saw Flapper sitting there.

"Hey, Flapper, it's great to see you again!" Knowing what he and Squeaky had done to save her made Skye love the cantankerous old pelican even more.

"How are you feeling?" Flapper asked.

"In a couple more days I'll be good as new, thanks to you and Squeaky."

"I'm just glad that CJ understood what we were trying to tell him and found you in time. You know I don't particularly care for that show-off, Squeaky, but if he hadn't remembered seeing the cabin while exploring, we couldn't have found you. I guess I'll have to be a little nicer to him from now on."

Skye had to smile at Flapper's reasoning. Changing the subject, Sky said, "CJ and I are going back to the Marquesas in a few days."

"What about that thing that has been killing people?" Flapper was worried for his friends.

"Since no one has seen it around for almost three weeks, CJ and I figure that it has probably moved on. Hardly anyone has been out on the water since Cap was killed, so it probably gave up trying to find food and found a better territory. I just hope someone destroys it before it kills again."

"Well, just in case, I'll let Squeaky know where you'll be, so he and I can check on you and CJ while you're out there. I'd better see if I can find him. I'll see you later, Skye." Flapper took to the air to find Squeaky.

The morning was clear and sunny as CJ and Skye loaded supplies on the *Money*. Lugging all the gear from the Volkswagen to the boat had made both realize how hot it was. Rivulets of sweat flowed freely from their faces. Their hair was wet, and both their tee shirts were sticking to their chests as if the shirts were glued to them. The temperature will be around ninety degrees by noon.

"Did you remember the bug spray?" Skye asked CJ.

"Yep, I don't want to get eaten alive. Been there done that," he laughed, remembering the year before.

When the teens told Poppy and the Jansen's that they were going to the Marquesas Keys again, none of them thought it was a good idea and tried to persuade them to wait until Skye had more time to recover. The truth was that even though the giant killer squid had not been seen by anyone for about three weeks, CJ's parents and Poppy were afraid for them to go. Michael had tried to get them to let him go with them, but at nearly seventeen and eighteen years old, neither wanted Michael tagging along treating them as if they were children.

With the boat fully loaded, CJ called his dad to let him know that they were leaving the dock. Michael already had the exact coordinates of where they were going.

"Please be careful, CJ. You remembered your pistol, didn't you?"

Sighing, CJ responded, "Yes, Dad, we have everything. Now stop worrying, okay?"

Undeterred, Michael said, "Call us when you get out there and call us each night before you turn in. If you have any trouble, I won't be far away. Just use your iPhone."

Assuring his father again that they would be fine, CJ hung up and turned on the engines of the old shrimp boat. Briefly remembering what had happened to Cap, CJ felt a little shiver at the base of his neck, and the hairs on his arms stood up. *Get a grip*, he told himself. *Everything will be fine. The squid is probably gone.*

Skye stood by CJ at the wheel and laid her head on his arm. *We've been through so much*, she thought, *and we're still together. I wonder what will happen when CJ goes away to the University of Florida this fall. Will he find a college girlfriend and forget about me?* Thinking about it made Skye sad because she knew if he did it would break her heart.

Forty minutes later, they arrived at their destination and dropped anchor. Gathering their gear, both shed the tee shirts covering their swimsuits. Pulling on his tank, CJ reached for his speargun just in case he might need it. Hearing a splash, he looked down and saw Skye already in the water. Spitting in her mask, rubbing it around on the glass and dipping it into the water, she fit it snuggly on her face and adjusted her mouthpiece.

"C'mon slowpoke, I'm waiting for you," she said as she laughed.

CJ said, "Let's go. There's gold down there waiting for us," and he fell over the side.

Using the same dive rules as they had on earlier dives, it seemed to take forever to get down to the ledge. Both shivered at the cold temperature the further down they went.

Though she wouldn't admit it to CJ, Skye was scared. *What if that killer squid is hiding somewhere down here?* Shaking off her fear, she concentrated on finding the gold as they reached the ledge.

Suddenly, out of the corner of her eye, she saw a huge brownish red tentacle moving toward her, and she screamed. CJ turned toward Skye and saw why she had screamed. He raised his speargun.

Chapter Sixty

"I've done it again, haven't I? I've scared you to death," said the giant octopus softly. "Please forgive me. I should have come up in front of you."

Because it wasn't aggressive, CJ realized it was probably the octopus he and Skye had seen on their first dive to the ledge. Skye would want to try to communicate with it. Still, he held the speargun cocked and ready in case it wasn't the one they had seen before.

Hearing the soothing voice, Skye turned. "Thank goodness it's you! I thought it might be that squid that has been killing people. Since no one has seen it in several weeks, we all thought it had left our area, but seeing your tentacle, I was afraid it was him."

"I haven't seen him around in a while either. Maybe he's moved around, but I don't think he's gone. The last time I saw you, you told me your name was Skye. That's a strange name for a human person, isn't it?"

"My parents were traveling in Scotland when my mother conceived me. Skye is a very popular name over there, so my parents decided to name me Skye. Do you have children?"

"Not yet. Shortly after we have our babies, we die. We have thousands of them. We usually only live four or five seasons."

"I'm so sorry," Skye said. That was the only thing she could think of to say. "I thought the giant octopus lives in the North Pacific. What are you doing here".

"I was raised in a big glass place where the water is cold. People came and looked at me. Not long ago, the glass place closed, and a human man with kind eyes, not realizing I need to be in cold water, had me transported down here where he lives. I found this deep, cold hole where I have been spending most of my time. The water around here is too warm for me. When the weather changes, I'll go up to where the cold water is."

"Wow! What an adventure! Oh, I almost forgot. Do you have a name?"

"We don't have names because we live alone in the sea. There's no one to talk to."

"Well, then, I'll call you Marina because it means 'of the sea,' and you are definitely from the sea."

"Marina? I like that name. What are you and your friend doing down here?"

"Do you know what gold is?"

"Gold?"

"Yes, it's glittery, yellow stuff that is sometimes in the water."

"Oh, yes, I've seen that before. There is a bunch below where you are standing. Is gold good?"

"Yes, humans like gold," Skye answered. "It makes beautiful jewelry and is worth a lot of money."

"Money?" Marina asked. "What's money?"

"Let's see," Skye said as she tried to figure out how to explain it to Marina. "Money is what humans use to buy food and clothes and boats, as well as other things. My friend CJ and I were just going to look for some gold when you arrived."

"Okay, I'll leave you now, but perhaps we'll see each other again soon. Please be careful in these waters. The bad thing may still be around. If I see it, I'll find you and let you know." Her long tentacles moved quickly in the water as she disappeared.

Marina's words sent a shiver up Skye's spine.

Looking at CJ, Skye saw him point to his dive watch. Their time was up for now. They would have to wait until the next dive to look for more gold.

Detective Callahan noticed Michael and Maria's car when he pulled into Poppy's driveway. *Good*, he thought, *I won't have to go to see them since they're already here.*

Poppy answered the doorbell and invited Sean Callahan inside. "Come on in, Detective Callahan. I've got a fresh pot of espresso brewing."

"Sounds great, Mr. Hudson*." I can use a cup, and Poppy certainly knew how to brew it,* he thought.

Sitting at Poppy's kitchen island, the entire group was sipping espresso, including Sonny Mitchell who had come back to the Jansen's for a weekend visit, .

"What brings you around these parts?" Michael asked.

"I just wanted to let you know what is going on with the three kidnappers. The good news is the FBI found remains behind the shack in the mangroves. It was Jack Watson, or at least what was left of him. Bill Marr turned state's evidence against Pete Samuels for a lighter sentence. Both will be sent to a federal prison because kidnapping for ransom is a federal offense, and the FBI plans to keep those two scumbags off the streets for a very long time."

"Now for more good news. At least I think it's good news. The giant squid hasn't killed again or even been seen in over three weeks, which probably means it has left our area. Of course, it could also mean that it is feeding in other areas and could come back here when more people start going fishing or boating again. Personally, I don't really think it will come back again. In any event, it doesn't look like we will have to worry about it anymore."

The whole group of friends gave a sigh of relief, knowing that CJ and Skye would be safe.

After having one of Skye's delicious sandwiches and a couple homemade chocolate chip cookies, CJ sat down on the deck, resting against the inside of the boat. Skye sat down beside him. Deciding that it was time to tell Skye how he really felt about her, he looked over at her and said, "I was so afraid that you were dead when we found you in the shack."

Before he could finish, Skye interrupted. "I thought I would die there too, but I kept willing you to find me. I kept asking you to come to me, and you did. You found me, CJ." Tears filled her eyes. "Before you found me, I thought I might never see you again."

Only thinking of one thing, CJ's long, tanned arms circled Skye's petite bikini-clad body, and he said, "I love you, Skye. I just wanted to tell you that. I've wanted to say it for a long time."

Skye just sat there thinking about what CJ had just told her, not knowing how to answer him.

Mistaking her hesitation in answering for rejection, CJ said, "I know you just want to be friends Skye, but I couldn't hold it in any longer."

Taking a deep breath, Skye looked up into CJ's beautiful, thick-lashed brown eyes, like his mother's eyes. "I love you too, CJ. I knew it the first time I saw you this summer. The only problem is I'm only here for the summers. You head off to UF in the fall for at least four years of college, if not more. I'll still be in high school another year. How can it possibly work?"

"It will work because we love each other, Skye. It doesn't matter where I am or where you are. You have my heart, and you always will." CJ leaned down, and for the first time he kissed Skye, softly at first and then with more passion. With his heart racing, he said, "We can make it work, Skye, as long as you love me too."

"I do, CJ, I do." With glassy eyes, she looked up into his eyes again, and right then she knew she would never love anyone but him.

———————

Preparing for their second dive, they smiled at each other, their feelings brightening their faces.

"Ready to go?" CJ asked.

"Yep, ready as I'm ever going to be. Let's go find some more gold." Both fell over the side and headed down into the cold, deep water.

Reaching the ledge at the same time, they felt around, stirring up the silt. CJ moved around to the back side of the ledge, and Skye was working from the front. Rocks were jutting out of the crevice below them. CJ shined his headlight down. Hanging on one of the sharp jutting rocks, he saw something glittering. Leaning over to get a better look with his light, he reached out to grab it. All of a sudden, he saw something that looked like a sharp spear heading straight toward him and fell back to get away from whatever it was while screaming to Skye, trying to get her attention. Fearing for his and Skye's lives, his body flooded with adrenalin. As he reached Skye and looked back, he saw it was only a swordfish, which lazily swam away. *Whew! Be still, my heart*, he thought, *as the Greek poet Homer would say.*

Returning to the spot where he had seen the glittering object, he reached down, this time taking hold of it. *Oh, my gosh! I can't believe it! Is it real?* In his hand, he held a large, heavy, solid gold crown filled with what looked like hundreds of diamonds and rubies. At the highest peak of the crown glittered what looked to be at least a ten-carat diamond.

Skye glanced over at CJ, wondering if he had found anything. Seeing what he held in his hand, she looked at his face. His eyes were wide open in either surprise or shock, she couldn't tell which, and slowly a smile appeared as he looked over at Skye.

She swam over to him, her face in awe of the treasure he was holding. He hadn't moved. He just kept smiling and looking at Skye in amazement.

Chapter Sixty-One

The giant creature slowly rose from the depths of the cold fissure. Its hunger demanded satisfaction. Since returning to the deep fracture, it had been unable to find sufficient food, other than some orange roughie's, when it had risen to shallower water. Seeing movement above, it cautiously and slowly made its way upward.

Thrilled at their new find, CJ and Skye climbed the ladder to board the old boat. It was almost dusk, and both were hungry again, but first they wanted to sit down on the deck and take a closer look at the crown. Unable to comprehend the value of the heavy gold and diamond headpiece, they just sat there touching it. Skye placed it on her head, but her face was so small it fell to the bridge of her nose.

"Do you think we should call your folks and Poppy and let them know what we found?"

"Yeah, plus we promised to check in each time we came up from a dive, and we didn't call them when we surfaced for lunch."

Picking up his iPhone, CJ pressed the number to his house and put the phone on speaker. His mother answered on the first ring.

"CJ, I was wondering when you were going to call. Your dad and I were starting to get a little worried because we hadn't heard from you and Skye. Are you okay?"

"We're fine, Mom. We just wanted to let you, and dad know that we're in for the night. We also thought you might be interested in our find today."

"Did you find another necklace, honey?"

"No, not this time, Mom."

"Oh, I'm sorry, CJ."

"It's okay, Mom." Smiling, CJ said, "We didn't find another necklace, but we did find a heavy gold crown with diamonds and rubies all over it. There's a diamond the size of dad's thumb at the crown's peak."

"What?" Maria couldn't believe what she had just heard.

"It's gorgeous, Mom. I'm going to text you and dad a picture of it. It's got to be worth several hundred thousand dollars, maybe even more. The diamond alone may be worth that."

"Oh, CJ, I'm so happy for you. Your dad is listening and nodding his head. I'll give Poppy a call and let him know too, okay?"

"Okay, Mom. That will be great. I love you. Skye sends her love too. We'll call you again tomorrow."

"Goodnight, Son." Maria hung up, looked at Michael, and broke into a huge smile. "I'd better call Poppy."

After Skye and CJ had eaten dinner, Skye went below to take care of her nightly routine, taking the crown with her and wrapping it in one of the towels they had brought with them for their trip.

CJ lay on the deck looking at the stars, thinking about Skye and the love and excitement she had brought to his life over the years. He was pleased with the results of their dive and satisfied from the good meal, and his eyelids grew heavy as the boat gently moved in the water.

The beast slowly rose in the water, hardly making a ripple. Seeing a light on the craft but no food, it was disappointed. Its hunger had to be satisfied. Raising an enormous reddish-brown tentacle over the side of the *Money,* the creature's limb made the boat list to one side.

CJ's eyes popped open. His heart began racing, and a shiver of fear raced up and down his spine causing the hairs on his entire body to stand at attention. Sensing danger was near, he turned and saw the huge tentacle on the deck, moving about as if searching for something. He quickly rolled away from the monster's feeler, his heart hammering harder in fear as he stood a little unsteadily. He momentarily froze. His throat was so dry he couldn't swallow. Shocked back to reality, he thought, *Skye. I can't let it hurt her.* He needed to get his gun. He knew he couldn't kill the squid, but maybe he could wound it enough that it would leave the boat so they could get away. Cap's screams abruptly came to mind. *I can't let that happen to Skye and me.*

Sensing movement, the creature's member quickly slithered on the deck toward CJ, knocking him off his feet. He bumped his head on the side of a cooler before he hit the deck. Screaming, he rolled, stood, and ran for the wheelhouse, grabbing his pistol from its storage. The tentacle followed him, searching in hunger. CJ quickly turned and fired twice, hitting the huge feeler both times. In pain and snapping its appendage as if it were a whip, the predator slithered toward CJ again. CJ fired again and again.

Hearing CJ's scream, Skye climbed the stairs as quickly as she could. Her heart felt like it was going to beat out of her chest. "Oh, my God, CJ, what's happening?" Getting no response as she reached the top of the stairs, she saw the enormous tentacle thrashing about on the deck, moving closer to CJ. The enormous whipping appendage caught CJ on the leg, and he fell to the deck of the wheelhouse. Skye screamed as CJ, trapped in the wheelhouse, took aim and fired until all the bullets had been spent. "Go back downstairs, Skye! Don't come up here! Call Dad! Tell him to come as fast as he can!"

"But CJ," Skye screamed, "I can't leave you!"

"Do what I tell you to do! Now! Hurry, and don't come back up here until I let you know it's okay. Promise me!" CJ knew there would be nothing his dad could do for him, but he needed to get Skye to go downstairs so she would be safe until his father got there.

Skye almost slid down the stairs. Shaking like a leaf and not sure if she could even speak, she dialed the Jansen's house. Michael answered. "Mr. Jansen, we need you! The giant squid is on the deck, and it's after CJ!" She started crying and couldn't stop, nor could she hear Michael tell her to stay where she was and that he was on his way. The phone disconnected.

Picking up his iPhone6 Plus, Michael called Detective Callahan. "Sean, Sonny and I need to get out to the Marquesas! CJ and Skye are in big trouble! It's the giant squid! What's the fastest way you can get us there?"

———————

The *Money* was silent. The boat still listed to the side. CJ hadn't called Skye to come back up to the deck. "Oh, God, she moaned, he's dead." She burst into tears and dropped to the bed. After a couple minutes, she sat up. Myriad thoughts ran through her mind. *If that monster has CJ, it can take me too.* She knew her life would never mean anything without CJ. Gathering her courage, she started up the stairs. When she reached the top, she looked toward the wheelhouse and saw CJ lying there. Blood was everywhere. "No!" she screamed.

Two seconds later, the enormous appendage slowly slid away

from CJ and over the side of the boat, correcting the list of the boat.

Dazed, CJ lifted his head, and seeing Skye running toward him, he smiled and said, "I thought I told you to stay below deck. You're the most hardheaded person I've ever known. Don't you ever listen to me?"

Chapter Sixty-Two

Detective Callahan made all the arrangements for the helicopter to transport him, Michael, and Sonny out to the *Money*. Seeing that Michael and Sonny were already standing on Poppy's dock waiting for their ride, Callahan told the pilot to set the helicopter down on the wide dock. Memories of the year before flashed through his mind as he remembered a private helicopter landing in the same place bringing the wealthy oil executive, John Duncan, to Skye's going away party.

As his thoughts quickly returned to the present, Callahan opened the door, got out, and motioned for them to get in. Michael's face was pale, drawn, and strained-looking as he headed toward the door. He walked as though he was in a fog. Sonny looked anxious as he stood next to Michael, afraid his friend might fall if he got too far away from him.

Please God, let the kids be okay, Callahan thought to himself. Lifting off from Poppy's dock, all three men sat stoic wondering what they would find when they got out to the boat. Michael stared out the window in a daze, wondering if his son was alive.

Sonny saw Michael staring, and he knew exactly what Michael was thinking. Michael and Maria had lost their first son, Jeffrey, who had been accidently struck and killed by a police officer's car. That's how Sonny, a former Miami police officer called to the scene, had met Michael. He didn't think either one of them could survive losing another child.

Fifteen minutes later, in the air, and using the coordinates that Michael had gotten from CJ before they left for their diving expedition, Callahan spotted the *Money*. Not seeing anyone on deck, his heart sank. Turning to look back at Michael, the detective said, "They probably went below deck. They'll hear the helicopter and come up, don't worry."

Michael didn't speak. He had already accepted the fact that he might never see his son again. Silent tears ran down his face. Sonny put his hand on Michael's shoulder and squeezed. "He's okay, Mikey. We'll see them in a minute." Michael didn't move. He didn't even look down at the boat again. His heart was breaking. He didn't know if Maria could manage another loss, but he knew he couldn't.

Suddenly, Callahan and Sonny looked down and saw the teens waving at them, jumping up and down with smiles covering their faces. "Michael, he's alive! They're both alive. Look!"

Michael's heart jumped with joy as he saw his beautiful son and Skye below them enthusiastically waving in happiness. *Thank you, God, for saving my son,* he prayed.

Callahan prepared the basket that would lower him, Michael, and Sonny, one at a time, aboard *Money in the Bank.* CJ remembered the instructions from the year before when the rescue diver, Curt Shields, had been lowered down from the helicopter so he could tend to Mr. Duncan before he was placed in the basket and lifted up to the rescue helicopter.

Detective Callahan was lowered into the boat first; next came Sonny Mitchell, and then finally Michael, where they were met by CJ and Skye. Michael grabbed CJ, looked him over and said, "Are you hurt, Son?" he yelled over the noise of the rotors.

Callahan reached up and waved the helicopter off. It circled around and headed back for Key West.

"No, Dad, I just got a bump on my head when the squid's tentacle knocked me down. I'm fine."

Then Michael reached over and hugged Skye, who was quietly

waiting by CJ's side. "I was so worried about you two. I didn't even tell your Poppy what had happened for fear of what we might find when we got here."

"It was really scary, Mr. Jansen. I thought the squid had killed CJ. I was freaking out when I called you."

Callahan and Sonny had given Michael some space with the teens before walking over.

"Everyone was so worried about the two of you. It was such a relief to see your smiling faces when we circled around and looked down the second time," Callahan said looking over at Skye and CJ.

"Little Missy, every time I speak with Michael, it seems like y'all are getting into trouble," Sonny said, smiling at Skye and then giving her and CJ a big hug.

She laughed and said, "Yeah, we've had some adventures, haven't we?"

"Yes, you have, and you need to slow down or you're going to give this old man here a heart attack," Sonny said, nudging Michael.

Sean Callahan asked CJ to tell all of them exactly what had happened.

Going over the events of the entire day, CJ told them what had happened below. First, seeing the giant octopus, then finding the gold and diamond crown, and then what had happened when Skye had gone downstairs to wash up and brush her teeth.

CJ looked over at Skye and asked, "Skye, why don't you tell everyone what happened next?"

Vividly remembering CJ's scream, the shots, and what she had seen when she got to the top of the stairs, she slowly told the story in detail, ending with finding CJ, surrounded by blood, lying in the wheelhouse. She told them she thought the squid had killed CJ until he opened his eyes and asked her if she ever did anything, he asked her to do. All three men laughed.

Then Sonny, looking seriously at Skye said, "You weren't afraid when you saw that octopus down below?"

"Of course not, we're friends now. Her name is Marina."

"What the heck are you talking about? What do you mean you're friends with a giant octopus?" Sonny asked.

Michael touched Sonny's shoulder and said, "I'll explain everything when we get home."

"But…"

"Later, bro, I promise."

Sonny wasn't satisfied, but he decided to wait until they got back to Michael's. He looked over and saw Callahan, who had a slight smile on his face, nod in agreement with Michael,

What does everyone know that I don't? Sonny wondered. He decided that as soon as they got back to Michael and Maria's house, someone was going to tell him everything.

Satisfied that they all knew what had happened during the squid attack, the men began walking around trying to recreate the scene. They found bullet holes in the deck where CJ had shot at the predator's tentacles, causing it to bleed profusely.

"We've got to kill this monster before it kills someone else!" Michael said angrily.

"Yes, we do need to kill it," Callahan said. "But how? That's the question."

Chapter Sixty-Three

The Jansen's house was the chosen meeting place to discuss ideas for destroying the predator. Michael had arranged the sun porch with seating for everyone. It had a beautiful view and looked out on the water. Maria had prepared coffee and had chilled soft drinks on hand. Skye had brought a large plate of her fresh-baked chocolate chip cookies. Detective Callahan, Mayor Morales, Sonny Mitchell and Poppy were present, along with Michael, Maria, CJ, and Skye. Poppy had asked to join the meeting and offered his boat and other resources to help in their quest to destroy the killer squid.

Mayor Morales was the first to speak. "I don't care what you have to do to kill this monster, just do it. If we don't kill it, our season will be over."

Michael interrupted. "Mayor, I think there's more here at stake than the season. People have been killed. Good people," he said, as he glanced at Poppy, who was staring at the hardwood flood thinking of Cap's death. "My son was almost killed by the same creature two days ago. I understand your need to save what is left of the summer season but destroying this monster, so it won't kill anyone else is the reason for this meeting."

Mayor Morales' face turned red, both from anger and from embarrassment at the rebuke from Michael.

Sean Callahan quickly stood up and spoke. "Okay, folks, we're here to discuss ways to eliminate the monster's threat to our community. Does anyone have any suggestions as to how we can do that?"

The room was silent. Finally, CJ stood up and said, "Skye and I have an idea."

Scoffing, the mayor looked at CJ and said, "You have an idea that will destroy a sixty-foot giant squid? Come on, son, let the adults make the decisions."

"But sir, if you'll just listen…"

Michael jumped up, his temper rising. "Mr. Mayor, my son was almost killed by this thing. I think he's earned the right to ask us to listen to his ideas."

Always the peacemaker, Callahan stood again and said, "Michael's right, Mr. Mayor. Other than the people who have been killed by this squid, CJ and Skye are the only two people who have even seen it, and they've seen it up close and survived. Let the young man speak."

"Thank you, Detective Callahan," CJ said. "What I was going to say is when Cap was killed by the giant squid, Skye and I spoke with Squeaky, a friend of ours, about finding a sperm whale to destroy the squid. That's the only thing that can kill it. Squeaky wasn't sure if he could find one, but he said he would try."

"And did your friend Squeaky say how he will convince the sperm whale to come here to kill the squid?" Morales said, laughing. "People can't talk to sperm whales, son, and I doubt your friend Squeaky is any different than most people. Does anyone else have any ideas?"

Not in the least bit discouraged, CJ spoke up again. "Squeaky can communicate with the sperm whale, sir."

"Come on, son, we're wasting precious time on this. Mr. Mitchell, you're with the National Security Agency. Do you have any ideas?"

Though Sonny had no idea where CJ was going with his suggestion, he looked at the mayor and said, "Let's listen to CJ, Mr. Mayor. I think he knows what he's talking about. Go ahead

CJ."

Morales just sat there fuming.

"Mr. Mayor, the reason I know that our friend Squeaky can communicate with the whale is because he's a dolphin."

"A dolphin? And just who communicates with the dolphin to ask him to go find a sperm whale and bring it back here to kill the squid?"

"Skye, sir. She has a very special gift. She can communicate with Squeaky, and a pelican named Flapper, and even a giant octopus she named Marina."

"I've never heard anything so ridiculous in all my life. I think all of you are crazy."

"It may sound ridiculous, but it's true, Mr. Mayor. I've seen it for myself," Michael said.

"So have I," Callahan chimed in, remembering the past summer when Skye had been talking with Squeaky and Flapper down on the dock the day of her going away party.

"My granddaughter does have a special gift," Poppy said. "It was hard for me to believe too, but Skye has never lied to me, and she told me she could communicate with them, plus I saw her myself talking with the pelican and the dolphin down on my dock."

Overwhelmed with testimonials from the group, the mayor sat in stunned silence.

Sonny Mitchell's mind was working at full speed. *Man, the NSA sure could sure use someone like that tiny little girl. Think of all the...* He stopped in mid-thought. *No, right now we need to focus our energies on killing the squid.* His thoughts threatened to come to the forefront of his mind again, but he concentrated on the major problem at hand, as he had learned from his years in the NSA. He sounded like an idiot, even to himself, when he said, "CJ, do you think Squeaky will help us?"

"Well, when Skye spoke with him about it the last time, he wasn't sure if he and his pod would be able to find a sperm whale, but he said they would try when we were ready. He also said he hasn't seen one around the Keys in a long time."

Still not believing the conversation that was happening, but willing to do anything to save the town's season, the mayor looked at Skye and said, "When do you plan to speak with the dolphin?"

"Well, it's late tonight. I'll call to Flapper in the morning and ask him to find Squeaky."

"And Flapper is the pelican?"

"Yes, sir. He's around Poppy's quite a bit when he knows I'm there. Both he and Squeaky saved mine and CJ's lives more than once."

Still thinking the teens were nuts, or were lying, the mayor asked, "Would you mind if I were there when you speak with the pelican and the dolphin?" *If they say no, I'll know they're lying.*

"Sure mayor. Squeaky is a show-off, and I'm sure he won't mind, but Flapper is a bit old and cantankerous. He may not like it, but we'll see." Looking at her grandfather, Skye asked, "You don't mind the company on your dock in the morning, do you, Poppy?"

"Nah, sweetheart, the more, the merrier." He smiled, thinking about the shock the mayor was in for tomorrow.

Everyone in the group agreed to meet at Poppy's at 9 a.m.

––––––––––

All the group arrived at Poppy's promptly at nine o'clock the next morning. On the wide dock, Poppy had set up a table with espresso and an assortment of pastries from Bob's Bunz Restaurant and Bakery for his guests. Always the southern gentleman, Poppy was prepared.

Skye and CJ sat in their usual spot on the dock, close to Flapper's favorite piling. Everyone watched and waited.

Skye said, "Flapper, if you're close by, please come to Poppy's dock. I need you."

Not more than a minute later, Flapper landed on the piling. "Hey, Skye. Sorry I didn't get out to the boat to check on you and CJ. Did you find more gold?" Looking around, he saw CJ, Poppy, CJ's mom and dad, and the stranger who had been in the boat with CJ and his dad when they went to rescue Skye. There was also a short, plump, grumpy-looking man standing there looking a little puzzled.

"Who are all these people?" Flapper asked Skye.

"Hi, Flapper. You know most everyone except CJ's Uncle Sonny," she said, pointing to Sonny Mitchell, and then turning to the mayor, she pointed and said, "This is Mayor Morales of Key West. What I called you about was to let you know the giant squid attacked CJ on the boat and almost killed him. We need your help. Could you go find Squeaky? These people are here to help us too."

Flapping his wings, he was a little upset that she had called him just so he could go find Squeaky. *What am I? A special delivery pelican?*

Everyone watched as the bird looked down at Skye and moved his head as if in anger.

"Why do you need to see that show-off?"

"We need him to go find a sperm whale to kill the giant squid."

Somewhat mollified by her answer, he nodded his head at Skye. "Okay, Skye, I'll go find Squeaky for you."

"Flapper, you've always been there for CJ and me, and we appreciate everything you and Squeaky have done for us. Come down here and give me a hug, so I'll know you're not upset."

Flapper jumped down from the piling, opened his wings and encircled Skye, waiting for his kiss on the beak. She kissed him and said, "Thank you, Flapper. Now go see if you can find Squeaky. The two of you may help save more lives than just mine and CJ's."

"Okay, Skye, I'll do my best to find him." With that, he lifted his wings and flew toward where he knew Squeaky's pod lived.

Everyone stood on the dock in shock, even the ones who had already witnessed Skye's gift. The mayor was speechless. No one said a word.

———————

About thirty minutes later, CJ looked out on the water, pointed, and said, "Here comes Flapper, and Squeaky is with him. Look!"

Still in shock from the interaction between Skye and the pelican, everyone looked toward where CJ was pointing. Sure enough, the pelican was getting close to the dock, and the dolphin was swimming toward them and doing flips for his audience.

As usual, Squeaky must show off when there's anyone around to see him. I still don't know what Skye sees in him. Oh, well, Skye and CJ like him, so I guess I'm stuck with him too, Flapper thought, landing on his favorite piling.

Squeaky did a couple flips, splashing water on everyone. Then he looked up at Skye, nodding his head and squeaking. "Hi, Skye, it's good to see you again. Flapper said you and CJ went out on the shrimp boat to find more gold. Any luck? Who are all these strangers?"

"Hey, Squeaky, it's good to see you again too. These people are friends of ours. I'll introduce them and explain in a minute why they're here. Yes, we had some luck, but that's not why I asked Flapper to go get you. Remember when CJ and I talked with you about finding a sperm whale? Well, we need one, and we need one in a hurry. The giant squid that killed Cap attacked CJ on Cap's old boat a couple days ago. He was lucky he didn't get killed. The only reason he survived is that CJ shot holes in the squid's tentacle with his gun, and bleeding profusely, it finally gave up."

Continuing, Sky said, "These strangers you don't know are Mayor Morales of Key West and Sonny Mitchell, CJ's uncle,"

Skye said, pointing first to the mayor and then to Sonny. "You know Mr. and Mrs. Jansen, Detective Callahan, and of course, Poppy. We've all gathered to see if we can find a way to kill the giant squid."

Squeaky looked at the group, nodding as if speaking and said, "I'm happy to meet you." Skye translated for him. Then looking at CJ, he said, "I'm so sorry you were hurt. I'll get my pod, and we'll leave right away to find a sperm whale." Skye again translated Squeaky's conversation to CJ and the group.

"Thank you, buddy," he said as Skye translated.

"Come on Flapper, we've got work to do, and I need your help," Squeaky said.

Flapper's chest puffed out in importance as he looked at Skye and said, "Maybe the show-off's not so bad after all." After having said that, Flapper lifted his wings and took to the air, with Squeaky swimming very fast below him, heading to his pod.

Skye laughed at Flapper's comment, but everyone else stood in stunned silence.

Finally, the mayor spoke, "CJ, I owe you and Skye a deep apology. I hope both of you will forgive me. You don't know how much I appreciate everything you're trying to do to help destroy the killer squid."

"Of course, we will, and thank you, Mr. Mayor. The first time I saw Skye talking with Flapper, I freaked out and so did she when she realized she could communicate with him. Poppy had a hard time believing it too, and mom and dad were both shocked when I told them," CJ said, looking over at his parents. Looking at his Uncle Sonny, CJ said, "What do you think, Uncle Sonny?"

Sonny's mind was a jumbled mess. He had just seen Skye speaking with a pelican and a dolphin. What could he say? "I'm speechless, CJ. I know what I just saw, but I had no idea something like that was even possible. It's amazing! That's the only way I can put it."

Poppy had replenished the coffee pot. "Coffee anyone?"

he asked. Suddenly the group all began talking at once. What they had seen was unbelievable, but they all knew it was true. Now, the question was, could the dolphin find a sperm whale, and will the sperm whale kill the giant squid?

Chapter Sixty-Four

Squeaky had his pod scattered up and down the coast from Miami over to Bimini in the Bahamas and down the Great Bahama Bank, then over to the Cay Sal Bank, and through Santarem Channel. Squeaky and several of his pod moved west beyond northwest Cuba through the Straits of Florida and then on to the Dry Tortugas. Flapper's job was to check out the waters from the sky and let Squeaky know if he saw any whales close by. Flapper finally felt like he was just as important to Skye as Squeaky was. *Maybe Squeaky and I make a good team after all,* he thought.

Unknown to the citizens of Key West, it was Squeaky who finally found the prize. Eighty miles northwest of the Dry Tortugas in fourteen hundred sixty feet of water, Squeaky picked up the echolocation of a sixty-five-foot, forty-five-ton bull sperm whale.

Squeaky and his buddies quickly headed for the whale. A few hours later, they surrounded the gentle giant. Squeaky had never met a sperm whale before and had been surprised when the very large whale seemed to take a liking to him and his buddies. The dolphin would zip by him, up and over as the giant slowly moved north. Every so often the whale would roll over and breach the surface imitating the dolphins.

Squeaky had communicated their purpose in being there to the whale. He told the whale about Skye and how he was able to communicate with her. He then asked the whale if he would follow them and kill the giant killer squid.

Thinking about what the dolphin had asked, the whale agreed to follow Squeaky and his pod back to the Marquesas Keys. *I think it might be nice to meet this special girl the dolphin is talking about. I wonder if she can communicate with me.*

———————

Three days later, Skye and CJ were sitting on the dock when Flapper unceremoniously dropped down and landed on his old familiar piling.

"Guess what? We found a sperm whale, and he's agreed to follow Squeaky and his pod back here. He also agreed to kill the giant squid. He only has one condition."

"That's great, Flapper! Thank you so much for letting us know. What's the condition?"

"Uh, he said he wants to meet you first. I think he wants to see if you can communicate with him like you do Squeaky and me. He's really nice, Skye. I think you should do it."

Skye translated Flapper's message to CJ. They both broke out laughing.

"Did I say something funny?" he asked, seeming a little offended and ruffling his feathers.

"Oh, Flapper, lighten up. It was just the way you said it, and the fact that a sperm whale wants to talk with me. Of course, I'll do it."

"That's great, Skye! I'll let Squeaky know. They're headed this way. They should be here in another couple of days. It's a little slow-going with the whale. He's huge."

"Thank you so much for everything you do for CJ and me, Flapper. I don't know what we'd do without you."

Flapper lowered his head and looked almost embarrassed at the praise. "You're my friends, Skye, and I would do anything for you

258

and CJ. I hope you know that."

"Of course I do, Flapper. I've got a bucket of fish with your name on it up in the outside refrigerator. Have you got a few minutes, so I can go get it?"

"Fresh fish? Oh, Skye, I've always got time for fresh fish." Settling on his perch on the dock piling, he waited for Skye to run up to the house.

Two days later, Skye was at CJ's house, helping him wash his Mako when Flapper landed on the dock close to them.

"Well, hello again little buddy," CJ said when he saw Flapper. Of course, Flapper could only communicate with Skye, but he had a pretty good idea what CJ had said because he looked happy to see Flapper.

"Hey, Flapper, what's up? Are Squeaky and the whale getting close?" Skye asked.

"Yep, Squeaky said to tell you they'll be out at the Marquesas Keys in the morning. He would like everyone to be there when they arrive."

"That's wonderful, Flapper! We'll let everyone know."

"You don't happen to have another bucket of fish, do you?" Flapper asked.

"No, sorry Flapper, but I'll make sure you and Squeaky each get a huge bucket when the squid has been killed, and we all get together to celebrate. Does that sound fair to you?"

Though he was a little disappointed, he nodded his head at Skye and said, "That will be fine, Skye. Squeaky sure deserves it after all he's done."

"Just remember, Flapper, he couldn't have done it without you." Skye knew that Flapper needed constant stroking and that there had been jealousy between him and Squeaky since she had known them.

Flapper puffed out his chest and magnanimously offered, "Sure, I helped, but Squeaky was the one who closed the deal."

Hmmm, Skye thought, *maybe the cranky old bird is starting to come around where Squeaky is concerned.*

Fifteen minutes later, CJ and Skye walked up to the house and told Michael and Sonny Flapper's news. Michael said he would call Detective Callahan, Mayor Morales, and Poppy. All three readily agreed to be present when Squeaky and the whale arrived. Michael would also let Maria know what was going on when she returned from the Winn-Dixie.

"I think the two of you had better head down to Key West and prepare the boat for tomorrow, don't you? We can all ride in it together out to the Marquesas if that's okay with you and Skye. After all, it's your boat now."

"Sure, Dad, that's a great idea. There's plenty of room. Skye and I can just go on down and spend the night on the boat at the marina."

––––––––––––

Packing all their supplies in the yellow VW, CJ and Skye headed for Key West. Out of the clear blue sky, CJ asked, "Skye, what will your major be in college?"

"Since it's only a little more than a year away, I've been giving it a lot of thought," she said. "Like you, I love the water, so I want it to be something where I'll be around the water. What about you? Have you decided what your major will be?"

"I've been thinking about underwater archeology. I love history, and I love diving, and I could do both with a master's degree."

"That's wonderful, CJ! We'll both be on the water."

For the next ten miles or so neither of them said another word. Finally, CJ got up the courage to discuss their future. "You know

I love you, and I want to spend the rest of my life with you. That means marriage. Will you marry me when we're both finished with college?"

Skye laughed and said, "Of course I will. What would you think about our getting married at Poppy's where we had the party last year? It's beautiful there, and there's room for lots of people."

CJ smiled broadly and promptly agreed.

Chapter Sixty-Five

Early the next morning, Skye poured them bowls of cereal and milk. CJ made a pot of coffee. Skye wasn't much of a coffee drinker, preferring hot tea, but CJ couldn't do without at least two cups in the morning.

Right after Skye had washed the dishes and put them away, they heard someone say, "Ahoy there! Your guests are here."

CJ walked over to the side of the boat and looked down at the jovial group standing on the dock. "Great! Come on up," he said.

His mom and dad, his Uncle Sonny, Poppy, Detective Callahan and Mayor Morales had brought coolers. CJ figured they were stuffed with food and drinks.

CJ's forehead wrinkled in thought. *They look like they're going to a party instead of going to see a sperm whale kill a giant squid. At least that's the plan. I hope everyone will be safe. It could get dangerous out there,* he thought. Unexpectedly, he shuddered, and it felt like giant ants were crawling up and down his spine.

The sky was clear except for some puffy clouds that reminded CJ of white cotton candy. There was usually a shower most afternoons that only lasted a few minutes, but so far, no rain had appeared. The sea was as smooth as glass, there was no breeze, and the temperature was in the low nineties. Everyone kept looking toward the sky, hoping for a reprieve from the sweltering heat.

Detective Callahan had rings of sweat under the armpits of his short-sleeved uniform shirt and was wiping his face with a paper towel he had found in the small galley.

Mayor Morales' face was beet red. Perspiration was rapidly soaking the white shirt that pulled tightly across his stomach enhancing the extra thirty pounds he was carrying.

Poppy found shade in the wheelhouse of Cap's old boat, which brought back fond memories of the times they had spent together. He also felt sadness that Cap's life had ended in almost the same spot he was standing.

Michael, Maria, and Sonny had all worn shorts and sandals, so they were faring a little better than the others. Everyone waited.

After having sandwiches and cold drinks for lunch, Mayor Morales was getting impatient. "Well, are they coming or not?" Even though he had seen it, he didn't understand how the girl could communicate with the bird and the dolphin, and he still wondered if it was all a scam to trick him that had been orchestrated by Sean Callahan.

"Flapper said they would be here. We just have to be patient, Mr. Mayor."

Almost as soon as Skye had spoken the words, she heard a voice say, "Hey, Skye, we're here." The dolphin did a couple flips and squeaked to everyone in the boat.

"Squeaky! I'm so glad you're here. Where's Flapper?"

"I'm here too," Flapper said as he smoothly landed on the top of the wheelhouse.

"Great! Thank you both so much for what you did. Is the whale with you?"

"Yep, he's out in deeper water. He wants to talk with you, Skye."

"I sure hope we can communicate. I'm sorta nervous. Where exactly is he? We can move the boat closer, so we'll be able to hear each other's thoughts."

"Sure," Squeaky said, "I'll swim out to him and let him know. You can follow in the boat."

There was excitement in everyone's voices as they all started talking at the same time. Each had seen Skye, Squeaky, and Flapper communicating, but all of them were wondering if she would be able to communicate with the whale.

Michael took control of the anchor detail, and within minutes it was secure on deck. CJ started the boat and slowly maneuvered the *Money* out into deeper water in the direction that Squeaky was heading.

"Hey guys, let me know if you spot the whale," CJ yelled over the engine noise. *Skye's going to talk with a sperm whale.* Just saying the words sounded ridiculous, even to CJ, who had seen it happen the first day she and Flapper had spoken. *Please, please, let this work,* he thought. *The monster has to be killed before it kills someone else, and if anyone can kill it, the sperm whale can.*

Abruptly, Michael pointed his finger. About three hundred yards to the east, in the direction Squeaky was heading, a dark gray sperm whale with a stream of air and vapor spouting from its blowhole was moving in what seemed like slow motion.

Squeaky swam up to the whale and started squeaking. He was letting the whale know that Skye was in the boat and was ready to try to talk with him. He told the whale that the others were family and friends of Skye's and that they were nice.

Skye directed her thoughts to the whale. "Hi, my name is Skye. Do you have a name?"

"Oh my gosh, I can hear you! I can't believe it! Uh, no, whales don't have names."

"Well then, we'd better give you one, hadn't we? That way I'll know what to call you. How about Willy? I saw a really cool movie about a whale named Willy."

"A movie? What's that?"

"Well, a movie is where you see moving pictures of people,

animals, sea creatures, and lots of things."

"Can you talk with them in the moving pictures?"

"No, you can't talk with them. They're real, but what we see are only moving pictures of them."

"Well, if you liked the whale named Willy in the moving picture you saw, I guess that name will be fine with me," Willy said almost shyly. "In fact, I kind of like it. It's sure better than Squeaky or Flapper. I'll have to let my pod know I have a name."

"Hey, wait a minute," Squeaky said, sounding offended.

Skye laughed and said, "Ah, c'mon Squeaky, he's just teasing." Then Skye's laughter stopped, and she became serious. "Willy, I know Squeaky told you about the giant squid that's been killing people around here. Can you help us get rid of it?"

"I guess you know that giant squid are the main staple of us sperm whales, don't you? We love to eat them. I told Squeaky I would kill it if you would talk with me, so I'll do it for you, but first I will need to find it."

"If you can just hang out for a while, I'll see if I can find Marina. She'll probably know where it is."

"Who's Marina?"

"Oh, she's a giant octopus I met while diving in the deep crevice over there," Skye said.

"You can talk with a giant octopus too?"

"Yep, she warned me the last time I saw her that the giant squid was close by. CJ and I will dive down into the crevice and see if she is around. Will you be okay out here for now?"

"Sure. Who's CJ?"

"CJ is my best friend. He's the one standing next to me," she said and touched CJ's arm. "Squeaky can keep you company while CJ and I get suited up for our dive. Is that okay with you?"

"That's fine with me. Willy, huh? I like my new name. I never had a name before."

Skye translated for the crowd, and everyone on the boat, including CJ, just stood there in awe of what they had just seen.

Chapter Sixty-Six

Suited up, CJ and Skye had checked their dive tanks and were ready to head over to the dive ladder of the old shrimp boat.

Michael was the first to speak. "Are you sure you won't let me dive with you, Son?"

Skye responded before CJ could speak. "Mr. Jansen, Marina might not come up if she sees a stranger with us. We'll be okay, don't worry. We'll only be down long enough to see if she's down there."

"Well, I don't like it," Poppy said. "What if that giant squid is down there?"

"If it is down there," CJ said, "it's probably very deep and won't even know we're there."

Callahan pulled an AK-47 rifle from under the bench seat. "I'll be ready if it comes up," he said, knowing that the rifle wouldn't make much of a dent in the monstrous creature, but it made him feel better knowing that he had it. He had also brought a Kimber Custom TLE II pistol. They belonged to the S.W.A.T. team in Key West, and he had borrowed them for the trip.

Maria walked over to the teens and hugged both of them. There were tears in her eyes as she said, "I love you both so much. Please promise me you'll be careful."

In unison, the teens said, "We will. We promise."

Still unsure whether he believed what happened even though he had seen it with his own eyes, Mayor Morales patted both teens on the shoulder and said in a soft voice, "You two be careful down there, okay?" He may not believe that Skye could communicate with the bird and the sea creatures, but he still didn't want anything to happen to either of the kids. *They're a lot braver than I am*, he thought.

With their dive tanks on their backs, CJ and Skye fell backward off the dive ladder of the *Money*. Staying close as they headed into the quickly cooling depths, both were looking down as well as all around them to make sure the monstrous squid wasn't close.

Reaching the crevice, Skye said, "Marina, if you're down there, please come up so we can talk." Nearly a minute passed. The teens were about to give up when finally, a soft voice said, "I'm on my way up."

When Skye looked down and saw a large tentacle, she felt an instant shiver of fear, not certain if it was Marina or the killer squid. Realizing she was holding her breath; she relaxed when she saw it was the giant octopus.

"Skye, it's so good to see you and your friend again, but it's not safe here for you. Why are you here?"

"That's what I wanted to talk with you about, Marina. Have you seen the giant squid around here lately?"

"The bad thing? Yes, from a distance. He goes down into this big hole every night. I make sure I'm away from here before he starts down there. Please don't stay down here long. You're in danger."

"We won't, Marina. Thank you for all your help. You stay safe. Maybe after tonight, you won't have to leave your nice deep, cold spot."

"What's happening tonight?"

"We found a sperm whale, and he is going to kill the giant squid."

"Oh, my goodness! I'd better leave here now. I sure don't want to be in the middle of all that."

"Yes, we have to leave too. We'll be out of air soon."

"I hope to see you again, Skye. I've never had anybody to talk with before. It's been so nice to be able to communicate with you."

"Thank you for all your help, Marina. We'll see each other again. Soon I hope."

Marina gently wrapped a tentacle around both Skye and CJ and said, "Please be careful. I don't want anything to happen to either of you."

Everyone was hanging over the side of the boat when CJ and Skye surfaced. Almost in unison, they breathed a sigh of relief, seeing that the teens were safe.

"Thank goodness," Maria said, "you're safe!"

After they were onboard and their dive tanks had been removed, Skye said, "We saw Marina. She said the squid goes down in the crevice every night. We'll have to let Willy know, so he can be ready."

Mayor Morales was almost in shock. *All this is like a science fiction movie*, he thought. *I'm going to wake up in the morning and realize that none of this is real.*

Poppy grabbed Skye and hugged her so tight she almost couldn't breathe. "Poppy, I'm okay. I'm okay."

"I know, little girl, I just need a hug." Poppy didn't want Skye to know how scared he had been.

Detective Callahan walked up to CJ and Skye and said, "You kids are much braver than I am. I could never do what you just did."

CJ said, "We just want to make sure the monster doesn't kill anyone else, Detective. Thanks to Skye's special gift, we know that the squid will be here this evening. Now the whale can get ready for the fight. Also, we're going to have to move away from this crack in the ground. We don't want to be caught in the fight, and we certainly don't want to be close by when the squid goes down for the night. He may decide he wants dessert, and I don't want it to be any of us."

"You're right, Son. It's three o'clock now. We need to move the boat in the next hour or so to be safe." Everyone started talking at once.

Mayor Morales said, "How can we see the fight if we are going to go leave?"

"We won't have to leave, Mr. Mayor. We just have to get far enough away from the fight so that we won't get caught up in it," CJ said.

Sonny had been pretty quiet all day. Finally, he spoke. "Skye, are you sure the whale can kill the squid? Do you think I should call the NSA and get some backup out here?"

Skye looked at Michael, "Mr. Jansen, what do you think?" Rubbing his forefinger and thumb over his chin in deep thought,

Michael said, "Sonny, I think the backup might be in more danger than they realize. They won't know what they're up against. None of them has ever seen a giant squid, and I'm sure none of them has seen a sperm whale. Besides, the sperm whale might be intimidated by a bunch of armed men. I think we should watch from a safe distance and keep the NSA out of this. No one has spoken to the press, have they, Mr. Mayor?" Michael said, looking pointedly at Morales.

"Well, not really."

"What do you mean, not really?" Callahan interrupted.

"Well, my secretary knows where I am. I had to tell her, and her husband works for the paper, but she gave me her word that she wouldn't tell him or anyone."

"Well, you'd better hope she doesn't, Mr. Mayor. The press showing up would not only put them in danger, but it also might scare off the whale."

Morales' red face turned even redder as he swallowed in embarrassment. He picked up his cell phone and dialed the office, but he got his secretary's voicemail saying the office was closed. Morales knew then, deep down in his gut, that the press would be coming. *I'll fire her tomorrow,* he thought. *I can't believe I was so stupid as to tell her.*

Chapter Sixty-Seven

It was dusk, and everyone was nervous. Even with what they were facing, everyone was mesmerized by the beautiful Key West sunset as it dropped behind the horizon.

Nervous, Michael started pacing the deck.

Sonny was staring out at the water as if he could already see the fight to come.

Anchored at what they thought was a safe distance, everyone on the *Money* watched as Willy moved in closer to the edge of the crevice, prepared for the battle. He disappeared into the depths.

Earlier, Skye had asked Squeaky to tell Willy that the rogue squid was supposed to be in the crevice by dark.

Everyone on the *Money* was on edge, waiting to see what would happen between Willy and the rogue giant squid.

Unexpectedly, a seventeen-foot boat almost flew past the *Money*, moving fast. A tall, slender, dark-haired man with a touch of gray in his temples stood at the wheel of the boat. He didn't even look over at the *Money*. His hand tightly gripped the wheel as he thought of the riches and fame he would receive when this was all over. He decided he might even write a book and win a Pulitzer.

Morales instantly recognized him. It was his secretary's husband, Noah. *Crap!* Morales thought. *They're going to screw up the whole thing. This was our one chance to kill this monster.* Another man holding a large camera was seated in the boat, panning the camera back and forth across the smooth water. His blond hair was blowing wildly in the wind from the speed they were traveling. He glanced up at the *Money* and smiled slyly as if to say, *You can't keep the press away. We're going to film this fight. Our ratings are gonna go through the roof.*

"Morales, your big mouth probably destroyed what chance we had at killing this thing," Callahan said, "and those idiots are probably going to get themselves killed."

"Now wait just a minute. You can't talk to me like that. I'm the mayor."

"Not for long," Callahan barked back at Morales.

The small media boat slowed to a stop and anchored on the opposite side of the *Money and* waited for the excitement to begin.

The massive predator rose slowly behind the boat that was carrying the press. Feeling the slap of the water against the small craft, causing it to rock back and forth, nearly turning over, Noah's eyes opened wide in shock, and he was momentarily speechless. As an enormous tentacle grabbed him, he let out a scream that was cut off as the gigantic limb wrapped around him so tightly it crushed his chest. Blood gushed from his mouth and his still wide open but lifeless eyes, as he was pulled from the boat into the water, disappearing with the squid.

Terrified, the camera operator threw down the camera and jumped out of the boat on the opposite side, thinking he could swim to the old shrimp boat and escape death. His heart was pumping so loudly he thought he could hear it. Pain gripped his chest as he swam for his life toward the *Money.*

Everyone on the *Money* was stunned. *Where is Willy?* Skye wondered. *Willy, we need you. Please hurry.* Michael and Sonny were yelling to the camera operator to swim harder. Callahan had tied a long rope on a life preserver and threw it out as far as he could.

"Hurry man! Swim!" Poppy yelled.

Suddenly, the giant squid rose up from the water close to the *Money,* and his huge tentacle grabbed the frantic swimmer. He didn't even have time to scream as he was pulled beneath the water. Bright red blood bubbled up to the surface.

Everyone on the larger boat froze and began backing away from the edge, wondering what was going to happen next.

Suddenly, severe chest pains gripped Morales as he grabbed his chest and collapsed on the deck, his face a sickly shade of gray.

Forgetting the squid, Callahan's emergency medical training took over as he checked for a pulse on the mayor's neck. There was none. Yelling to Michael to give him a hand, he ripped open the mayor's shirt and started counting as he clasped his hands together and began pressing them to the unresponsive man's chest. His training told him to try to give the man a hundred compressions a minute. After about eighty, he asked Michael to take over as he stood from his cramped position. He walked over to the bench seat and grabbed the AK-47.

"What's going on?" he asked CJ, who was slowly creeping back to the edge of the shrimp boat to see what was happening with the squid.

"I'm not sure. The squid got the camera man. Did you see it? He didn't have a chance."

"Yeah, I saw it. CJ, relieve Michael when he's tired, okay?"

"Sure, no problem."

Sonny walked over to the bench seat and grabbed the Kimber pistol. He had a feeling he was going to need it. He headed to the side of the boat; the pistol gripped firmly in his hand.

Always curious, Skye slowly crept to the side of the *Money.* She had to see what was going on. As she looked over the edge of the boat, two massive tentacles grabbed onto the boat, causing the boat to tilt and Skye to fall into the water. She let out a bloodcurdling scream. With the pistol in his hand, Sonny started firing at the tentacles as Callahan fired the AK-47. The tentacles were sliding back and forth and snapping in the air in anger. Finally, both bloody limbs slid back into the water. The predator was heading to the safety of the cold, deep water of the huge crevice.

Hearing Skye scream, CJ left the mayor lying there and ran to the edge of the boat. Michael took over again. Finally, Mayor Morales took a quick breath and then a long, deep one. A little color began coming back into his face. "What's happening?" he asked weakly.

"Don't talk now, Mayor. Just lay there and save your strength. You had a heart attack. Sorry, Mayor, but Skye just fell overboard. I've got to help CJ get her out of the water."

Without thinking, CJ jumped into the water and swam toward Skye, whose eyes were frozen in fear. "Skye, I'm coming." There was no response. *Shock. She's in shock*, he thought. *I need to get her back in the boat and get her warm.* As he reached for Skye, she started screaming, "No, no, go away."

"Skye, it's me, sweetheart. It's me." Instantly her eyes focused on CJ, and she began crying. Grabbing onto the life preserver, he put it over Skye's head, told her to grab hold and began pulling her toward the rear ladder. Michael, Sonny, and Poppy were there waiting for them. Callahan was making rounds around the perimeter of the boat, checking for the predator. It had disappeared.

Still shivering in fear as she boarded the boat, Skye said, "Where's the squid, CJ? Where is it?"

"Everything's okay, Skye. It's gone. Uncle Sonny and Detective Callahan shot at it, and it went back into the deep crevice."

"Is it dead?" Skye said, her voice shaking and her face very pale. "Where is Willy?"

"He disappeared into the crevice, and we haven't seen him since."

With two tentacles injured, the giant squid had fled to the bottom of the giant crack, where, unknowingly, Willy, the sperm whale waited.

At an unbelievable sixty feet, the predator was almost as long as the sperm whale, Willy, who topped off at sixty-seven feet. Seeing the whale coming in for the kill, the predator began the race to the surface where both shot up out of the water at the same time, to the surprise of everyone on the *Money*.

"Move the boat away!" Willy yelled to Skye in the midst of the fight to the death.

"CJ, start the engine! Quick!"

"Huh?" CJ said, looking over at Skye.

"Willy said to move the boat out of the way. Go!"

Realizing that Willy was communicating with Skye, CJ ran to the wheelhouse and started the engine, moving the boat about three hundred yards away from the fight. Even at that distance, the boat rocked in the waves caused by the fight between the massive creatures.

All aboard the *Money* were mesmerized as the two battled. The monstrous squid wrapped its tentacle tightly around Willy's head and squeezed as hard as it could as jets of dark ink shot out from the squid.

Unaffected by the ink and much stronger than the squid, the sperm whale, his head a little battered, opened his mouth and powerfully suctioned off one of the tentacles, then another. The squid tried its best to flee from the huge whale, but after a couple minutes the battle was over, almost before it had begun. The killer squid was dead, and Willy dragged it to the cold ocean floor to finish his fine meal.

———————

Standing in the boat close to the rear ladder, Skye spoke to Willy for the last time. "I don't know how to thank you, Willy, for everything you did, not only for CJ and me, but for everyone in the whole area. Without you, the squid would have continued killing people and may never have moved on. No one would ever have been safe on the water again. The squid almost got CJ one night on this boat. Did I tell you that?"

Embarrassed at all the praise, Willie spoke to Skye, "No, you didn't tell me that. I'm so glad your friend is safe. I think he means a lot to you. Skye, you'll never know how good it feels to be able to communicate with a human person. I can't thank you enough. I was so jealous when Squeaky told me that you had started speaking to him and Flapper last summer. I still can't believe you can talk to me. You're a sweet girl with a very special gift, and I'll never forget you. Maybe if you don't mind, I'll come back to see you again. Is that okay?"

"Of course, it is, Willy. I love talking with you, and I will miss you very much. I think Squeaky and Flapper will miss you too. Just let Squeaky know when you're coming, and CJ and I will come out here to the crevice and meet you. You take good care of yourself. You're my hero, you know."

"Oh, I don't know about that," Willy said, shyly. "After meeting and talking with you, I just knew I had to do what I could to help, plus that squid was the biggest meal I've had in quite a while."

With heavy hearts, Willy and Skye both were sad to say goodbye, but it was time for Willy to go back to his pod, and it was time for the *Money* to head back to the marina in Key West.

Chapter Sixty-Eight

Nearly the whole town showed up for the celebration. Completely recovered from his heart attack and on a strict weight loss plan, Mayor Morales was in rare form as he laughed and shook hands with everyone he saw. The mayor's re-election campaign had already begun, and no one had any doubts that he would be re-elected. *Thanks to those teens, I'm a town hero.*

Most of the crowd was gathered all the way down Duval Street past the Pier House to the large wooden deck over the water where bands sometimes entertained in the evenings. Others were sightseeing until the merriment began.

Waiting for the festivities to start, a group from the crowd headed down to Sloppy Joe's Bar for a cold beer. The bar had been around since 1933, and the famous writer, Ernest Hemmingway, had spent quite a bit of time there during the 1930's.

Skye, CJ, Michael, Maria, Poppy, Sonny, and Detective Callahan were seated on the deck at a large round table. A podium was in front of the group, unmanned for another hour.

Hearing of the amazing incident the week before, hundreds of visitors had come to Key West to be part of the commemoration. It would remember those who the giant squid had killed and honor those who were instrumental in the killing of the squid. The celebration would officially begin at sunset. Many of the attendees were on boats or landmark tours enjoying the beautiful scenery until the appointed time.

It had been whispered around town, though no one could confirm it, that newly elected President Shannon would attend the celebration, so people had come from all over the country, hoping for a glimpse of him. Key West hadn't seen that much action since the overseas highway had been refurbished in the 1950's.

"I'll be glad when all this is all over," CJ said. As usual, he was uncomfortable from all the attention, letting Skye do most of the talking for both. He had always been shy.

Glancing over at CJ, Skye said, "Yeah, me too. This is a beautiful place, but today it's a madhouse, and I'm ready to go back home to Poppy's."

"Dad, Mayor Morales sure looks better than he did last week on the boat, doesn't he?"

"Yeah, Son, he sure does. He was lucky. He seems to be enjoying himself today. I think he's changed since the incident in the water and on the boat. I sure hope so. He seems like a nice guy now."

"Thanks to the mayor and the NSA, the media were only told that the giant squid was killed by a sperm whale," Sonny said. "They know nothing of your ability, Skye. After talking with the mayor and Poppy, we felt it was better not to let the public know about your special gift or how the whale knew the squid was around these waters."

"Thanks, Uncle Sonny. I sure don't want to be hounded by the newspapers nor end up on the front page of the *National Enquirer*."

Detective Callahan looked at both the teens and said, "Well, it looks like you two are heroes again this summer. I just want you to know how much I appreciate what both of you did for the sheriff's office and this community. Will you be back next summer, Skye?"

"Nothing could keep me away, Detective," Skye said, smiling as she looked at CJ as though they shared a secret, which they did.

"Well, speaking as an old man, it's close to dark, and I'm ready to get this thing over with and hit the road. Us old folks like to be in before dark," Poppy said. Everyone laughed.

"Why don't we spend the night here at the Pier House and head home in the morning? The mayor offered us rooms at the city's expense," Maria told the group.

"Sounds like a good plan to me," Poppy agreed.

The exquisite sunset was slowly sinking beneath the horizon. Total sunset would be in about five more minutes.

Mayor Morales walked up to the podium and asked for everyone's attention. The mass finally quieted. Those returning from the tours were back and had integrated into the crowd. The media was front and center, wildly snapping pictures of the mayor and the group behind the podium that had stood at the request of Mayor Morales.

The mayor looked out into the throng of people and said, "Ladies and gentlemen, first I would like to name those who were lost to this community by the giant predator." The crowd was somber and quiet as he listed the deceased. Cap's name brought tears to Skye's eyes.

"Next, I would like to introduce you to the small group of people that pursued the killer squid and were present when it was killed. First, allow me to introduce Skye Somers and CJ Jansen, the most incredible teenagers I have ever met. The information they provided to my office, as well as the Monroe County Sheriff's Office, was invaluable. For such a young girl, Skye has exceptional intuition." The mayor looked at Skye with a small smile, letting her know he would always keep her secret. "CJ," he said, putting his hand on CJ's shoulder, "always fearless, drove the shrimp boat, *Money II*, to the spot where the squid made a home in several hundred feet of water, almost losing his life when he was attacked by the creature. In fact, they both lost a good friend to the squid, Captain Mark Anderson, whom I mentioned earlier."

The mayor continued, "Standing next to CJ are his parents, Michael and Maria Jansen, and CJ's uncle, Sonny Mitchell, who is with the National Security Agency. Michael helped to save my life on the boat when I had a heart attack. Standing to the left of Skye is her grandfather, George Hudson, a resident of Islamorada. Skye spends every summer with Mr. Hudson. And last, for those of you who don't know him, I would like to introduce Detective Sean Callahan with the Monroe County Sheriff's office. Detective Callahan and Sonny Mitchell had the courage to face the predator, shooting at it until it released its hold on the boat and slid back into the water, after trying to attack us. Detective Callahan also assisted in saving my life. I probably would not be here if it had not been for Michael Jansen and Sean Callahan, and I am sincerely grateful to both of them."

"Now, I would like to ask Skye and CJ to come up to the podium." CJ and Skye stood beside the mayor. "If I may, I would like to present" a long pause ensued, "the President of the United States of America, John Shannon. Mr. President." Everyone gasped in shock, and the crowd started looking around excitedly. CJ and Skye were speechless.

"Oh, my gosh, the president is here!" Maria said, surprised. "Do you see him, Michael?"

"I can't see anything for the crowd," he said.

The roar of the crowd grew louder as they all turned one way and then the other looking around for the most powerful man in the world.

About fifteen seconds later, a U.S. Secret Service entourage, clearing space through the crowd for the president to walk, surrounded him in protection and walked toward the deck where the mayor and CJ and Skye stood.

John Shannon, light-haired and handsome, blue eyes sparkling, and a big smile on his face, walked up to the podium, reached out his hand to Mayor Morales and gave him an enthusiastic handshake.

"Thank you so much for inviting me to your celebration," he said in a rich baritone voice. The crowd roared and then quieted as

Mayor Morales motioned for silence. The mayor was thrilled as he shook the president's hand.

"Mr. President, it is I who am honored to have you attend today. May I introduce CJ Jansen and Skye Somers. These two, along with their crew standing behind us, risked their lives and were indirectly responsible for killing the giant squid which had taken several citizens and would have taken many more if it hadn't been for them."

The president offered his hand, first to CJ and then to Skye. "It is an honor to meet you both," he said with a broad smile.

CJ glanced at Skye as if to say, "Help."

Skye looked up at the tall, handsome man and said, "Sir, we lost a good friend to the squid, and we knew if everyone around here could ever hope to feel safe again, we had to find a way to kill it. We couldn't have done it without CJ's dad and uncle, my grandfather, the mayor, and Detective Sean Callahan, and, of course, the wonderful support of CJ's mother."

The president turned and shook each of the groups' hands. "Thank you for your bravery and service," he said to the group in unison. Then he turned back to Skye and CJ and said, "It would be mine and my wife and son's honor if all of you would join us for dinner at the White House two weeks from today. I'll send Air Force One to Key West Naval Station, and they will fly all of you to Andrews Air Force Base where Marine I, my helicopter, will bring you to the White House."

The mayor, CJ, Skye, and the whole group broke out in big smiles.

Finally, CJ got up the courage to speak, "Sir, I know I can speak for everyone here. It will be our pleasure to join you. I've always wanted to see the White House."

The president turned toward the large crowd that had gathered. "I also wanted those of you who lost loved ones to know that you will be in our prayers. Thank you for coming today to honor this small group whose bravery and courage made this celebration possible. Now, everyone enjoy yourselves. My ride is waiting, and I've got a little business I need to take care of in the Middle East with some folks who call themselves ISIS."

Everyone in the crowd clapped wildly. With that, he stepped away from the podium, and he and his security protection walked to a waiting limousine.

Epilogue

Gathered around a table at the Green Turtle Inn, their favorite restaurant, Skye, CJ, Poppy, Michael, Maria, Sonny, and Sean Callahan talked excitedly about their visit to the White House three days before. Sonny was the only one who had ever been to the White House, and that was on NSA business, not to get a personal tour as they all had on their visit.

As the discussion wound down, Michael looked over at CJ and Skye and said, "Well, I heard from the state earlier today, and they said the gold is yours to keep or sell. Including the gold and diamond crown, the total of what you found is worth four point six million dollars if you decide to sell it. You could probably get more than that if you sell it to private collector."

Everyone gasped in shock. CJ just smiled and looked at his dad and said, "We haven't decided for sure what we'll do with it, but we are leaning toward selling it. Skye and I discussed it, and because of how you've all supported and helped us, and what you all did on the *Money* the day Willy killed the squid, we want to give each of you a share of it. We want to split it seven ways. That will give each of you just over sixty hundred-fifty thousand dollars."

Each one around the table just sat there, stunned at what CJ had just offered them.

Finally, Callahan spoke, "Kids, I can't take your money. For what the two of you have done for all of us in the past couple of summers, you both deserve it all."

Sonny looked over at the teens and said, "I agree with Sean. You all nearly got killed finding that gold, and you should keep it."

Skye looked at all of them and said, "Look, we're a family and families share. No arguing now, everyone is going to receive a share. You can do whatever you want with it. That's up to you. It's yours."

Poppy looked over at his granddaughter and CJ, who felt like a grandson to him, and he said, "I've never been prouder of you two than I am today. You're the bravest kids I know and the most generous. I love you both more than I could ever say." With that, tears filled the old man's eyes.

————————

CJ and Skye sat on Poppy's dock. CJ's parents and Poppy stayed inside to give the teens time alone on Skye's last night in Islamorada. Both sat in silence for a while, just enjoying each other's company.

CJ was the first to speak. "I guess you know I'm going to miss you so very much. I won't know what to do with myself. I can't imagine waking up on Monday and not being able to drive down to Poppy's to pick you up for another adventure." Tears filled his eyes, but he held them in check. He didn't want to cry like a baby, but he sure felt like it.

"Oh, CJ, you'll be so busy at the University of Florida you won't have time to miss me."

"I'll miss you every day until I see you again next summer."

"Well, you won't have to miss me until next summer. My parents are coming to visit Poppy during Christmas vacation, and they told me they would take a flight into Jacksonville and rent a car to drive down to Gainesville, so I can see you. Maybe you can drive down with us to Poppy's. Won't you be on Christmas break too?"

"Oh, wow! That's great news! Yes, I'll be coming back to Islamorada for Christmas break, and it would be fun to spend time with your folks. After all, in five years they'll be my in- laws." He laughed as he said it. He still couldn't believe that Skye had agreed to marry him when they graduated from college. They had also talked about working on their graduate degrees after they were married.

Early the next morning, CJ would take Skye to the airport in Miami for her flight to Boston, where her parents would meet her for the drive down to Connecticut, just like last year. The only difference was this year Skye wouldn't have to worry about the worn-out muffler on CJ's ancient yellow VW Thing. He had used a small part of his share of the money from the gold and had bought himself a brand-new Corvette Z206, so Skye knew she would be riding to the airport in style this year with the young man she loved. She thought to herself., Yep, *I'm a very lucky girl.*

The End

A Preview

A Miracle for Tristan

By J Thomas Stovall

Chapter 1

Miami
Friday, July 10, 2015

The nearly deafening thwap-thwap-thwap of the rotor blades from the Marathon-based Trauma Star helicopter hovering over the rooftop landing pad caused the visitors in the parking lot to look up. Some people wondered if the patient aboard would survive, and others wondered if it could be someone they knew and prayed it wasn't.

Though unaware of the identity of the person on the gurney as it was being lifted from the emergency helicopter, almost everyone in the United States would recognize the name of the critically injured man being rushed to the high-speed elevator. The fifteen-second ride would transport him to the resuscitation room of the Ryder Trauma Center at Jackson Memorial Hospital in Miami, Florida. Every second was crucial for the patient. Severely injured patients receiving emergency treatment within the first sixty minutes or less had a much higher chance of survival.

Notified of the incoming patient by the Trauma Star paramedics on their two-way radio, the trauma team at the state-of-the-art hospital, stood in place. Four of the trauma center's top board-certified surgeons, plus an anesthesiologist, a neurologist, and several critical care nurses waited. Two anxious Army Forward Surgical Team members stood silently against the wall of the resuscitation room, ready to assist if called upon to help.

Ten units of the injured man's blood were being rushed by jet and should be arriving within minutes.

During the helicopter transport, paramedics applied occlusive dressings on the two gunshot wounds to the man's chest, each taped on three sides. The open sides allowed air to escape. One of the paramedics kept squeezing a bag valve mask, placed over the patient's face, every two seconds. Two large-bore IV bags dripped into the critically injured man's arm. With pale, clammy skin, he was hypotensive from severe blood loss. The paramedics had not expected him to survive the trip to the Level I Trauma Center.

The pneumatic doors to the resuscitation room swooshed open as the paramedics rushed the gurney through the entryway. The trauma team immediately took over and quickly began assessing the injuries. Shouts of instructions filled the room. Blood from several wounds seeped heavily through the sheet covering the unresponsive man. A dark red substance had congealed and matted on the scalp and in the hair. Blood trickled from the corners of the patient's mouth. His bloody right arm lay broken, and his right knee shattered.

The trauma team had been notified in advance of the identity of the incoming patient. They were shocked at the death-like pallor on his face. Each wondered how the man had remained alive.

Though the group of medical professionals, some of the best in the country, had helped many critically injured patients survive, this team knew the significance of saving this particular man's life. John Shannon, the President of the United States, had to live..